PRAISE FOR THE NOVELS
OF ASHLEY MARCH

Romancing the Countess

"Ashley March is a glorious new voice in romance. From the first page, *Romancing the Countess* captivated me with a smart heroine, a sexy, brooding hero, and a sophisticated romance that vibrates with sexual tension. Ashley March is the goods!"
—*New York Times* bestselling author Elizabeth Hoyt

"Powerfully sensual, beautifully told, compulsively readable—Ashley March has created a hero and heroine meant for each other and a romance meant to be savored."
—Julie Anne Long, author of *What I Did for a Duke*

"Riveting, sensual, and hauntingly beautiful. Ashley March entrances."
—Laura Lee Guhrke, author of *Trouble at the Wedding*

"March's elegant style is a joy." —*Publishers Weekly*

"Wit and repartee add zest to March's theme of a second chance at love. A fresh new voice, she twists and turns the classic plot into something new."
—*Romantic Times* (4 stars)

"Her writing is addictive, superb, and hopelessly romantic." —The Romance Reviews

continued . . .

Also by Ashley March

Seducing the Duchess
Romancing the Countess
Romancing Lady Cecily
(A Penguin e-Special)

My Lady Rival

ASHLEY MARCH

A SIGNET ECLIPSE BOOK

SIGNET ECLIPSE
Published by New American Library, a division of
Penguin Group (USA) Inc., 375 Hudson Street,
New York, New York 10014, USA
Penguin Group (Canada), 90 Eglinton Avenue East, Suite 700, Toronto,
Ontario M4P 2Y3, Canada (a division of Pearson Penguin Canada Inc.)
Penguin Books Ltd., 80 Strand, London WC2R 0RL, England
Penguin Ireland, 25 St. Stephen's Green, Dublin 2,
Ireland (a division of Penguin Books Ltd.)
Penguin Group (Australia), 250 Camberwell Road, Camberwell, Victoria 3124,
Australia (a division of Pearson Australia Group Pty. Ltd.)
Penguin Books India Pvt. Ltd., 11 Community Centre, Panchsheel Park,
New Delhi - 110 017, India
Penguin Group (NZ), 67 Apollo Drive, Rosedale, Auckland 0632,
New Zealand (a division of Pearson New Zealand Ltd.)
Penguin Books (South Africa) (Pty.) Ltd., 24 Sturdee Avenue,
Rosebank, Johannesburg 2196, South Africa

Penguin Books Ltd., Registered Offices:
80 Strand, London WC2R 0RL, England

First published by Signet Eclipse, an imprint of New American Library,
a division of Penguin Group (USA) Inc.

First Printing, May 2012
10 9 8 7 6 5 4 3 2 1

ALWAYS LEARNING   PEARSON

Chapter 1

London, April 1849

*I*t was not a hearse. Hearses were dark and gloomy things. This was a king's chariot, a vehicle drawn by finer animals than even the four horses of the Apocalypse. Angels probably sat up top beside the coachman.

Alex ran his hand over the black squabs he sat upon. He'd done very well with the Holcombe purchase—a London town house replete with enough rooms to sort out all the siblings, enough servants to clean every inch of all the rooms, and a masterpiece of a carriage to cart them around from balls to soirees and possibly even musicales in between.

"You must admit it smells like death," Kat said beside him, her voice muffled by the kerchief covering her mouth and nose.

Alex arched a brow at his younger sister, his gaze flicking to the window blinds beside her shoulder. Black blinds. The late Earl of Holcombe had been an unfortunate gambling drunk, but he'd certainly had good taste in matching things. Black carriage. Black squabs. Black blinds.

If it *had* been a hearse, Holcombe could have done no better.

"Nonsense," he replied, smiling indulgently. "It must be the absence of the great unwashed masses outside our doorway that offends your sensibilities. The carriage doesn't smell like death. It smells of life, of wealth!"

"The house holds a stench, too," Susan Laurie said from the opposite side. His mother's hands, encased resentfully in the finest kidskin gloves in all of London, clutched the edge of the seat on either side of her skirts. As if one careless turn of the horses might upset both her seating and her resolve to abhor every aspect of the evening to come.

"Oh, but you are mistaken, Mama," Jo said at her side. "It is simply that you are unaccustomed to the scent of life, of wealth!" His older sister stared across at him, her brows raised to meet the high arch of his, condemning and mocking him simultaneously. Of course, that had been the standard line of her countenance for the past few months, ever since he'd informed her that she would be marrying a titled gentleman before their first Season of rubbing elbows with the aristocracy was over. "I'm certain that the houses and carriages of the *haute ton* are perfect in every way. Just as we soon shall be, too. Isn't that correct, Alex?"

"No need to grumble, Jo," he said with a wink. "Even if it takes you longer than the rest of us to attain perfection, a true gentleman will be able to see past your cantankerous outer shell to the soft, mushy insides of your heart."

"I'm one and thirty. You mean he'll see past to the dowry you gave me."

He decided to ignore the reference to her age. Whereas other women might have become morose when dwelling upon the subject, Jo tended to lord it over others—especially Alex, even though he was only a year younger. "Ah, yes. The banknotes are soft and mushy, too." He gestured toward her. "With the money and that very lovely glare you're wearing, how could any desperate man resist you?"

"Alexander," his mother reprimanded. He gave her his most charming grin, but she just shook her head. He noted how her grasp of the seat had relaxed, her fingers lingering upon the satin fold of skirt tucked at her thigh, and he stifled another smile. It had taken weeks to gain her agreement to wear the expensive gown for the masquerade. Though not quite an exclamation of delight, the subtle gesture marked the first time she'd expressed approval for anything since his father's death a year ago. Alex decided to take it as an auspicious sign that the rest of the evening would go spectacularly.

But then she turned her head toward the window. "I agree with Kat. The carriage stinks. And the house does, too. More than fifteen servants and it smells worse than a privy."

"Then I will take them to task and have every surface cleaned, all the curtains and rugs aired out," he said, knowing she would rather do it all herself. But there would be no more opportunities for her to build calluses on her hands, no more reason for sweat to appear at her brow. Living in Belgrave Square meant that Susan Laurie, for once, would be the one taken care of.

Kat tugged at his arm. "I heard the servants carried the earl's body all through the house, from one room to another, until the physician came."

"That explains the stench," Jo said. Even not looking at her directly, Alex could *hear* her glare.

His mother nodded.

Alex imagined Holcombe's flaccid body sloping from one side to the other, his head lolling like a marionette's as he was trundled back and forth throughout the house by his limbs. "A ridiculous story," he pronounced. "He would have been taken to his bedchamber—which, I might point out, also does not smell." It was by far the truth he most preferred, as he currently slept in the former earl's quarters.

"Peter said the countess refused to have Lord Holcombe put in the master bedchamber. She didn't want him set so close to her."

Alex narrowed his eyes. "Peter, you say?"

In the dim light cast from the lamp near his head, Kat's cheeks reddened. She shrugged, retrieving her hand from his arm. "That's why they had to carry him from room to room. Lady Holcombe followed them around, crying whenever they put him down."

"The *ton* does not gossip with servants, Kat." Nor did they have cause to blush when speaking the first footman's name.

Alex was usually an amiable man, but at the moment Peter's continued employment at Holcombe House came into question. He had no tolerance for the male servants acting inappropriately toward any of his sisters. Jo he could throw to the wolves without care, as she would always be able to defend herself well. But he didn't need to think of secret whispers and stolen kisses in regards to his other sisters—and *especially* not if any of it involved Kat. Not after her almost elopement with the cobbler's apprentice last year.

From across the carriage came an amused chuckle. It was amazing the condescension Jo could ascribe to any sound. Of them all, she who loathed the aristocracy most would probably fit in best.

He gave his head a little shake and lifted his gaze to the dark expanse of the carriage ceiling in supplication, causing Kat to giggle. "Yes, Jo? You believe I should encourage her to gossip with the footman?"

Jo waved her mask before her face, as if moving the stagnant air could relieve its offensive properties. "You are the only one who pretends we are equal to the aristocracy. Even these"—she fluttered the rose mask, its white feathers rippling in response—"are not enough to disguise the fact that we are inferior."

"You know we're not. And remember our soft and mushy banknotes." Alex wagged his finger. "The members of the *ton* would never dare say such a thing while they try to court our good graces."

"But it's what they believe. Do you think a mask will hide the pattern of my speech? No number of Miss Ross' lessons will keep them from recognizing my common blood as soon as my mouth opens."

"Please don't make me dance, Alex." This, pled by Kat. "I've tried as best I can to remember all the steps to the quadrille and to be graceful when I waltz. But I'll forget. Poor Mr. Doiseau's feet must be bruised from all my mistakes. Please, let's return home. In a few weeks, after I've practiced longer—"

"No. We are going to the masquerade." Sometimes one simply needed to be blunt. He knew that their fears would always give them cause to delay entering Society, and now that the period of mourning for his father was over, there was no reason to wait.

Alex glanced at his mother, certain she would be next in the queue of complaints. She met his gaze with the same dark brown eyes most of the eight Laurie siblings had inherited, including him. Then she raised her mask to her face and tied the ribbons behind her head, and Alex vowed to give her a dozen more pretty gowns that she could secretly admire. And one of them would be the same color as the gown in the

Queen's Madonna portrait with Princess Louise. All he had to do was successfully re-create the dye.

Soon the carriage slowed before the Winstead town house, the sound of the horses' hooves and the vehicle's groans smothered by a swell of voices.

"We're here," Alex announced cheerfully, tying on his mask. The silence which greeted his announcement was decidedly *un*cheerful. Jo didn't make a sound—not even so much as a sigh—as both she and Kat followed suit. Ready or not, willing or not, they were all at their first event of the Season. Their first ball, their first masquerade, their first test to see if they of common-born origins could be accepted—even anonymously—into this realm of idle nobility.

The metal snap outside signaled the groom's unfolding of the steps. Then he opened the door, and a waft of West End London air rushed in—scented with flowers and coal and perfumed bodies. It was a distinct smell Alex still hadn't become accustomed to, even after two months, and refreshing in contrast to the—supposed—stench of death permeating the late Lord Holcombe's carriage. But it wasn't at all welcoming when compared to the scents of his youth—of ink so thick upon the air one could nearly taste it, of burnt fat from the tallow candles as his father worked into the early morning, of the lye heavy upon his mother's hands, strong and yet still unable to mask the odor filtering in from the streets outside.

He inhaled the West End London air into his lungs. This was their future—that of his family and of the dye-making business his father had created from little more than scribbles on advertisements and late-night dreams. Joseph Laurie might have died and left Alex to take his place, but he would not prove a failure. Although his father had wished for investments from those with exalted titles, he had never dreamed of establishing ties with the aristocracy through marriage. But the Lauries deserved the best, and once their merchants' money lured in the proud but destitute, they would never be snubbed again.

The groom appeared in the opening. "Mr. Laurie? Will you come out, sir?"

Alex grinned at Jo and held out his hand. "Shall we go pretend to be their equals, then?"

She snorted and stood, clasping his hand momentarily before moving to take the groom's. "Give me a moment to lower my intelligence and morals."

"Only a moment?"

She paused, her eyes flashing with laughter behind the mask as she looked at him over her shoulder. "You do have your good points, you know. And I love you, even if I despise you for making me come tonight."

Alex placed a hand over his heart. "Soft and mushy, Jo. Soft and mushy."

Alex handed their invitation to the Winstead butler, then waited as the man sniffed and peered at the script. It was a ceremonial gesture; no names would be announced tonight at the masquerade ball.

"He let us in," Kat whispered as they walked past

the butler to the landing which overlooked the ballroom.

"Of course he let us in," Alex replied. "We had an
invitation." He would have reminded himself to
thank Lunsford for arranging their attendance but
was fairly sure his friend would have no qualms in
prompting his gratitude at the first opportunity.

"Did you hear him sniff?" Jo asked. "If that smell
from the carriage is clinging to our clothes, then I'm
leaving right—"

"Good heavens." His mother stopped short, three
feet before the first stair. The hand lying over his arm
tensed, her fingers digging into his coat sleeve.

Directly in their line of sight hung a row of four
grand chandeliers, each sparkling with crystal tear-
drops and heavy with the flame of what seemed a
hundred candles. The scent of candle smoke filled his
nostrils as thin black streams lifted from the chandeliers to waft toward the ceiling.

Ten marble pillars, five on each side, stretched from
the ceiling to the floor below, where a host of masked
men and women milled about the perimeter of the
dancing. Their movements were stuttered, their numbers allowing only small steps in any direction. Heads
bobbed from left to right as the guests greeted others
who brushed against their shoulders by virtue of the
crowd's crush; feathers stacked high on masks waved
from each corner of the room, and half faces ob-
scured by silk and velvet disguises drew attention to
the mouths beneath: laughing, smiling, pursing, frown-

ing, drinking, gossiping, shouting to be heard above the din of gaiety. Strains of music floated overhead from the balcony, pushing and pulling the dancers in the center of the ballroom, their mouths huffing for breath.

The noise should have been overwhelming, the wealth intimidating in its brash opulence of crystal and gold, marble and jewels. The sight of so many people, each with the potential to sneer or unmask him for the common upstart he was, should have been at least the tiniest bit disconcerting.

Instead, it felt like a welcome.

Alex smiled and bent his head toward his mother's ear. "I was hoping at least for elephants to ride upon. Or a river of gold. Harem girls would also have been nice—"

"I don't want to hear about harem girls," Susan said, her skin pale and the corners of her mouth pinched.

Behind him, a finger jabbed his ribs. "They're pushing us back here," Jo complained. "Keep going!"

Alex led his mother down the stairs, pointing out the strange and ludicrous to ease her nerves. "There appears to be a bull over there by the terrace. See his horns curved above the mask? No, don't smile—he'll surely see us and charge."

Halfway down. "Ah, a unicorn! And it appears she even applied some sort of paste to her face. Now, that, Mother dear, exhibits a fair amount of creative dedication."

"Hmm." His mother's hand still clung to his arm, as if she would tumble down the stairs to her death if he were to withdraw his support. He had never seen her afraid, not once in his life, not even after his father had died. Yet now her touch held the slightest tremor—she who had always been his definition of strength and bravery—and he felt like a damned monster for forcing her to come. She'd refused at first, hadn't she? She hadn't wanted to relinquish her widow's weeds for a ball gown, her melancholy expression of mourning for one of pretense. But he'd coaxed and charmed as he did best until she agreed to attend the masquerade, knowing that neither Jo nor Kat would come without her acquiescence to his plans. She'd agreed for his sake. Alex's jaw clenched. God help anyone who dared to scorn her tonight.

"It might take a bit of creativity if she were the only one masked as a unicorn," Jo said snidely behind them. "There's another one by the refreshments. Do you suppose they're unicorn lovers?"

"Were we meant to dress as animals?" his mother asked.

"I wish I was a swan," Kat said.

"No, not at all." Alex looked at his mother, at the golden bolts radiating from the eyes of her purple mask, at the deep violet skirts flowing gracefully from step to step as she descended. Regal, he'd told the modiste. Though he still hadn't replicated the color of the

Queen's Madonna gown, which she adored, she deserved to look like royalty. And she did. "He would have approved," Alex murmured.

"Thank you." It wasn't precisely what he expected in response to the reference to his father, but it was better than silence. And she didn't immediately try to exit the room as she did at home. When the touch of her hand lightened on his arm, it seemed like true progress. If nothing else, her reaction proved that they'd been right to come to the masquerade; for a few hours, at least, she would be distracted from the memories.

They reached the bottom of the stairs and Alex drew her to the side, trusting that Kat and Jo would follow. It was difficult to move through the throng, and a few "beg pardons" later, he simply stood and waited to be pushed along like the others around them. Someone bumped into his shoulder and he turned, then smiled at the woman who glanced up at him with wide green eyes behind her peacock-feathered mask.

"Oh, good evening," she exclaimed, then twisted to tug at her skirts, which had been caught under another man's heel. "I'm certain he did that on purpose," she told Alex. "If that's not Sir Alfred Crowley, then my name's not . . ." She paused and winked, her smile mischievous.

"What *is* your name?" Alex asked.

She shook her head and leaned closer.

"What *is* your name?" he asked again, more loudly.

"Why, Lady Peacock, of course, sir. And you must be Mr. Midnight."

Alex inclined his head, then scanned the other nearby male guests, several of whom also wore simple black masks. "There appear to be many Mr. Midnights at tonight's ball."

"I think you all do it deliberately, so we— Oh!" Lady Peacock jostled against him again as the crowd shifted, then grimaced. "I must go before I'm trampled. A pleasure to meet you, Mr. Midnight."

"And you as well, Lady—"

She had already turned, holding her hands to her mask to protect the peacock feathers as she shoved her way through the crowd.

"She was nice," his mother said beside him, a tight smile on her lips as she nodded at the greetings directed toward her.

"Yes, very nice." If one could draw such a conclusion from a minute of conversation.

"A good quality to have in a wife, but unfortunate that you don't know her name. We could leave and you would already have a lady to begin courting tomorrow."

Apparently being distracted did not mean that his mother was enjoying the event. Alex smiled. "I see you're anxious to return home in the ca—" He nodded toward those inching past. "Good evening. I beg your pardon. Yes, good evening to you." Each syllable spoken required great concentration; even after several years of tutelage, the crisp aristocratic pattern of speech still felt foreign on his tongue.

His mother sniffed. "The carriage?"

"Yes, the carriage."

"Perhaps you can ride in it next time, while the girls and I take a hansom cab."

Alex grinned. "I'm heartened to hear you say there will be a next time."

"You know very well I meant later this evening."

Loudly, a few feet away, over the other voices: "No, I won't dance with you!"

Heads swiveled toward Alex's left. He groaned.

"Surely you're not surprised," his mother said.

Of course he wasn't. Why should he have been surprised to find his older sister shouting a refusal to a man who'd probably complimented her on how lovely she was and then kindly asked her to dance?

He tugged his mother toward Jo, intent on intervening and reminding Jo of her good manners, even if he did have to wade through a sea of peacocks, bulls, and unicorns to do so—when another woman crashed into his side.

He stumbled, lifting his hands to steady himself and the masked stranger. He half expected to see Lady Peacock again, with her large green eyes and wide smile. Instead, as the woman removed her head from his shoulder and looked up, he found himself staring into blue eyes—eyes the color of the ocean, surrounded by a landscape of diamonds and bordered by gold. She glanced away, laughed, then looked back, her eyelashes sweeping. "Oh, I do beg your pardon!"

He knew her.

The thought was faint but immediate, a shock of familiarity. How did he know her? Was she someone he'd met on the Continent, or the daughter of a duke Lunsford had pointed out during a ride in Hyde Park?

The mouth beneath her mask curved, waiting for his response. But before he could reply, she said, "I believe this is the part where you assure me it wasn't my fault."

Framed by the sleeves of her violet gown, her shoulders were slim beneath his hands. A fool would have mistaken their slenderness for fragility and not sensed the strength poised beneath his fingertips. He had hoped his mother's purple dress would make her feel like royalty, but it was apparent the woman before him needed no such ruse. Though the crowd had made her clumsy, "strength" and "poise," "grace" and "charm" were all words that he associated with her after only a moment's passing. "Beauty," too, if he were to judge based only on a study of her lips and eyes.

And he had no doubt that if he gave her an apology she would dismiss him and be on her way.

"I assure you, my lady, it was entirely your fault. After all, you were the one who crashed into me."

Her chin lifted. Behind her excessively gaudy mask, he imagined that her eyebrows did the same. "You believe I bumped into you deliberately?"

Alex didn't remove his hands from her shoulders. He knew she was also very aware of this fact, and yet neither of them gave voice to the impropriety. The crowd kept them close, gave him reason to hold on to her for balance for both their sakes. "Or perhaps I saw you veering toward me and made it inevitable that you would fall into my arms."

She lifted her fingers to his wrists and freed herself from his touch. His arms fell to his sides. "My apologies for the collision, my lord. I will take the blame." Her voice held the musical air of bells, softening the aristocratic syllables into something warm and inviting. It lingered like an echo in his mind, and Alex sifted through memories, intent to locate her. Any hint of a recollection dissipated at the slow, intimate turn of her lips. "I also bear the responsibility of taking pleasure in such a meeting. If you see me again later in the evening, my lord, please—feel welcome to crash into me next."

The short exchange ended, the rest of the ball attendees surging and pushing and edging past them. But whereas he'd turned away when the Lady Peacock left, Alex's gaze remained on the woman with the ocean blue eyes for several minutes, following her path as she threaded her way through the other guests.

"She seemed nice, too," his mother said behind him. Alex glanced over his shoulder. A wisp of humor, so faint others might not have seen it, hung at the corners of her mouth.

Alex smiled. "Possibly even nicer than the first." He offered his arm again. "Now, let's try to find Jo lest she offends half of London on only our first night. I'd expected it would take at least three."

But as they gradually shuffled through the crowd of ill-conceived animal costumes, gods and goddesses, and a few random historical figures, his mind held fast to the vision of a slender blond beauty gowned in violet. A woman with ocean eyes, gracefully slim shoulders belying her strength, and a mask that offered the most overt display of wealth he'd ever seen.

The Lady in Diamonds.

Chapter 2

Willa Stratton blamed her presence at the Winstead masquerade on Mr. Andrew Woolstone. He was supposed to have been at his bachelor's residence. He was supposed to have sold the information about the Madonna dye as soon as she offered. Instead, he was missing, and Willa didn't have a clue as to his whereabouts. Yes, it was true he didn't know who she was, nor had he expected for her to come to England to meet him, but those facts weren't as important as the very distressing realization that Woolstone had *disappeared*.

Of course, her suspicions immediately focused on Alex Laurie, current owner of the competing dye maker Laurie & Sons. He was the son of her father's former business partner and now her father's rival. Three years ago he'd become *her* rival as they competed for the same investor. And although she hadn't heard that he was interested in acquiring the dye for himself, if there was anyone who could ruin her plans quite so thoroughly, it was Alex Laurie.

Instead of celebrating her possession of the dye and informing her father that she had no intention of returning to America to marry Harold Eichel, she'd come to the masquerade as her father had always intended. He expected her visit to England to result in swaying Alex's greatest investor to their side, but Willa had other plans. Or rather, she didn't have plans any longer, now that Woolstone was missing; she had *desperation*.

She danced; she smiled; she laughed. She didn't simper, of course—Willa Stratton *never* simpered—but she certainly engaged in more than her fair share of flirting with Mr. Lunsford, Alex Laurie's largest investor and close friend. After a cotillion, they stood on the perimeter of the dancing, Willa pointing his attention to another couple in the quadrille closest to their position.

She knew her companion was Mr. Jack Lunsford, second son of the Viscount Carews, though they hadn't shared their names. Even though he was masked in a red domino tonight, she could have drawn his every feature almost as clearly as a mirror's reflection. She'd long since memorized the portrait she'd been given of him, the accounting of his habits and vagaries a tuneless litany in her head.

She didn't care for any of it now; all she wished

was to somehow charm Lunsford into telling her what Alex Laurie knew of the Madonna dye. And whether he had anything to do with Woolstone's disappearance. The *blackguard*.

Of course, that was assuming that Alex *was* involved. If he wasn't, then she must work even harder to find Woolstone before he did.

Although they danced and flirted back and forth just as expected, it didn't seem to take long for Lunsford to realize that Willa didn't engage him out of amorous interests. And Lunsford, she knew, was a man who cared greatly about amorous interests.

His suspicions were evident when he suggested they escape from the heat of the ballroom. "It's a lovely evening, my lady. Shall we take a stroll on the terrace to find relief from the crush?" Though his gaze lingered on hers with all sincerity, there was a knowing tilt to his smile that convinced her that the question was but a test. There was also a slight mocking to his voice, though he covered it well with the tones of consideration.

Upon arriving at the Winstead masquerade she'd been desperate. Upon recognizing Lunsford she'd been determined. And now, unfortunately, after having crashed into the man in the black mask a little while ago, she was distracted. Her attraction to a complete stranger who was of no consequence at all couldn't have come at a worse time.

Willa, who understood very well what occurred on terraces out in the moonlight—from experience—

refused. Her business flirtations didn't extend into that distant a territory. Or rather, they had once, but she preferred to learn from her mistakes.

"No, thank you," she said, another line of perspiration rolling between her shoulder blades. "I'm very comfortable." She liked Mr. Lunsford. She enjoyed his banter and sly observations of the guests milling about them. But she knew enough of his love for women—all women—to wish to keep her lips from becoming yet another pair to pledge their surrender.

The other side of his mouth lifted in a curl, presenting the full extent of his smile—a smile which would have made other women consider fainting, if only for a chance to be caught against his chest.

"I am not the sort of man to complain when a woman wishes to spend the entire evening with me," he said. His smile grew wider, yet still she didn't feel at all like fainting. "I enjoy spending time in your company, my lady. Yet I find myself suddenly questioning why *you* prefer *mine*."

"I think you very handsome," Willa said automatically, obviously, flirting with the ease of practice. She regretted it at once, nearly laughing when his eyes narrowed. Perhaps some level of enthusiasm was called for.

"Do you?"

"The *most handsome* man I've ever seen," she added, fluttering her eyelashes. It was the closest to simpering she'd ever come.

"And I suppose you've gathered all this from staring at my mask tonight?"

Well, blast.

It was the lack of breathlessness, she decided. She needed to affect a loss of oxygen in the quality of her voice whenever he looked at her. Heave her breasts a little to distract his attention. She should feign something similar to the way she'd truly felt earlier in the evening in the company of the other man.

As she'd done at least a dozen times since leaving him, Willa's gaze swept through the throng of masks for a simple black domino tied to a dark head. There were many such men nearby, and none of them him. She knew this, for not one caused her breath to stutter in her lungs, or her heart to race as it had done before, when his brown eyes had captured hers and his strong, warm hands remained settled on her shoulders.

Foolish. Tonight she was here for the Madonna dye, nothing more.

Willa tilted her head as if to consider Mr. Lunsford's attributes. "Your chin is very fine," she acknowledged.

"Ah, but many men have fine chins," he said. "You claimed me to be the *most handsome* man."

She pressed her lips together. "Your nose is nice as well."

"The one behind my mask?"

"It's the only one you have, isn't it?"

He chuckled, his gaze stretching over her shoulder.

"And what of this approaching fellow?" he asked. "Shall you say that *his* nose is nice, too?"

Willa turned to find *him* approaching, the man with the black domino and the dark hair. She shouldn't have allowed her gaze to linger, should have returned her attention quickly to Lunsford. But the stranger succeeded in distracting her yet again, and as he neared, thoughts of everything else fled from her mind. Her palms perspired in her gloves. Her chest heaved. And she became *breathless*.

He halted before her, his gaze flicking to Mr. Lunsford. He nodded, then met her eyes. And the thought came, swiftly—and yes, foolishly—that perhaps if all else failed when it came to the dye, she might marry an aristocrat. A rich one who loved her, to be sure, one who didn't need her father's money, for Daniel Stratton had made it abundantly clear that she would have neither dowry nor inheritance unless she married Harold Eichel.

"I beg your pardon, sir," the man addressed Mr. Lunsford, his gaze still locked on hers. He had brown eyes. Dark and rich—she could almost feel herself melting into their warm depths. "I believe she agreed the next dance to be mine."

To Willa, he lowered his voice and said, "You shouldn't have turned around. I had every intention of accidentally running into you."

She smiled, disarmed by the simple pleasure of hearing these words. They'd met before for only the space of a minute, and yet already they shared a secret jest. "Shall I turn again and wait to be knocked to the ground?"

From behind her, Mr. Lunsford said, "I suppose I'll simply stand here and pretend as if I'm also included in the conversation."

She should have been distressed at offending him. He could be her key to Alex Laurie and any connection he had with the dye. And yet . . . for once Willa didn't want to have to think about all the reasons she shouldn't do something she wanted. Getting the dye was something she had to do. Dancing with a handsome man who made her heart beat faster was much more appealing than spending the rest of the evening trying to avoid Lunsford's amorous interest. If she didn't come up with an alternative plan to find Woolstone in the morning, she could speak with him again. After all, she knew where he lived and dined and raced, all of the invitations he'd accepted for the next month. Mr. Lunsford would be the easiest man to locate in all of England if she wanted to; the stranger in the black mask would not.

She peered at Lunsford over her shoulder and lied. "I apologize, sir, but I did promise him the next dance. I'll see you again soon, I hope. I'd very much like to continue our discussion."

She was placating him. She couldn't even remember the topic of their conversation. And he knew she was placating her. But instead of becoming offended or dismissing her as easily as she had him, Lunsford only smiled and then waved them away.

He—the man she *wanted* to spend the rest of the evening with—took her hand in his. She thrilled at this, knowing enough of English Society to understand it was a forward gesture. Her toes even curled in her slippers, and only as a result of the touch of his gloved fingers. Perhaps later, if *he* were to invite her to the ballroom terrace for a breath of air, she wouldn't refuse him as she had Mr. Lunsford. And if he accidentally bumped into her again in the dark of night, she might also allow him to steal a kiss. Or two.

For now he drew her to where other couples waited for the beginning of the music. The first notes of a waltz lifted in the air. He clasped her hand and settled the other at her waist, and she became his captive once more.

Alex liked the way she fit in his arms, more natural than a stranger should have. *Had they danced together before?*

"Do I know you?" he asked.

The Lady in Diamonds laughed and her head tipped back—not far enough to be immodest, but enough to hint at abandonment. The movement drew his gaze to the slender length of her neck, teased his imagination with the thought of her head tipped the same way in his bed, her mouth parted in pleasure instead of laughter.

He normally didn't indulge in such lascivious thoughts. Interesting that she should be the exception.

"No, my lord, this is my first Season in London."

My lord. Clearly she didn't know who he was, either. He could have been mistaken . . . or perhaps she simply reminded him of someone else.

"But I feel as if I should know you also." She paused, angled her chin to the side; a blond curl grazed the side of her neck. She pursed her lips, revealing a dimple hidden at the side of her mouth. "Perhaps this is a sign that we are kindred spirits, that we are meant to become friends."

Alex smiled and bent his head toward her, creating an intimate space he knew from his dancing lessons to be as improper as taking her hand instead of offering his arm. He wanted her to remember him. "I should like very much to be your friend, then."

And more. The unspoken words echoed between them.

Like her shoulders, her hand was small yet strong in his, her touch warm through their gloves. And her ears—those were delicate, feminine, perfect for a man to shape his mouth around as he tugged at her lobe.

Her hair was dressed intricately: a pile of golden locks held together by a violet ribbon, its ends woven throughout the strands and disappearing somewhere mysterious beneath. With her head angled to the side, he realized that the ribbon in her hair was the same one holding her mask in place.

Clever, she was, for she must know this made a man wish to be the one who revealed her identity by removing both the mask and the ribbon from her hair. *Alex* wanted to be that man, imagining even now how the golden locks would feel threaded through his fingers.

Though the mask she wore glittered with diamonds, her violet gown was as plain in style and decoration as the mask was ornate. The contrast fascinated him; the mask and its ribbons begged for a man's touch to unravel her, while the gown alluded to a woman of chastity and reserve.

The shadow of memory loomed again, and Alex knew she couldn't be anyone Lunsford had pointed out in their drives about Town, when Lunsford attempted to identify those he should know before the Season began. Even if he recognized the shape of her face or a certain way she moved, there was something else about the Lady in Diamonds that resonated inside him. Many women were beautiful, many women were charming, but this particular woman was both of these as well as achingly familiar. He *had* spoken with her before, *had* danced with her . . .

"What is your name?" he asked.

She smiled up at him. Her lips were as lovely as every other part: a ripe, dark pink. Not thin and not too full, they were lips of action, shaped as if she spoke often, laughed often . . . His thoughts wandered further, and he wished to know the intimacy of her lips as they moved beneath his own.

She studied him for several moments. "I'll tell you my name after we dance."

He grinned. "You're teasing, aren't you?"

"Perhaps." Her lips pressed together, as if suppressing another smile. "Will you tell me your name also? You didn't offer, but I assume you meant to do so. A name for a name is only fair."

"I can tell you my name now." He leaned in close as they turned. "Mr. Midnight."

Her head tipped back again as she laughed. Alex wanted to plant his mouth against her throat, to feel the sound as it moved through her. "Mr. Midnight, you say? Not my Lord Midnight? I'm not sure why, but I believed you to be very lordlike."

Alex shrugged and pulled her closer still—much closer than Mr. Doiseau would have approved. "It was a name given to me by another woman earlier this evening. Because of the black mask, I believe."

"Another woman? Shouldn't you be aware, Mr. Midnight, that you're not supposed to speak of other women while we waltz? You're only to speak of me, to think of me, and rain down compliments upon my greedy ears."

Alex tilted his head—to one side, then the other. "Your ears don't appear very greedy to me. In fact, they appear quite delectable."

Her reaction left him more curious than regretful over the scandalous comment, wondering when a blush failed to paint her cheeks below the edges of her mask.

Instead, she mimicked his movements, tilting her head from one side to the other as she evaluated his ears. Those same ears burned—damn it, *and* his cheeks. *He* was blushing.

"You're blushing," she said, smiling. "Oh, how delightful! I've never made a man blush before."

"You were looking at my ears," he muttered.

"Yes, I was," she agreed solemnly. "And they're very fine, masculine ears, I might add."

"Masculine?"

"Yes." She tugged her hand from his and touched his left ear, drawing a finger over the shell's arch. A hot flush ran down Alex's spine. "They're larger than mine, of course, but beautiful. And you have this little sharp point at the curve—"

Alex covered her hand with his and returned it to its proper place—shoulder-level beside their bodies, far away from his ears and every other *masculine* extremity.

"Don't touch my ears," he said, and she laughed again.

Willa liked him. She liked him very much. And his ears were quite adorable—as adorable as ears could be, at least.

He danced as if he needed to protect her: his touch strong and supportive, the hand at her waist and the one clasped around her fingers like anchors as they swept from one corner of the dancing square to the next.

His eyes were steady on hers, watching her through each step. As if she was a curious toy—unpredictable and fascinating. She liked the idea that he was fascinated by her; it had taken only a short while, but she'd already become thoroughly enchanted by him.

"I have a confession to make," she said.

"I do hope you're not retracting the statement about my ears. It's a compliment I intend to take with me to the grave."

"Earlier, when I crashed into you, it wasn't by accident."

A moment passed. "It wasn't?" A new deepening of his voice hinted of his pleasure at this admission.

"Oh, no. It was very deliberate. I wanted to meet you, you see."

"I've underestimated myself, then. How irresistible I must be to make you risk bodily injury in order to gain an introduction, even if it is a nameless one for the moment." His dark brown eyes gleamed. Another woman's skirts brushed hers as he led her backward.

"It's not something I do all the time, you understand."

"No? Then I must know—in what way was I irresistible? Is it my fine figure? The allure of the lower portion of my face? Perhaps you heard me speaking and were impressed by my obvious intelligence?"

Willa bit her lip.

"Come now, my lady, you must tell me the truth."

"The truth? Are you certain?"

"Very."

"You were . . . there."

She'd been searching for Mr. Lunsford among the ball attendees when a woman shouted. Willa's head had jerked toward the sound and then *he* was there, pushing through the crowd with another woman, who, from their similar coloring and chins and difference in ages, she assumed was his mother. He'd held on to her tightly, as if she needed to be protected from something dangerous and unknown. Until Willa had seen him, she hadn't known how much she yearned for someone to hold on to, for someone to protect her from monsters if need be. Or at least, she hadn't admitted it to herself yet.

"I was . . . there?"

Willa nodded. "In my path."

"A random man in your path. Not very irresistible after all." His thumb circled the back of her hand. His lips curved in a half smile. "Shame on you, my lady, for teasing my vanity."

"I would never tease your vanity, sir. For after I saw you, I was unable to turn away. You were very striking." She said too much, even in flirtation. He watched her carefully, as if seeking out the truth in her words.

"Then I count myself fortunate," he murmured after a moment. "Although I don't advise you to accost random men at future balls simply because they appear in your path."

"Of course not. I promise to accost only you."

They smiled at each other and he led her forward. She purposely stepped amiss, curious to see his reaction at having his toes crushed.

Oh, very well—she was desirous of having a

reason for their bodies to brush against each other again.

He muffled a startled *oomph* as the ball of her foot came down, and then his eyes widened when she lurched into him, her breasts pushing against his chest. But he was a perfect gentleman, otherwise; he didn't point out her mistake, nor did he offer a subtly suggestive comment.

"Oh, I beg your pardon." Willa lowered her gaze to the end of his nose, just visible below his mask; to the firm, subtle curves of his mouth; the hard line of his jaw. Then she looked up again. "I must admit that I also did that deliberately."

"You stumbled on purpose?"

"I did."

He laughed, a sound that shouldn't have pleased her as much as it did. It also made her pulse leap.

She knew his laugh.

She'd heard it before. Not here, at the Winstead masquerade, but somewhere else.

"Are you always this forthright, my lady? Or is it the mask speaking and acting for you tonight?"

Willa's heart raced. Like he'd done earlier, she wanted to ask how she knew him. For a moment she considered the possibility that he was . . .

But no. Alex Laurie didn't usually move among the *ton* circles. Even if he did have the wealth to ingratiate himself, and even if his friend and investor Lunsford could have arranged for invitations . . .

Flustered, she admitted, "I wanted to lean against you again."

"I see." The hand clasping hers shifted, loosening, then tightening, as if he wasn't certain whether to keep her captive or let her go—

His hand stilled. His eyes lowered to her mouth, then rose again. Ah then, he'd decided to keep her. Willa was tempted to smile. No, he couldn't be Alex Laurie. Despite some of his improper words, his reactions seemed almost modest. And Alex was certainly not the modest sort; he'd known her for only a few hours in Italy before kissing her.

"I find your honesty intriguing, my lady. Most people aren't as willing to expose their true motives. Why not have me believe that the stumbling was an accident? Why not allow me to think our meeting a happy coincidence?"

It took a moment for her to make sense of his words. In her mind, she was running down a list of the cities and countries she'd visited since she began working for her father seven years ago. There were dozens, at least forty.

And she'd met plenty of Englishmen in her travels abroad . . . although there was an oddness to the way he spoke. She'd dismissed it earlier as an aristocrat's dialect from another part of the country, but now she considered that he could be a foreigner who'd studied the speech of the nobility as he studied the English language.

"My lady?"

"Do you not tire of the facade we make for ourselves? The half-truths, the flattery, the elaborate presentations we make for others' benefit?"

Who are you behind this current facade?

She hoped he wasn't one of her father's investors whose advances she'd been forced to reject in the past.

Mr. Midnight's mouth slowly curved. It was a wicked curve, his bottom lip full of sinful promises, delicious in the prolonged draw upward. Willa was captivated, drowning in his slow smile. She couldn't imagine ever having turned him away.

"You seem to have forgotten that we are attending a masquerade," he said. "Your wish for transparency would be more appropriate were we both not presently concealing our identities."

Willa smiled, conceding the point. "But as you said, my dear Mr. Midnight, it is the mask which is helping me to act and speak so freely. If it were removed, I fear I'd return to acting merely charming, not also revealing my truths to you."

He pulled her closer; Willa felt the lessened distance in the loss of her breath.

"Then allow me to also tell you a truth of mine, my Lady Diamonds." His head bent toward hers. "I'm devilishly glad you accosted me."

The waltz ended. Willa wouldn't have known except that he ceased dancing, then steadied her when her feet would have continued. Around them, the other pairs strolled away, making room for the next set. No music played, but still it echoed in her ears, as clearly as the smooth baritone of his voice. She swayed toward him, smiled when he used the motion to bring her closer.

"Tell me your name," he said, lowering their clasped hands. He released her, though his fingers slowly threaded through hers as he withdrew.

Willa stepped back. She shook her head and offered him a close-lipped smile.

"Surely you haven't forgotten your promise," he said, but he smiled, too. He enjoyed this as well: the flirtation, the teasing, the mystery and excitement. "Do you not remember? After the dance—"

"Oh, my apologies. I meant after the third time we dance, of course."

"Ah. The *third* dance?" His dark gaze burned into her. "Then let them be two more waltzes."

Willa, her throat suddenly dry, swallowed. The third waltz for the evening was the midnight waltz; after the dance the guests were to remove their masks. Yet her pulse didn't leap because of this; it leapt because she would have the pleasure of spending two more dances tonight in his arms. She nodded. "Farewell for now, Mr. Midnight."

Then she turned on her slipper, toward the bevy of masked men and women meandering along the sides of the ballroom.

Don't look back. Don't look back.

She reached the edge of the dance floor, nodded at a woman wearing a peacock mask nearby.

Don't look back.

She peeked over her shoulder to see if he was still standing there, watching her.

He was.

Willa smiled.

Chapter 3

"*H*e's still watching."

Willa glanced at the woman with the peacock mask. "It was a very nice withdrawal, wasn't it?"

"Indeed." The woman returned her smile. "I met him earlier in the evening. He doesn't seem very familiar to me, but then neither do you and I recognize most everyone even with their masks on. Is this your first Season?"

"It is." Her first London Season, at least. She hadn't visited London since she'd left England as a child. "You must tell me if I make any mistakes." Willa never made mistakes; she said this only to be friendly and make the woman sympathetic toward her. She believed in dealing in kindness as much as possible. Except when it came to Alex Laurie; *he*, she dealt with in smiles, leaving him to guess the ruthless motive behind each one.

"I'd be happy to help. I absolutely *loathed* my first Season. But I would ask you to help me in return. I was trying to escape someone"—her nose wrinkled—"most detestable. In fact, I feel it's my moral duty to point him out to you now lest he try to charm you and win you over. You should be prepared."

She tapped the shoulder of a woman to her side wearing a rose mask with white feathers, arms crossed over her chest and glaring at the assemblage. "Jo here would have fallen prey to his tactics if I hadn't warned her. But I saw him approaching and told her not to dance with him." The peacock woman smiled triumphantly. "She refused him outright! I shall always cherish the moment when she shouted at him, his expression of horror—"

Jo shrugged. "I would have refused him, anyway. I don't want to dance with anyone." But her air of nonchalance disappeared as a tiny, smug smile turned her lips. "The neat little O his mouth formed was very gratifying, though, especially if you say he's as awful as—"

"The very worst of scoundrels." The peacock woman nodded, frowning. "There he is now, speaking with your beau from earlier," she said to Willa, pursing her lips to the right and darting her gaze in the same direction. Her eyes narrowed, her voice lowering with the crispest of syllables. "Mr. Jack Lunsford, second son of the Viscount Carews. The devil's minion sent to plague the earth."

"Oh, I spoke with him only a little while ago," Willa said, amused to find that the charming Mr. Lunsford had an enemy. "He seemed nice to me. He made me laugh." Even though she'd scarcely been paying any attention to him.

"Ah, yes. You should be careful, then. Lunsford often starts with the laughter before he tries for seduction."

"Hmm." Mr. Lunsford probably had more to fear from Willa with her charms and flirtatious glances than she did from him. Instead she focused on Mr. Midnight, admiring him openly as he stood beside Lunsford on the opposite side of the room. So the two men knew each other, did they?

They made a striking pair—both tall, Mr. Midnight as dark as his temporary appellation next to Mr. Lunsford's golden countenance. Mr. Midnight was built with more muscle—Willa remembered his strength, the solid hand at her waist as they danced, guiding and turning her with the music. Mr. Lunsford was leaner, more elegant—and although the peacock woman appeared to believe he was the greatest of rakes and Willa's own sources had told her this, it seemed from her interaction with him much more probable that he encouraged the label only for his own amusement.

Her gaze returned to Mr. Midnight anxiously, as though it couldn't bear to be parted from him for even the slightest length of time. He alone held her attention. Confident, but not overbearing. He knew his appeal to women, and yet he blushed when she complimented his ears.

It was true that Alex Laurie had dark hair, and though she couldn't remember the exact color of his eyes, she believed that they were dark, too. He'd been tall. Muscular.

Not the sort of man to blush, though. And yes, he'd been confident, but he had also acted more than overbearing as they'd competed to win the favor of the Italian investor three years ago.

Willa had won, of course. She smiled at the memory.

Behind her, someone let out the long, unmistakable sound of a yawn.

Willa glanced at Jo, who surveyed her from head to foot, then cocked her head at the pair of men. "Strike your fancy, does he?"

"Surely not Mr. Lunsford!" said the peacock woman.

And then, because Willa simply couldn't bear to think of her any longer as "the peacock woman," she held out her hand. "I think we should be introduced. My name is Miss Willa Stratton, from New York."

The peacock woman stared at her hand, then reached out and took it. "But your speech is flawless," she said, her brows knit together. "You speak like one of us."

"Yes, my father—" Willa stumbled over her thoughts. No need to tell the woman how her father had taught her to believe that the best way to sneak past a person's defenses was to take on that person's habits and customs, and even his or her accent if possible. She needed to cease thinking of Mr. Midnight, to focus on what was before her. Smiling quickly, she released the woman's hand. "And you are?"

The peacock woman smiled and answered, "Lady Althea Redding, and although some prefer to torment me by using my full name"—she sent a withering glare across the ballroom—"please call me Thea."

"Jo," said Jo, stretching out her hand to Willa. Though the introduction was short and terse, her eyes crinkled at the corners inside her mask. "A pleasure to meet you."

Willa took her hand and shook it, and something indefinable passed between them—an understanding, it seemed, although she didn't know quite what it might be.

"The man you were dancing with," Jo said, smirking. "What did you call him?"

"Mr. Midnight," Thea and Willa said together.

"He mentioned a woman from earlier this evening gave him the title—"

"Yes, it was me," Thea said. "Suits him well, I think, especially when he's standing"—she craned her neck to peer around a passing shepherdess—"next to Lunsford. Do you know, Lunsford once told me that he doesn't believe that the earth revolves around the sun?"

"What does he believe it revolves around?" Willa asked.

Thea scowled. "Him."

Willa and Jo exchanged glances; then Willa looked across the ballroom again.

"Mr. Midnight is very handsome, isn't he?" Jo murmured, almost as if speaking to herself.

Willa nodded. At that moment, he glanced away from his conversation with Thea's dastardly Mr. Lunsford and stared—directly at her.

Willa smiled, gave a short curtsy, then laughed as Thea compared Mr. Lunsford's head to an overripe orange.

"Who is that lovely woman standing next to the curmudgeonly Lady Althea and your sister?"

Alex dragged his gaze away from the Lady in Diamonds. "You've met Jo?"

Lunsford rocked back on his heels and took another sip from his punch—a tepid, nasty concoction he actually seemed to enjoy. "Ah, yes, Miss Laurie. I made the mistake of asking her to dance—which, if I recall correctly, you asked me to do and I so kindly agreed—only to have her shout at me. She even raised her hand halfway." Lunsford lifted his own hand. "As if to slap me, Laurie."

Alex coughed. Then, when Lunsford only continued to stare at him, he cleared his throat. "Yes, well . . . Jo is . . ."

"Terrifying. Surely that's the word you were searching for. Further invitations might be difficult to arrange if she continues behaving so."

"Which is probably what she's counting on," Alex

muttered. He and his dearest older sister would need to speak regarding her efforts of sabotage after the masquerade. He should have expected she would do something to undermine his plans for the family.

"And a word of advice if you will, Laurie. Keep her away from Lady Althea."

"Is she the Lady Peacock?"

Lunsford darted a glance to the group of women, then back at Alex. His tone, heretofore affable even when speaking of Jo's rejection, changed to one that could only be described as devious. It came along with a sly smile. "Lady Peacock. Yes. Yes, she is."

Alex looked at the Lady in Diamonds. Her hands were now moving rapidly across her body as she spoke, the bell of her violet skirts making her waist seem impossibly small. Only because it was the natural path for his eyes to follow, Alex trailed his gaze over her bodice. Her breasts were lifted up and out, a nice, full curve for his imagination to round as he continued toward the top of her head. She was smiling again, and laughing.

"Good God, stop it."

Alex started and glanced at Lunsford, then back at the Lady in Diamonds again. "What?"

"You're staring at her like a little boy peeking through a shop window full of treats."

"Do you know her?"

"No. If you'll recall," Lunsford drawled, "I asked the same thing of you only a moment ago. I still haven't forgiven you for stealing her away from me earlier. I was just about to convince her to take a stroll with me through the gardens."

Alex lifted a brow. "Apparently you weren't convincing enough if she went along with my lie about the dance."

Lunsford narrowed his eyes. "I suspected as much. I certainly won't forgive you now. I might not even tell you the name behind the Queen's Madonna gown."

"You will."

"Perhaps I should wait until you're finished. I don't like to repeat myself, and you keep staring at her."

Alex deliberately—reluctantly—turned his back to the trio of women. He couldn't help it if his mind continued wandering to the Lady in Diamonds, or that the nape of his neck prickled with the thought that she might be staring at him now.

Still, after facing away from her it became easier to focus on the subject of the Madonna dye. He'd tried so hard to replicate it himself, but if there was finally word on the identity of the dye's creator, then he wouldn't act the stubborn fool. He would buy the damn dye information.

"Go on," he said. "This is the first I've heard about a name being attached. You believe you know who it is?"

"Oh, I'm certain I know who it is. His name is Woolstone, and he boasted at the club about being commissioned to create it by Prince Albert."

"Woolstone?" Alex frowned. "The name doesn't

sound familiar." But then, he still didn't recognize half the names of the peerage.

"Ah, but this man isn't just any man named Woolstone. He is Mr. Andrew Woolstone, the second son of the Marquess of Byrne and brother to the Earl of Uxbridge."

"A very important man, I presume. Someone I should have known about before this evening."

Lunsford inclined his head. "Well, yes, but one can't memorize all of our names in a few months. It's taken everyone else a lifetime. Of course, I can memorize facts and details instantaneously, but I don't expect you to—"

"Woolstone, Lunsford."

"Indeed. Andrew Woolstone is the son of the Marquess of Byrne, a fact which is all the more important to remember because Andrew may not be the heir, but he is certainly the spare. And the Marquess of Byrne does not tolerate family dabbling in trade, even if the dye was commissioned for the purpose of art by the monarchy."

Alex shook his head. "Trade. So coarse and unworthy of the aristocracy. Best to leave it to the commoners."

"Yes, and let us reinvigorate our inheritances by making all of our money off of your hard work. Or expand our allowances, as the case may be." Lunsford leaned in and whispered, "But the news now is that Woolstone's disappeared."

"Disappeared?"

Lunsford snapped his fingers. "Into thin air, if you will. A week ago the marquess is said to have had a row with him about the dye and such, and then, three days ago—gone. No one knows where, and honestly, no one cares, as they all think he'll show up with a bad head within a few days—"

"Has a tendency to drink much, does he?"

"Like a fish. His disappearance isn't commonly known yet, so do keep it quiet. But I thought you would want to know his name . . . what with your lack of success in re-creating the color, you see."

Alex lifted a brow, then realized Lunsford couldn't see it behind his mask. Sometimes it seemed his friend enjoyed baiting him far too much. "Thank you, Lunsford. Your kindness in helping me move past my failures is very much appreciated."

Lunsford shrugged modestly as he suppressed a smile. "If you can find him and he wishes to make up to dear old Byrne, then he might feel generous enough to share his secrets with you and be done with it. And then you and I, my friend, will be even wealthier than we are now."

Alex recalled the last few months of frustration and desperation, of nights passed without a second's sleep as he revised calculations and pored over every ingredient his father had ever used. Still, no shade of blue or violet Alex had concocted afterward resembled anything similar to the Queen's gown.

He needed Woolstone. Beyond giving his mother

a gown that would please her and make her the envy of all of London, he wanted the acclaim that replicating the dye would bring. The Lauries might soon be sought after in marriage for their wealth, but he wanted more interest for their company, too. With the dye and his invention—which *would* eventually work—every aristocrat with hopes of renewing the family fortune would see his successes and invest in Laurie & Sons. His family *and* his family's business would be the talk of the *ton*—in the best of ways, if Jo could behave herself and Kat could refrain from befriending all the servants. And he would have to purchase new transportation, too.

God, Holcombe's carriage truly had smelled like death.

"Thank you again for the information, Lunsford." Alex turned, as did Lunsford beside him, and he quickly located the Lady in Diamonds across the ballroom.

"As for the mysterious woman beside your sister and Lady Althea—"

"Lady Diamonds."

"Oh, Lady Diamonds, is she? You've named her?" Lunsford laughed.

"Lady Diamonds. Lady in Diamonds." Alex shrugged. "I believe the musicians are opening for another waltz." He tried to decide if the right or left would be the faster route to her side.

"You're leaving? I meant to tell you a tale of my

superior wit and charm the other day. Of course, there have been many such occurrences since then, but I didn't wish to boast over—"

Alex waved him off as he strode away. "Not now."

The Lady in Diamonds placed her hand against his, then set her other at his shoulder. "I didn't think you would come for me."

"You knew I would."

Her mouth tilted at the corners. "Perhaps."

"Hmm." Alex looked over the top of her head, pretended to focus his attention on someone else in the distance. "I believe I know why you crashed into me."

"It's not because you were in my path and irresistible?"

"No. You obviously know who I am, have developed a hopeless *tendre* for me, and are now trying to make me feel the same for you before you reveal your identity. You want to ensure my feelings before you declare yourself openly."

He knew it was a conspicuous attempt to learn her name, but still he tried. Instead of complying, she laughed and drew Alex's attention back to her mouth.

"And what are your feelings toward me right now, Mr. Midnight?"

He bent his head. "Perhaps my feelings are just as much a mystery as your name, Lady Diamonds."

"Or perhaps you want to kiss me," she said.

Alex stumbled in the turn of the dance. "A kiss might be a good place to start," he allowed.

Although this was his first official event of the *ton*, he'd attended many balls and other such affairs with aristocrats and businessmen throughout the Continent for the purpose of securing more investors for his father's company. Most of the women he'd danced with then had been married, some interested in him for more than an innocent waltz. He hadn't expected the ladies of the London *ton*—especially the unmarried ones—to be so bold and direct with their invitations. Hell, she was even more direct than the Italians and the French. They, at least, were subtle with their suggestions; she was brasher, bolder, more like the Americans he'd met on his travels.

He didn't much care for the Americans he'd met on his travels.

"The question is," he continued, "where exactly that first kiss should be." He stared into her eyes—beautiful eyes they were, the color of the ocean . . . as he'd thought before, as he'd thought the first time they met in Italy . . .

Dear *God*.

He glanced at her chin, her lips, her ears, as if doing so could assure him that yes, he *had* put all of the pieces to the puzzle together correctly. It was obvious now—the way she tipped her head back when she laughed, the startling color of her eyes, that singular combination of outward confidence and the hint of inner reserve . . .

Willa Stratton. She was Willa *bloody* Stratton.

Her eyelashes swept down and her chin angled to the side—if he didn't know any better, he would have considered it a bashful gesture. But he did know who she was now, and he knew each dark, manipulative twist of her devious little mind. She'd *sabotaged* him. And she'd *won*. He wasn't sure which was worse, but one thing was very much certain now: he knew *her* identity, yet she had no idea of *his*.

Alex smiled.

"Here," she said, reminding him of their topic of conversation: a kiss.

He stared at the tender, vulnerable skin bared for his view, a sweet spot that began at the curve of her collarbone. She expected him to woo her, did she? Ah, but she *liked* him. No, rather—she liked Mr. Midnight.

Alex pressed his lips together lest his smile widen into a full grin. "Hmm," he offered, still staring at the place she indicated for a kiss. Leave it to his baser nature to find the temptation of his enemy appealing.

When he didn't speak further, she lifted her eyes. "Mr. Midnight?"

"I'm certain kissing you—there—would be delightful," he said slowly. And then he remembered that she'd made him blush with the comment about his ears. He'd *blushed*, for God's sake! And so, after a moment's consideration, he continued. "However, I think a kiss first on your hand would be far more appropriate." Unlike others, he saw no weakness in having a desire for revenge. After all, he'd been raised with Jo for an older sibling; revenge was a necessity for self-preservation.

"You do?" Her mouth pursed. Willa bloody Stratton wasn't pleased with his self-discipline.

"I do."

He wasn't pleased that she would offer herself so easily, no more than he was in Italy when he realized that she'd kissed him to distract him from his pursuit of the Conte di Contarini as an investor for Laurie & Sons. He also didn't believe she meant her present offer, for she had nothing to gain from him this time.

Alex swept her around the far end of the floor. He well remembered her claim afterward that *he* had been the one to kiss *her*. All he knew was that she'd been waiting for him in the moonlight and that she'd risen to her tiptoes and leaned toward him. It was the first of her many works of sabotage in winning Contarini for her father, and it had succeeded. He'd been thoroughly distracted that first night. Thankfully, though, he was intelligent enough to stay away from her in the following days. But still she'd *won*, and that kiss had been the beginning.

Alex hummed a little under his breath, happy. Ah, revenge. She would be the one fooled into thinking she was wanted tonight. "You, my Lady Diamonds, are not someone to be flirted with one moment and discarded the next, nor someone with whom men should exchange illicit whisperings while you dance.

When your hand touches mine, it should be because I am bowing before you. I would take you for afternoon strolls and rides through the park. We would converse about the things that amuse you—" He paused thoughtfully. "What things do amuse you? Painting? The pianoforte and the like?"

She was silent for a moment, studying him. "I'd prefer to know which hobbies you prefer."

He recognized this, the way she turned the reins of conversations over to men. How she made them speak the most, how she played their egos as skillfully as instruments. "Ah, but I asked you first."

She gave a small sigh, a touch of impatience to the sound. "Languages. Though I paint a very good blob, and my talent at the pianoforte has nearly reached the level of a two-year-old."

"A very prodigious two-year-old, I would imagine," he said, smiling as he took note of her weaknesses. "Very well, then. We would converse about languages and even do so in different languages. I speak French, Italian, and German. You?"

She gave a shrug—one that seemed almost Gallic. Alex narrowed his eyes. This must be the reason why he hadn't recognized her fully before. The Gallic shrug, the perfect British accent: she was a master of disguises.

"A few," she said, then: "What makes you believe I am the sort of woman who prefers to be courted instead of kissed?"

He remembered the first time he'd ever seen her, how the air had seemed to sparkle with the radiance of her smile. Not seductive, not sinfully provocative, but *clean*. He was a man who'd been raised among the worst sort of filth—a description to fit both the people and the streets—and she had reminded him of sunshine on the best of days and rain that washed it all away on the worst.

"You have an air of innocence about you," he replied, realizing it was something she must have cultivated well: more lie than perception, more perception than truth. His fault for once believing it. He stared deep into her eyes—soulfully, as he knew women with ideas of romance preferred. He doubted Willa Stratton had a romantic bone in her body.

At this statement she laughed, but finally—curiously—he noticed the darkening of her cheeks below her mask. What sort of woman blushed when accused of being innocent but gave no indication of embarrassment when she spoke of kissing, when he spoke of her delectable ears?

"You're the one who is blushing now," he said softly.

When she looked up at him again, her eyes seemed brighter than before. The rose of her cheeks might have been becoming if she were someone else. "The waltz is almost over," she murmured.

His hand tightened even as a *Thank God!* rolled through his mind.

"I've never danced three waltzes with the same

woman in one evening," he said. "Should I prepare myself to soon be scandalized?"

"No one is watching us. They are all concerned with their own affairs."

"Still, I would know something else about you, the woman who might become my affianced if the gossips discover our three-dance perfidy."

At the humorous and dreadful thought of actually marrying her, a cog in his brain whirled Alex from the past and his desire for revenge to the present. Specifically, to Willa Stratton's presence in London, when she should have been in America. Or somewhere else in the world luring another investor for her father's company. Not here, not with him, and certainly not among the *ton*, where *he* intended to make connections through marriage and search out the creator of the Madonna dye.

He sucked in a breath, the air hissing through his teeth. "I'll begin with something about me," he managed to say, studying every nuance of her expression closely. "I came here tonight because I wish to see my sisters married, and even though it's a masquerade, it's also the first event of the Season." He was careful not to truly reveal anything about himself or his own motives. "And you, my Lady in Diamonds? Why did you come to the Winstead masquerade?"

"Oh, that's simple," she said, dimpling. Not even pausing to consider her words. "To find you, Mr. Midnight."

He nearly growled. Jo would have applauded.

The waltz ended. Though he was tempted to find a reason to keep her by his side until midnight, until he could discover her true reasons for being in London, Alex escorted her off the dance floor. "Minx," he murmured in her ear, then turned and walked away.

Chapter 4

Willa held her palms to her cheeks. "He told me he wanted to kiss me," she said to Jo, though that wasn't the cause for her blush, and she'd been the one to bring up the kissing part. But Jo didn't need to know that.

"Oh, he did?" Jo's gaze snapped across the ballroom.

Willa nodded. She wished he hadn't called her innocent, though. She'd done things in the past that had left her conscience black. Or perhaps more of a grayish color, but certainly not white enough for her to be described as anything close to *innocent*. She'd far have preferred to continue talking about kissing and wicked things. He would be good at kissing. He had a nice mouth, Mr. Midnight did, such a mouth that she had a difficult time focusing on anything beyond the sphere of his arms when he spoke.

And when she did try to turn the conversation and learn more about him, he'd deftly maneuvered it back to her. Clever man.

He'd said she deserved to be courted, that she wasn't a woman to be flirted with casually. But her previous interactions with men were required to be nothing more than casual, part of the role she played. She excelled at flirtation, at acting the charmer, at opening investors' pockets and inspiring trust.

"Well, are you going to kiss him?" Jo asked.

"Kiss? What did I miss?" Thea asked, pushing forward with three glasses of punch.

"Mr. Midnight." She willed herself not to look behind her. She knew he was there, somewhere. Perhaps watching her, perhaps not. But she shouldn't look.

Truthfully, she shouldn't even remain at the masquerade any longer. She should return to her rooms at Mivart's Hotel and prepare more plans for how she was going to find Woolstone and the Madonna dye. And, if it was true Alex Laurie had gotten to him first, how she was going to get the dye away from him.

Eight months. Nearly eight months she'd spent searching out clues for the identity of the Madonna dye's creator—a dye which could bring the owner a massive amount of wealth and which would be the key to her freedom. Eight months, only to discover the possibility that Alex Laurie might have swooped in before she could meet with Woolstone. Excessively galling and infuriating, that's what it was. She could only hope she was wrong and that Woolstone had gone missing for an entirely different reason. Not because he was murdered—that wouldn't have been good, either . . . although at least she wouldn't have lost to Alex then.

Willa felt her conscience turning a darker shade of gray. No, *of course* she wouldn't prefer for Woolstone to be murdered. Even she wasn't that focused on winning. Perhaps.

Besides, if Woolstone was murdered, she might never find the dye, and then she'd have to marry Eichel after all. Somehow this still felt entirely too selfish.

"I liked Mr. Midnight earlier," Thea said, frowning.

At this mention of the dashing Mr. Midnight, Willa swiftly sent up a plea that Woolstone was alive and far, far away from Alex Laurie, then returned her attention to her companions.

"Why do you not like him now?" she asked.

"Because then I saw him speaking with Lunsford. And anyone who willingly speaks to Lunsford must be reconsidered, I believe. Even if he is very nice, and even if he does have a very nice mouth and wants to kiss you."

She didn't like the thought of Thea noticing Mr. Midnight's mouth. Although it was difficult to notice anything else at the masquerade, she wanted to hide him away for her own pleasure. She alone would be able to look at his mouth and have him hold her in his arms while they danced and then tell her nice things like she was an innocent who deserved to be courted.

"Perhaps . . . ," she began, then hesitated. Charming women was just as useful as charming men, and it wouldn't do well to offend her new friend. "Perhaps Mr. Lunsford only reacts badly in your presence. There's a possibility he's usually as nice and decent as Mr. Midnight."

"Oh, I'm certain Lunsford behaves poorly specifically around me and nicely to others. It's a pretense he's perfected, and one he knows that I've seen thr—"

"*No*, thank you."

Willa glanced toward Jo, who was glaring at a man wearing a navy cape lined beneath with silver, a matching navy and silver mask tied around his head. The man currently had Jo's hand lifted halfway to his mouth.

Jo tugged at her hand. "Let me go."

"I don't see why she came to the masquerade if she doesn't intend to dance with anyone," Thea murmured to Willa.

Jo gave them an exasperated glance, then stomped on the man's foot. Thea gasped.

"Bloody hell," he cursed, immediately dropping her hand. He backed away, matching her glare.

Jo turned and shrugged. "He shouldn't touch people's hands when they haven't given him permission to do so."

A corner of Willa's mouth tugged upward. "I'm sure he'll think better of it next time."

"Jo . . . I believe you just tried to maim none other than the Duke of Aulburn," Thea said.

All of the blood leached from Jo's face. "A d-duke?" she whispered.

Thea nodded. "Everyone knows who he is," she said, drawing her finger along the right side of her cheek, past her mask to the tip of her jaw. "The scar. Most certainly the Duke of Aulburn."

A mutinous glint lit Jo's eyes, her chin firming. "I don't care who he is. He shouldn't have touched me."

"I will be sure to not make that mistake in the future, fair lady, lest my toes too become in danger of being crushed."

Willa's heart leapt to her throat when she spied Mr. Lunsford. She lifted to her toes and peeked over his shoulder, searching for Mr. Midnight, but he wasn't anywhere nearby. With her heart sinking to its appropriate location once again, she smiled in due form when Mr. Lunsford shifted his gaze from Jo to Thea—his mouth gave a tic at the corner as he scanned past her—then to Willa.

"Here we meet again, my Lady Diamonds."

She nodded. "I'm glad you found me. We were discussing the fine qualities of your chin, if I recall correctly."

Thea snorted.

The tic showed itself again, but he otherwise ignored her. "No matter. Those can be discussed another day."

From behind his back he withdrew a bouquet of flowers—well, in truth, it actually appeared to be a branch from a purple begonia plant—and extended his arm toward her. "From Mr. Midnight."

Willa accepted the branch hesitantly, holding it as far away as possible. There were still bits of soil hanging from the petals and leaves. "He couldn't bring it himself?" She felt something . . . familiar.

"Ah, but it's all in the anticipation," Lunsford replied. Then he shrugged. "Besides, it was the perfect opportunity to visit the area of the ballroom where evil doth reside." He wagged his fingers in greeting at Thea. "Lady Althea."

After Willa had won Contarini as an investor, Alex Laurie gave her flowers.

"Oh, my dear Mr. Lunsford!" Thea said brightly, smiling wide. Then her brows lowered and she scowled. "Please don't feel inclined to stay any longer on my behalf. Please, go. Go now," she said, shooing him with her hands.

No, he hadn't given her flowers. He'd asked Contarini to give her the flowers at the ball the last evening in Italy. She'd seen him do it. From another man it would have been a sign of admiration. As she'd taken the flowers from her new investor, Willa couldn't help but think that Alex Laurie was trying to kill her. She'd told him, early in their stay, of her reactions to flowers when he suggested a walk in the villa's gardens.

Willa's head snapped up from the begonia. She searched the ballroom, but she couldn't find him.

"A pleasure, as always. Your lovely countenance warms the cockles of my heart," Lunsford was telling Thea.

Jo extended her arm toward him as he backed away, holding her glass by her fingertips. "I've finished with my punch."

Thea laughed and linked her arm through Jo's. "Yes, you're right. Though I'm certain that *is* the only use he has, I doubt he—"

Lunsford held up his hand. "Now as you well know, I *do* have many other uses, Lady Althea." He gave her a narrow smile when she stiffened. Then, with a bow, he ignored the glass and turned away.

Willa caught his eye as he left. "Please be certain to thank Mr. Midnight for the kind gift," she said. Then, with her nose itching, she promptly searched for a place to dispose of the amputated begonia flowers.

Alex and Lunsford covertly stared at the trio of Willa Stratton, Jo, and Lady Althea.

"I really don't like that woman," Lunsford muttered as he sipped from a new cup of punch.

"Lady Diamonds, Lunsford," Alex repeated for the third time. He hadn't yet revealed her identity to Lunsford. He wanted to keep that information to himself for now. But he *had* employed Lunsford in the delivery of the begonia branch, a gesture meant to keep her interested in him and to toy with her a little before the next waltz. The final waltz.

He'd expected Lunsford to be back before he finished checking on his mother and Kat—they were fine, grudgingly admitting they were enjoying themselves—but it had taken Lunsford an eternity to return from his mission. After speaking with Willa, apparently he'd stopped at the refreshment table and then proceeded to flirt with half the women in the ballroom on his way back. He seemed especially enamored of one of the unicorns. "What did the Lady in Diamonds say?"

"Oh, her." Lunsford waved his hand. "She said thank you and wanted to know why you didn't bring them yourself."

Lunsford obviously didn't know that when Alex asked what she said, he also wanted to know how she'd *appeared*. Had her eyes lit with pleasure? Had her mouth curved? Did any of it help to foretell the extent of her dismay when his identity was finally revealed? He knew, of course, she would have no reason to reveal the truth about her attendance at the masquerade that evening.

"What did you tell her?"

"Some nonsense about anticipation." Lunsford glanced behind them to the now much less healthier-looking potted begonia. "Has anyone noticed anything amiss with the plant yet?"

"No, but I was just thinking it might be best to move to another part of the room."

"Good idea."

Several minutes later they stood at the far end of the ballroom, still opposite Willa, Lady Althea, and Jo. Jo was staring at him. Alex inclined his head, and she looked away. For the first time, he became concerned that she stood beside Willa. Surely Jo wouldn't tell her who he was. She must not have identified Willa as their enemy, since she continued speaking with her.

But then . . . then Jo turned back and smiled at him. *No*, he mouthed. Dear God, he *knew* that smile, part satisfaction and part mischief.

He shook his head.

She shrugged her shoulders, as if telling him that she had no idea what his gesture meant. For the next few minutes he watched as she continued speaking to Willa, but nothing amiss came about. Willa went on smiling and laughing, and Alex let out a little sigh.

Lunsford took another sip of his drink, his gaze flicking to something beyond Alex's shoulder. "If you're curious, there's Woolstone's sister, Lady Marianna, to your left, just beyond the corner of the dancing."

Alex shifted his attention toward a black-haired woman dressed in bright, rose pink silk. Her mask was pink as well, complementing her lily-of-the-valley skin. He returned his gaze to Lunsford. "Need I know about Lady Marianna?"

Lunsford shrugged. "Need to know? No. I, however, make it a habit to take time to appreciate all things beautiful when they come my way. And Lady

Marianna happens to be exquisitely beautiful." He paused, cast another glance her way, then sighed. "But she is of no importance. Woolstone is the one with the dye. However, if you *do* wish to hear more about her, I included her on Jo's guest list—"

Alex nodded, his attention slipping. He was keenly aware that the next dance was the third waltz, and the pleasure at seeing Willa appear the fool when their masks were revealed began to lessen as he continued considering her reasons for attending the masquerade.

She could be here to marry a title, as other Americans had crossed the Atlantic to do. That reason seemed the most obvious and unfortunately did not bring Alex any peace. For if Willa Stratton intended to marry into the aristocracy, then that meant she might legitimize her father's company in their eyes, too. *She* might make connections and new investors that otherwise would have been *his*.

As he remembered her flirting with Lunsford earlier, Alex scowled. He'd been thinking about his potential investors, but she might also try to steal his current investors away.

Yet beyond these two very real possibilities, the last reason he considered was the one which concerned him the most. She could be here for the Madonna dye. And if that were the case, then he must take care to discover what she knew before the night was over, before she slipped away. The only thought that offered any consolation was that if she'd had anything to do with Woolstone's disappearance, she wouldn't need to be here at the masquerade. Perhaps she'd come here looking for the dye's creator instead. Perhaps she—

Lunsford's fingers snapped in front of his vision.

He looked to his friend, who stared at him quietly, expectantly. Alex winced. "Apologies. You were speaking, weren't you?"

Lunsford waved a hand. "Oh, only for the past five minutes or so. And you were thinking of the Lady in Diamonds, were you not?"

Alex nodded. Indeed, he was. Or rather, the woman on his mind certainly wore enough diamonds to display her ill-begotten wealth for all to see, but she wasn't a lady at all. She was a miss. With the proper adjective, she was Miss Willa *bloody* Stratton, and no matter the reason why she'd come to London, this time he'd be damned if he let her get in his way.

This was the last waltz of the evening, the midnight waltz, and for the moment Willa Stratton was his again. Alex thought about shoving her away.

She shouldn't have felt so perfect in his arms, shouldn't have come to just the right height to put the top of her head at his shoulder. When she looked up at him, the light from the chandeliers above reflected in the blue of her eyes. If she were another woman, whom he actually *admired*, he would need to lower his head only a few degrees in order to touch his mouth to hers . . .

"You needn't continue pretending," she said. "I know who you are."

He stumbled, his foot landing on the hem of her dress and nearly sending both of them crashing to the floor.

But he successfully righted them again—her fingers digging into his shoulder and hand rather unnecessarily, he thought—and met her narrowed eyes. No, her *glaring* eyes.

"Why did you send the flowers?" she hissed.

For the first time ever in their brief acquaintance, Alex considered the possibility that Willa Stratton might be a bit mad. Usually a woman was pleased to receive flowers. They made her happy; it was a flattering gesture, as if comparing a woman's appearance to that of the beautiful specimen she received.

But Willa was obviously neither happy nor flattered as he'd intended so that she would remain unguarded. He might have believed she'd become offended at the bedraggled state of the begonia, but the obvious answer presented itself immediately: *Jo.*

Jo had told her who he was.

Though he wasn't certain why she would, unless she did it only to aggravate him. It wouldn't be the first time tonight she'd taken pleasure in being contrary.

"I asked you a question, *Mr. Midnight*," Willa said, her voice smothering his alias with equal parts mockery and disdain.

Alex patted his mouth as he feigned a yawn.

"Hmm. If you are correct in having uncovered my identity, my *Lady in Diamonds*"—he could inflect his voice with arrogance and condescension, too—"then I must say that I'm entirely surprised to find that *you* are the one angry with *me*."

"You gave me flowers when you know that they make me ill."

"I know no such thing."

"I told you in Italy." *Ah. It hadn't been Jo, after all.* "I'm sure you remember, because you—"

"I know it's rude to correct a woman's assumptions, but I can promise you that I remember nothing. Your words are not such pearls that I collect each and every one as treasured mementos. However, I'm sorry if the begonia made you ill."

She glared at him. "No, you're not."

Alex allowed a slow, wide smile to spread over his face. "No, I am not."

She tried to tug her hand away from his, but he held it firm as they continued dancing. "It's a shame that we have to remove our masks in a moment," she said, "for I don't believe I'll like you very much then."

"Oh? I was under the impression that you didn't like me very much now."

Her lips tightly pressed together. "How very true."

"It's just as well, I suppose, for I don't like you, either." And then, because he couldn't resist besting her: "In fact, I happen to dislike you far more than you dislike me."

She sniffed, and it somehow turned her entire expression into one of haughty boredom. "I believe the word you're searching for is *despise*, Mr. Midnight. You *despise* me."

Alex stared. "Surely you didn't just correct the wording of my insult."

Her teeth flashed, white and gleaming, before she returned to her unwavering glare. "Shall I repeat it?"

"No, I can say it for myself. I *despise* you, dearest Lady in Diamonds."

Willa refused to be the first to look away. A minute or more passed. Neither spoke, and damn him, he didn't look away, either. As the musicians continued playing the third waltz and Alex led her about the ballroom floor, Willa had nothing to do but to memorize the color of his irises: a mahogany with depths, not so dark as to be indistinguishable from his pupils, but dark enough that the longer she gazed into them, the more she felt as if she was seeing a shadow of a shadow. She stared so long she became certain that after this evening she would never forget their color again.

How could he have known first? She'd even begun to convince herself that she'd imagined the familiarity, to believe she had simply *wanted* to know him better. "How did you know it was me?" she asked. "We haven't seen each other in three years."

"Ah, but how could I forget you, my Lady Diamonds?" He shook his head and smiled. "Or should I say—my Lady Rival?" The waltz was ending. *One-two-three. One-two-three.*

She laughed, tilting her head back as if he'd said something far too amusing for her mirth to be contained. When she finished and lowered her chin, he was staring at her with his jaw locked, his eyes fixed on her lips.

She smiled. The same trick had worked on him in Italy, too.

Notes were drawn out, a long conclusion to the piece.

As soon as the last note died they broke apart. The ballroom became hushed with expectation. Lady Winstead stepped onto the ballroom floor. Above, on the landing, a servant rang a gong. "It is midnight, dear ladies and gentlemen," she announced. "You may now remove your masks!"

They each hesitated, knowing that the person to remove his or her mask first would be the first to become vulnerable.

"Well?" he said after a moment. "Do you intend to run away, or are you going to take the mask off?"

"I never run away. I always have a strategy. Perhaps if you hadn't underestimated me in Italy you wouldn't have lost Contarini to me."

She smirked; he scowled. Around them, all of the other guests were removing their masks. There was much laughter and glee.

Willa tilted her head. "However, if you're afraid to go first—"

"Of course not. I was merely trying to be polite by giving preference to the person of the lesser sex."

"You mean fairer."

"Hmm?"

"The fairer sex."

He smiled indulgently. "Of course I did. My mistake." He lifted his hands to his head. "I can see you are breathless to look upon me again. And since you insist—never say I lose my manners when forced to be near you—" He drew the mask away and bowed. "Here I am, at last."

Chapter 5

When he straightened, Willa's heart gave a hard thump in her chest. Yes, he was there. It was him. Alex Laurie.

He might be her rival, but he was still one of the most beautiful men she'd ever met.

Beautiful?

Yes, beautiful. Masculine beauty carved into his cheekbones, chiseled into his jaw. His nose was the slightest bit crooked, as though he'd broken it once or twice, and his forehead was high. His was a face of resolve, of ruthless purpose hidden behind that casual smile. . . . He wore his own masks of expression, his civility and charm a disguise for the strength of his desires and determination. One woman might have called him handsome, another rugged, and yet another as ordinary as a solid oak tree. But to Willa he was beautiful. She wanted to put her hands to his jaw, to run her palms across every plane and hollow, to smooth her thumbs over his eyebrows.

Instead she lifted her hands to her head to untie her mask, too.

But before she could begin, he frowned and made a little swirl with his finger in the air. "Your hair— Do you need—"

"No, it's only an illusion." Reaching beneath the intricate coiffure, Willa found the ends of the mask's ribbons and untied them. She drew them forward, already feeling the weight of the gold and diamond mask lift from her skin. "Here I am, at last," she announced, the words and the curtsy she then gave a deliberate echo of his own unmasking.

His brow lifted. "I expected you to look older. Is deception not supposed to age a person's appearance?" Though he drawled the words, his gaze was piercing enough to poke tiny holes all along her skin.

"I suppose I shall need more practice, although a kiss does not seem very deceptive to me. A kiss, for any length or manner, is only a kiss, isn't it?" She raised her mask again, peered at him through the space carved for her eyes. He plucked the mask away. The ribbons dangled from his fingertips, as precarious as her careful facade of nonchalance.

Willa let her gaze drift. She smiled, pretending to see someone beyond his shoulder she recognized. Looking up at him again, she shrugged. "It was business, Laurie. Nothing but business. You mustn't take it personally."

He stared at her without responding, swinging her mask to and fro by its ribbons. Willa waited, her heart pounding. She could walk away now—he did not block her; she could easily escape from here, in the middle of this large and crowded ballroom. Even if he pulled her deep into the shadows of the massive pillars or against the wall—even if he dragged her out to the terrace—there would always be others to see them. Because of this she stayed, her breath fractured as she watched him watching her. She would never run from him.

After another full minute of his silence she sighed loudly, darting a glance at him through her eyelashes. Yes, he still appeared as if he'd like to strangle her. The musicians were preparing for another set. "I'd like to thank you for the waltzes and for the pleasurable company, Mr. Laurie. Unfortunately, now that your identity is revealed, I must be away. There are other, more important matters I must attend to while I am in London."

When she walked toward the perimeter of the ballroom, he took her hand and placed it on his arm. They strolled together, her fingers captive beneath his hold. Only she realized too late that he was steadfastly guiding her toward the shadows which clung to the far corner of the ballroom, partially hidden by one of those massive pillars. Yes, others would be able to see them if they peered closely enough. But no one was looking. No one at all.

He stood in front of her, his shoulders eclipsing her view of the room. "I am well aware of the matters you think you seek. I am also aware that you will not find them."

"You seem very certain of this. I would caution your habit toward overconfidence. It did not serve you well in Italy, either." She would not be intimidated, though he leaned his body near hers. And he knew this; he knew she was not scared of him, just as she knew he was the type to use ruthlessness with words rather than fists. It was this understanding that caused her pulse to flutter, for there could be only one reason why he stood so near. It was the same reason why she'd decided to kiss him in Italy, when never before and never since had she used such a tactic to get what she wished. "I have been searching for matters long before you ever were, Mr. Laurie. I daresay I know much more about such matters than you do."

"I know the name," he said, then narrowed his eyes when she stilled. "I see that you know it, too."

She shifted, trying to see past him, irritated that she gave so much away. If he was here at the masquerade and he knew Woolstone was the dye's creator, could that mean—

"He's not here."

Her gaze lifted to his again, though not before taking a contrary detour to his mouth first. "I do not understand your presence at the masquerade. Is it truly because you wish to marry your sisters to titles? I did not think you were so fond of the aristocracy."

His lips curled. "I hesitate to admit or deny lest you run back to Papa and tell him my plans."

Willa felt her cheeks burn. True, most everything she'd done in the past seven years had been on behalf of her father and his company, but she was here in London for herself. Luring Mr. Lunsford to her father's company was the agreement she'd made in order to delay the wedding to Eichel. It was of no concern to her if she actually succeeded. No, she was here for the Madonna dye. And this time, the competition was between Willa and Alex alone.

"There you go underestimating me again, Mr. Laurie," she said softly. "I sincerely hoped you had learned from the last time. My father does not control everything I do. And you need not fear having me as competition, for I have no desire to become a pawn in marriage for my father's alliances." If she did, she would have been happy to take Eichel, for he was young and rich and handsome, more so even than the man standing before her.

He placed his hands on either side of shoulders, bracketing her inside his arms with her back pressing into the corner. When he spoke, his breath stirred the curls at her temples and ears. "I truly don't care, actually. There's only one thing that matters to me that you should know."

For a moment before he pulled back her breath lodged in her throat. "And what is that?"

His eyes bore into hers, his lips mere inches away from her own. "I will finish what was begun in Italy. *I* am the one who will win this time, Miss Stratton."

Chapter 6

The next day, Willa smiled across at her English companion, the lovely widow Lady Sarah Carlyle, as the carriage borrowed from Mivart's Hotel stopped in front of the Marquess of Byrne's house, the residence where Lady Marianna, Woolstone's sister, lived with her parents.

"Like this?" she asked Sarah, speaking through her teeth.

Sarah leaned forward slightly, a line creased between her brows. "No, I'm afraid that's still too much. I can see nearly the entire upper row of teeth. Try to become more subdued."

Willa rolled her lips inward.

Sarah laughed. "No, that's not it at all, I'm afraid. Here, cease smiling. No, don't frown. Try a natural expression, as if you were by yourself and hadn't a care in the world. Yes, very good. Now, think of something only slightly amusing. It's a secret you want to keep to yourself, not to share with others. But all the same you wish them to *know* that you have a slightly amusing secret that you couldn't possibly share with them, and—yes, that's it!"

Willa let the smile freeze on her lips as she memorized the shape and feel of it. Then she sighed. "It's no wonder I haven't come to England in so many years, and no wonder you left all that time ago. I never realized the English cared so much about their smiles." The voice of the coachman soothing the horses to a standstill came as the carriage ceased moving. Willa's smile turned sly. "Of course, after seeing so many people laughing at the masquerade last night, I can well understand the desire to keep their teeth covered when possible."

She grinned at Sarah's choked gasp of laughter. The footman opened the door.

"Willa—"

"No need to fear, I will behave myself with an immense amount of decorum. And I promise to not show my teeth—not even once." Taking the servant's hand, she stepped out of the carriage. She threw cursory glances at the imposing Byrne town house and the black carriage sitting on the street near their own, then looked back toward Sarah. "I neglected to ask. Is Lady Marianna Woolstone's younger sister or older?"

"What does it matter?" Sarah walked toward her as the footman closed the carriage door. Out of the corner of her eye, she saw the door of the other carriage open.

"It may indicate how protective she wishes to be, how much information she cares to give us." After Willa's mother had died when she was fourteen, she'd become both mother and sister to her younger brother, Jeffrey. Even though he was a grown man now, she would never cease worrying about him.

"I believe she's younger."

Willa nodded. "Good. That means—"

A voice at the other carriage stilled her thoughts. Willa's head turned, her gaze searching . . .

She scowled. Or rather, on the inside she scowled. On her face she wore that slight, secretly amusing smile Sarah had taught her as she met Alex Laurie's eyes.

He nodded a wary greeting. Willa turned. "Come," she whispered urgently, then proceeded to rush toward the Byrne town house's door.

She could have cursed. Somehow he must have devised the same ingenious plan: get close to Woolstone's sister to discover if she knew of his whereabouts.

Sarah's skirts rustled behind her as Willa climbed the steps. "Why are we— Oh, good afternoon, sir."

"Good afternoon, madam." He bounded up the steps beside Willa, cutting her off at the door. "Miss Stratton."

Willa drew herself up instantly to avoid crashing into him yet again. He thought himself very clever;

she was certain his eyes laughed at her before he turned his back to her. Though she nearly teetered off the edge of the top step, she managed to draw her skirts close to her legs and edge beside him. Her shoulder brushed his arm. "I believe we arrived first, Mr. Laurie. Kindly move out of the way."

"I would of course concede if you were correct, Miss Stratton, but you are wrong. My carriage arrived before yours."

Sarah poked Willa's arm. When she glanced over her shoulder, her friend's brows were lifted inquiringly.

"Oh yes. Lady Carlyle, allow me to present to you the back of Mr. Alex Laurie."

"I apologize for my rudeness, Lady Carlyle. It is not my habit to be offensive."

"You do not have to forgive him. This is, of course, the one I told you of before."

"Spreading lies about me again, madam? How very unoriginal of you."

Willa almost laughed. He thought she'd told *lies* about him to Contarini?

"On the contrary, I find lies wholly unnecessary. And please be assured that I will tell you if I ever feel the need to court your opinion of my actions."

He said something beneath his breath which she couldn't hear. She would have been tempted to ask him to repeat it louder, if she didn't believe he did it for the sole purpose of irritating her.

She sensed Sarah's quiet assessment of him as

Willa knew he must appear to her: the breadth of his shoulders, the jaunty tip of his hat, the fine tapering of his waist and legs. She didn't wish for her companion to be undone by his appeal; it would not do to have her friend enamored of her enemy.

Though she professed to speak of him to Sarah, she hadn't told her companion much of anything regarding Alex Laurie. She knew that they were rivals, of course, and that he was also after the Madonna dye, but Sarah didn't know about their dancing the previous evening, as her services as chaperone had not been required at the masquerade. And she knew nothing about their kiss three years ago. Some things must be kept a secret from everyone.

Willa shifted. It seemed to be taking an inordinate amount of time for a servant to come to the door and allow them entrance.

Beside her, Alex raised his fist. As if they shared the same thoughts. It was an infinitely disturbing thing to contemplate.

"If we are to go in by order of our rank, then I believe Lady Carlyle should stand before us both."

He paused, his head turning toward her. "Why must we go in according to our rank?"

"Because it's the custom that is expected and usually observed among the *ton*." And because she hoped Sarah would be able to ask Lady Marianna about Woolstone's location before Alex ever had a chance to speak to her. "Is that not true, Lady Carlyle? Would you care to educate Mr. Laurie on the matters of precedence?"

Behind them, Sarah cleared her throat. "The usual precedence is—"

He leaned toward Willa, his words overlapping Sarah's. "I know what precedence is. And I find it odd that you are ordering around a lady if you are so bloody concerned about it."

Willa lifted her chin. "She is my hired companion." She paused, because Sarah had remained with her for far too long to be thought of as a mere companion. "As well as a dear friend. And in truth, I wished for her to go before us because I would have a private word with you before we enter."

His eyes narrowed. He saw her attempt at distraction, and yet he was intrigued. It was altogether dizzying, how well she could read him at times and yet how he remained an opaque mystery to her at others.

"Please," she added. More of a perfunctory request than a pleading. Her tone the same as if she'd just needlessly attached the word to the end of a command addressed to a servant. He tried to hide it, but still she saw the slight curl at the corners of his mouth.

"Very well," he said, then retreated down the steps and gestured for Sarah to replace him at the door. Willa followed, then turned toward him. He imitated her movement. They stood facing each other, no more than a foot apart. "Yes?" he asked, his voice lowered. "What is it you wished to say?"

At last the door opened. They both watched Sarah disappear inside. It remained ajar, the footman waiting for their entrance.

More time was needed for Sarah to speak with Lady Marianna. Willa took a deep breath. She made her voice soft. "I'm sorry. For the kiss."

All traces of a smile disappeared from his face. "You admit now that you were the one who kissed me?"

Such arrogance. As if his lips had not been involved, as if his tongue had not courted hers. "No, I admit no such thing. I am only sorry that it happened. I hope there will be no repeating of the occurrence this time." Then, simply because she knew it would aggravate him to no end, she said, "I might need to save every kiss for Woolstone when we meet."

His expression hardened and he stepped closer. Six inches away. "Leave England. Go anywhere else to increase your family's fortune. Snare all the investors you like. Better yet, return to America and stay there forever."

Willa inhaled deeply again, this time at his nearness. Of course he would try to give himself the advantage by dressing as he did in his tan trousers and jacket, the color of which only emphasized the dark brown warmth of his eyes. The cut of his clothes showed off his broad shoulders, the leanness of his hips, the muscular length of his legs. He knew his appeal to the fairer sex, and he used it well.

Lifting her lashes, she realized her mistake when she found him watching her. She'd done what she said she wouldn't; she'd been caught ogling him. When Alex's eyes narrowed and his gaze began to fall below her face, Willa crossed her arms over her chest.

"I must admit that I would like more than anything to return to America and never see you again," she said, then nearly shook her head. She'd become quite the proficient liar since Italy. Not only did she have no intention of ever returning to America; she hadn't felt so alive since he'd kissed her. "But I think it will be difficult at first, especially since your sister has invited me to her dinner party on Thursday."

His attention snapped upward. His mouth opened—

"Yes, Jo invited me to Holcombe House last night when we were at the Winstead masquerade."

"I assume you coerced her somehow."

"Actually, there was no need to coerce her."

"She knows who you are." He'd made sure of it on the return home in the carriage. They'd also discussed her attempts to sabotage the evening.

"Of course she knows who I am. We're friends."

His brows slashed downward. "You're not friends."

"We are. I call her Jo; she calls me Willa. We laugh together, talk together, and get along merrily."

"Ah." He rocked back on his heels, smirking. "I would have believed you if you'd omitted the parts about 'laughing' and 'merrily.'"

"It might have been an exaggeration," Willa acknowledged. "She does smile quite a bit, though."

Alex's mouth thinned. "You're not coming to the dinner party. You don't have a written invitation."

Willa smiled her secretly amused smile. "See you tomorrow evening," she said as she climbed up the steps, her voice full of cheer.

As she was magnanimous, she forgave him for the grumbling curse he sent after her as he followed her into the Byrne town house.

Alex strode up the steps to Holcombe House, his jaw clenched. Nothing beyond an introduction to Lady Marianna had been accomplished today. And although it seemed Willa hadn't fared any better in soliciting information from Woolstone's sister, either, he'd seen her gaze light with suspicion when Lady Marianna greeted Alex. When she mentioned how she looked forward to visiting Holcombe House for the dinner party.

He startled when the door was opened before him; he still hadn't become accustomed to the servants' presence.

Handing his hat to Tribbley, he asked: "Where is Jo?" He didn't feel much in the mood for long-winded, effusive sentences. He was presently maintaining the barest control on his temper; in only those three words spoken aloud, he internally inserted a string of ten epithets.

Tribbley brushed away a speck of dirt from his hat. "I believe she's in the sitting room with the others, sir. Miss Ross is here."

"Thank you." Spinning on his heel, Alex ran up the stairs to the first floor, then shoved the door wide open as he entered the sitting room.

"Alex!"

"Alex!"

"Alex!"

His three youngest siblings scrambled from where they'd been sitting cross-legged on the floor like the little heathens they were and rushed him. Laughing, Alex swept David and Victoria into his arms, grunting with the weight of the nine-year-old boy and cursing inwardly when five-year-old Victoria accidentally kicked his groin.

"Hullo to you, too, rascals." Setting them down, he strode forward to Philippa, who was waiting nearby. Crouching at her level, he reached up and mussed her carefully plaited hair. "There. You look much better—more like my sister, at any rate."

Pippa grinned a gap-toothed smile, her sightless eyes fixed somewhere near his ear. "You would be very proud of me, I think. I haven't yet once today screamed at Miss Ross."

"That is a vast improvement. I'm certain she appreciates your restraint." Taking her hand—he and Tor were the only ones she allowed to do so—he led her forward to the middle of the collection of chairs and settees.

"Good afternoon, Miss Ross," he said, nodding to their dialect tutor.

"Mr. Laurie." She glanced away, a hint of pink rising to her cheeks.

To her left, his mother sat with Anne and Kat. She frowned at him. But he hadn't come here for today's speaking lesson; no, he had come to find the very annoying and contrary older sister seated to Miss Ross' right.

He released Pippa's hand as she sat with David and Tor, then stepped forward to stand in front of Jo. "Come."

Her brows rose first, arching higher and higher until they reached the appropriate height of disbelief. Then her chin lifted, and she stared at him. "Did you just order me to your side like a dog?"

Miss Ross cleared her dainty, ladylike throat.

"I'm certain a dog would be far more obedient. Now, Jo."

Heaving a great beleaguered sigh, she rose and swept ahead of him out of the room.

He bowed to the rest of his family and Miss Ross. "I beg your pardon. Please excuse us."

On the floor, the children giggled.

Jo waited for him outside the door with her arms crossed, the fingers of one hand drumming on the opposite forearm. "You do know we're the ones who need to be in there most of all? Unless, of course, you've given up this ridiculous plan to secure a lofty and aristocratic spouse for each of us."

"I wish you to rescind the invitation to Miss Stratton."

"Who?"

Alex curled his hand. Inside his fist, he held the last remaining shred of his patience. He squeezed it tightly. "Miss Willa Stratton, the woman with the diamond mask that you met at the Winstead masquerade ball. Do you remember her? Perhaps she was lying and you didn't invite her to the dinner party."

Jo waved her hand with a sly smile. "Of course I remember her. No, I invited Miss Stratton. I liked her very much, actually. And I had assumed that you did as well. You did dance with her three times, didn't you?"

He glared. "I want you to rescind your invitation. Immediately."

"Rubbed on your nerves, did she?"

"She's Willa *Stratton*."

"Willa *Stratton*? Why didn't you say so?"

"She's trying to compete with us."

"With us, or with you?"

"God, Jo, do you have to question everything I say? Can't you—just once—do as I ask without questioning my decisions?"

The spark in his sister's eyes dimmed. "Miss Ross wouldn't be very pleased to hear you speak in such a manner, my dear fellow," she said, in English more perfect than even the aristocrats could speak.

Alex narrowed his eyes.

"But yes, I'll do as you say. Thank you for asking so nicely. Now, if you are feeling generous toward me at the moment because I acquiesced so easily—"

Jo had never done anything *easily*.

"—then I'd like to renew the discussion of the accounts. Where did you hide them?"

Alex frowned. "Tribbley told me you were up in

the middle of the night searching again. We've already spoken about this. Ladies who marry a titled nobleman do not review ledgers."

"If I ever do marry—which I'm not sure I will, and I hope to God it's not to one of your pansy-faced nobs—I would hope that he'd be happy to allow me to look over his estate books. I'm sure I'd have much more of a talent for it than he or anyone else would."

A grizzled, gray-haired old man, his skin as tough as leather, spun his grown daughter around the room. "That's my girl, Jo! What would I do without you? Alex, Jo thinks if we can find only eleven more investors with a thousand pounds each—"

Alex shook his head. "Father wouldn't have wanted you to continue taking care of the accounts this long, Jo."

It was the excuse he gave her, though not the true reason. Like his mother's mourning veil, the accounts were his sister's monument to their father. She intended to grieve for him for years, perhaps decades. She would give up the rest of her life to remain close to the things he had loved.

Her chin lifted. "He trusted me. I took care of them before he died. Before you returned from your last trip. When you weren't here." She struck low, but blindly. Unfortunate that her anger was accurate. He didn't allow anyone to see that he, too, continued grieving. It was more difficult than he'd thought, to know his father was dead only by his prolonged absence. To not have said his farewell, to not have seen him stilled, without breath.

"Where are the ledgers, Alex?"

"I've assigned them to someone else."

Her mouth tightened, and not for the first time since he was nine and she was ten, Alex was grateful for the advantage of his height. She was petite, her head coming only to the center of his chest, and it was difficult to be intimidated by a slip of a woman that he could most likely carry under his arm if he wished.

"We should return to Miss Ross' lesson," she said. "Your accent has slipped a few times just in the last several minutes."

"We are agreed that you will rescind Miss Stratton's invitation?"

"Yes." Jo turned away and opened the door. "But I will find the ledgers," she vowed. "That we have *not* agreed upon."

Willa took the hand of the servant and stepped down from the Mivart carriage. Sarah soon followed, and together they stared up at Holcombe House, the current Belgrave Square residence of the Laurie family.

"Well," Willa said. "It's beyond me why he's still so upset about the incident in Italy. He's obviously very wealthy even without Contarini as an investor."

Sarah studied the Holcombe mansion—for truly, the term was far more apt than "house." "They've improved it since Holcombe died," she said. "Or at least, had someone clean all the windows of cobwebs and scrubbed the dirt from the exterior. New servants, perhaps?"

"Perhaps." Or, more likely, a new master who refused to let anything stand in his way, including a layer of grime and attitudes of carelessness.

As they climbed up the steps, Willa murmured to Sarah, "I'm not quite sure of the reception I'll receive. If he threatens to throw me bodily out the nearest window, I trust that you'll be able to make it back to the hotel by yourself?"

"If he throws you bodily out the window," Sarah replied, "I will be returning to my home, not the hotel."

"Very well, then. You must do as you will—I only ask that you remember me kindly. None of that nonsense about forcing you to take strolls with me in the park at ungodly hours." Willa peeked toward both sides of the doorstep and was very relieved to find bushes beneath the windows. And they didn't appear very prickly. Her gaze lifted. But, of course, if one were thrown from the drawing room upstairs, the bushes weren't likely to cushion a fall very well. She had no doubts that Alex would be furious that she'd come, even after she received a note from Jo rescinding her previous invitation. But he was a fool if he believed she would let him alone with Lady Marianna for a few hours.

The door opened at their arrival. A handsome, dark-haired footman welcomed them inside. "If you will follow me, I will escort you to the drawing room, where the butler will announce you."

Willa exchanged glances with Sarah. She might have been correct about new servants, after all. This one sounded as if he were reciting lines.

The sweep of the staircase led them in a semicircle from the ground floor to the first, and as they climbed, their view wended around the grand marble-checkered entrance and the painted dome above.

Good heavens. She'd always believed her family to be wealthy, but this residence was twice as grand as her father's house. As they reached the first floor and followed the footman toward the drawing room, Willa said to Sarah, "You remember what we discussed in the carriage?"

Sarah nodded. "Keep Mr. Laurie distracted as much as possible. I will attempt to bear the burden well."

During their return to the hotel following the call on Lady Marianna, Sarah had spent the entire time commenting about something or other Alex had done at the Byrne town house. Her questions concerning him had been endless, too. It was not something one would wish for in a friend or companion, this interest she took in Willa's enemy. "I have the greatest amount of faith in you," Willa chirped, then smiled at the butler as the footman stopped at the drawing room.

"Good evening," he said, bowing. "May I have your invitation?"

"I could tell you our names," Willa offered, giving

him the twinkling grin that once worked wonders on her father.

Unfortunately, the Laurie butler merely stared at her. "My apologies, but I must have an invitation."

The door was open beyond him. She could hear the conversations of the other guests, see men and women milling about the room. "Lady Carlyle," she said, turning to her companion. "You have it in your reticule, don't you?"

It took Sarah a moment to catch on. Willa stretched her smile wider for emphasis. "Ah. Yes," she agreed. "Yes, I believe I have it—just one moment . . ."

With the butler focused on Sarah while she dug through her reticule for the imaginary invitation, Willa rushed past him into the room.

"Miss!" he hissed after her. "You cannot—" She heard his feet stutter to a halt behind her.

Willa beamed across the room at Jo, then scanned the crowd currently staring at her. She was looking for . . . searching for . . .

Ah, yes. There he was. Glower and all.

She hadn't thought it possible for her smile to stretch any wider, and yet it did.

"Miss," the butler, dutiful servant that he was, tried again. "You can't be here without an invitation."

Twisting to look at him, she said, "But Mr. Laurie extended an invitation to me at the Fontenots' a few days past. I'm afraid I don't have an invitation to provide to you, but I'm certain he will vouch for me."

She glanced at Alex. "Mr. Laurie?"

His eyes spoke of dark, murderous things. Nevertheless, a roomful of guests stood between them, people who were watching and waiting on every word to see if the Laurie dinner party would provide excitement in their otherwise dreary lives and give them gossip for the next day. *Evicting someone from the dinner party? How thrilling. And how appropriately wild of Mr. Alexander Laurie, the head of the middle-class upstart Laurie family.*

Alex extricated himself from the group of guests he'd been standing among and strolled toward her. *No, better yet to dull the moment and avoid such rumors.* "She's correct, Tribbley," he said to the butler. "Miss Stratton came at my invitation."

"And Lady Carlyle," Willa said happily, watching the knot form as he clenched his jaw.

His gaze skipped beyond her shoulder. "And Lady Carlyle," he said more softly, then returned his attention to her abruptly.

"Ahem. Lady Carlyle and Miss Stratton," the butler announced belatedly with a bow, then backed out of the doorway.

A loud silence followed as the other guests seemed willing to wait for the expected drama to unfold, but when Jo moved to greet Willa and Sarah, they all returned to their discussions and jests.

Alex merely continued to glower at Willa as his sister stepped forward.

"Miss Stratton. Lady Carlyle." Jo smiled. "Welcome to Holcombe House. We're so glad you could come."

"I thought you said you would rescind the invitation," Alex muttered to his sister, still glaring at Willa.

Jo laid a hand on his upper arm. "How charming he is—don't you agree? Please, allow me to introduce you to the others."

"Would you mind accompanying Lady Carlyle?" Willa asked Alex as she moved past to walk beside Jo. "Thank you."

Jo motioned to a balding man with spectacles standing near the hearth. "Have you met Mr. Soward, the heir to the Caldwell-Black baron or some such gibberish? No? Come, I'd be happy to introduce you. He has a terrific lisp. But bite your tongue when you hear it—it wouldn't do to offend him by laughing."

Something—or rather, someone—caught at Willa's sleeve. Then a strong masculine grip tugged her to a stop and caught her hand, placing it over his arm. "Jo, why don't you introduce Lady Carlyle to Mr. Soward?" he suggested. "Miss Stratton and I will move about the room in the other direction. We have matters to discuss."

Willa's heart sped as Alex looked down at her, his dark brown eyes narrowed with menace.

And so the battle begins.

Chapter 7

Alex could feel Willa's curious stare as he steered her away from the more populated side of the drawing room and from the people he didn't want her speaking with. Her hand lifted from his arm and she tried to escape, but he ever so gently—insistently—tugged it back down.

"Do not think for a moment that I mean to release you upon my guests. You are like a wild animal—you will devour the men with your charm and leave them bewildered when you flit to the next one. You have come against my wishes, Miss Stratton, and we will both pay the penance for it."

"And what penance would that be, Mr. Laurie?"

He looked down at her. "You will not leave my side all evening." He paused, noting how his arm heated everywhere she touched it, from the light placement of her hand over his to the press of her forearm on top of his forearm. Alex sighed. "It does seem to be rather more of a punishment for me, though."

"Oh, come now, Mr. Laurie. We both know what pleasant company I can be. Would you like me to flatter you? Let's see, what shall we begin with?"

"I'd rather you didn't. In fact, have you never heard that silence is most pleasing on a man's ears?"

She tapped her chin with her free hand, her gaze assessing as she studied his face. Frowning, she said, "I admit, flattering you does seem to be rather difficult. I usually try to find something which is honestly appealing and simply extrapolate upon its fine qualities. Hmm. No, I can't find anything. My apologies." She shrugged.

Alex grinned. "You're lying," he said.

"I beg your pardon?"

"You are lying, Miss Stratton. It's plain to see that you find everything appealing about me and are simply at a loss as to where to begin. It's why you decided to come to the dinner party, is it not?"

"If I were to lie to you, Mr. Laurie, then I would do so by telling you how very nice your chin is."

"My chin?"

"Again, please note that I am lying. Not the best sort of flattery. You're the second man whose chin I've complimented recently, and a chin is always the last resort for a compliment."

"You can't even try to be original in your flattery? I am offended, Miss Stratton."

"One should only hope," she muttered, so low he wasn't sure if she'd intended for him to hear it or not. He glanced at her sharply, then nodded at Lady Penelope and her sister, Lady Amelia. They were daughters of the Earl of Pennock, if he recalled correctly. Each equally suitable as a potential bride. Both ladies smiled as he passed, then giggled.

"Ohhh," Willa breathed, twisting her neck to glance back at them. "I believe they *like* you, Mr. Laurie."

"It's my chin. As you pointed out, it is very fine."

"Yes, so it is. Masculine and firm. I wish I could touch it."

Alex choked on air. "Now, that, Miss Stratton, is by far the worst proposition I have ever received. Did you say that to the other man, too?"

Something in her gaze changed, a new sort of smile tugging at her lips. For a moment Alex thought it might have been a seductive expression, but then . . . No, it was a smirk. "I must confess I didn't. Only your chin seems to hold me so enthralled. But should you like me to proposition you, Mr. Laurie?"

"Isn't that what you were attempting to do in Italy when you stole Contarini away from me?"

They both knew it was unfair. Alex might have cared had her skirts not just brushed against his legs while they walked. For a moment he was tempted to pivot abruptly so that she was forced to lean into him. Instead he took a deep breath and extended his elbow from his side to keep her at a greater distance, all the while calling himself a fool. It hadn't even been an involuntary caress of her fingers against his sleeve, or the curve of her breast brushing against his arm. It was her *skirts*, for God's sake.

Of course, he should have known she wouldn't let the comment lie. "Oh, I stole him now? I thought I merely distracted you with a kiss. My evilness surely knows no bounds."

"It's because you're half American. I don't blame you entirely, for it's part of your nature, something which I understand you can't control."

"Such insults and accusations!" She was all charm and airy flirtation in contrast to his dark bitterness. He resented her even more for it. "Perhaps you're angry because I never properly thanked you for the kiss and your role in my success with Contarini? My apologies, Mr. Laurie. And thank you."

He glared down at her. "I should dearly like to— Good evening, Lord Dutton, Lady Dutton." Alex's expression became placid as the couple stopped to greet them. If he had been paying attention, he would have seen their approach and could have well avoided their path. But he was focused on Willa and her damnable skirts and that damnable kiss, which had left her forever imprinted on his memory. "I don't believe I mentioned, my lady, how exceedingly lovely you look tonight. Lord Dutton—"

"You appear lovely as well," Willa interjected, smiling.

Lord Dutton chuckled and patted his wife's hand.

"Thank you, my dear," he said to Willa, then looked at Alex.

He could sense Willa beside him, waiting expectantly. He did not want to introduce her to one of his potential investors. Even though she was firmly attached to his side, he could not hide the bright curve of her smile or the intelligence in her eyes, her most useful instruments of persuasion.

Lady Dutton raised a brow. "Would you mind introducing us to your guest, Mr. Laurie?"

Alex swallowed a curse and attempted to appear affable instead of tormented as he stood beside his rival. "Lord and Lady Dutton, may I present to you Miss Willa Stratton?"

"Oh, you're the American girl," Lord Dutton said, pleased with himself.

Alex feared the man's vision was irrevocably impaired. Willa Stratton was obviously a woman, with a woman's breasts and a woman's backside. Or perhaps he simply hadn't studied her as closely as Alex had, taking time to imagine the lines of her shape beneath the restrictions of her corset, crinoline, and skirts. Alex also had the advantage of having once had her pressed up against him, her breasts full against his chest, her arms linked behind his neck—a man could go mad comparing the memory of how she felt to the mystery hidden beneath her gowns.

Willa smiled, seeming happy to hear that Dutton knew of her. Alex smiled and pretended to be happy, too, as she replied, "It's true I've lived in America since the age of eight, my lord, but I was born in England. Here in London, in fact."

"You're Daniel Stratton's daughter, aren't you?" Lord Dutton continued. "I've heard about his successes from Lord Kilbourne—"

"I believe Miss Stratton has returned to England to find a husband," Alex said smoothly. "Another rich heiress come to steal a title for herself." He chuckled as if it were the quaintest thing. There would always be common men like him whose vulgar wealth young ladies of good *ton* could settle for, but there were only a few titled lords for them to fight over first.

Willa's fingers dug into his arm. "Actually, Mr. Laurie—"

"Oh, I didn't realize. Of course you've come to marry." Lady Dutton's previously friendly demeanor shifted as she glanced toward Lunsford, where her daughter Lady Miranda stood enraptured with other young women. When her gaze returned to Willa, she sniffed. "A pleasure to meet you, Miss Stratton. My lord, I believe I see the butler about to hit the dinner gong."

"Miss Stratton. Mr. Laur—" Lady Dutton tugged Lord Dutton abruptly away before he could finish.

Willa turned toward Alex as they marched off. "That wasn't very nice," she said, brows lowered. "I haven't come to marry anyone, as well you know."

"And as I said before, it doesn't matter to me what you do. Even though you've come here against my wishes, I will still win."

The dinner gong sounded.

"You shouldn't frown so, Miss Stratton. It makes the wrinkles in your forehead deepen."

Willa gasped as her fingers flew to her face, as if to smooth them out, then scowled and lowered her hand to her side. "I don't like you, Mr. Laurie."

Alex flicked at a speck of dust on his coat sleeve. "This is becoming repetitive. Isn't this the moment when I tell you how much I despise you in return?"

Her eyes glinted. "You were right about me, you know. I did kiss you to distract you from Contarini. But let's put aside the flattery for now, shall we? The kiss was terrible. It nearly made me cast up my accounts. Afterward I had to rinse my mouth with brandy to flush the taste out, and I don't even *like* brandy."

"For once, Miss Stratton, I believe you're actually telling the truth." Alex watched as the guests began to pair up for dinner, Jo as hostess with Lord Dutton first.

"Good." She paused. "You do?"

He nodded. "That kiss has remained in my memory if for no other reason than that it was wholly unpleasant. Such fumbling and awkwardness; I took pity on you to try to teach you better. Hearing you admit that you didn't want to kiss me relieves me now. I should hate to think that your future husband— God bless his eternal soul—might have to endure such a chore once you are married."

Willa opened her mouth. Closed it. Opened. Closed.

Alex smiled to himself. "I see you're trying the silence I suggested earlier. Well done, Miss Stratton. Come, it's time for dinner now."

Willa decided to ignore Alex with the same dedication with which she applied herself to consuming every spoonful of the first course. Not that he tried to make conversation with her, as the discussions of the other guests and the width of table would have made it difficult for them to speak to each other . . . But if he had, she would have given him the cold shoulder. As it was, he sat across the table and talked to the lady on his right, while she focused on the man to her left, Mr. Lunsford.

Fortunately, once she paid attention to him, Lunsford was a much more charming and amusing dinner companion than he'd been a dancing partner.

As the soup was taken away and replaced with the second course—a veal in mustard sauce—Willa turned to him and said, "Mr. Lunsford, you seem to be a very nice man."

"Oh, I am, my dear Miss Stratton. Don't believe anything Lady Althea says." He'd already expressed his dismay during their consumption of the soup that Jo had, without his knowledge, added Thea to his pre-approved list of guests for the evening.

"Very nice," she continued, "which is why I don't understand how you and Mr. Laurie get along as you do. Is it only because you are his investor and the promise of fortune binds you together? Or perhaps you have a charitable heart which recognizes someone in need of your friendship? How do you tolerate him so well?"

Lunsford chuckled. "I believe you are the first woman I've met who hasn't fallen directly in love with Laurie, Miss Stratton. Although I suppose you did leave my company so you could dance with him at the Winstead masquerade."

Willa ignored the foolish reminder of this latter part and scoffed at the former. "First woman not to fall in love with him? Surely not."

"Ah, but 'tis true. You would think that with my superior form and vast charm I would have the advantage—not to mention that I dress much, much better than he does—but while I may attract ladies to my side initially, it is he they clamor for at the end."

"You're also the son of an earl, while he is a no-body," Willa added.

Lunsford waved this away, the light from the candles sparking a reflection off of his fork. "As to your other question, we are friends now, but I was first only an investor in Joseph Laurie's company. Alex and I met in Moscow while I was on holiday—"

"You went to Moscow on holiday?" She'd been twice to Moscow, once in the winter and once in the summer, and both times the weather proved to be unbearably dreadful. She couldn't imagine anyone visiting the city for pleasure.

Lunsford smiled, lowering his gaze as he took a sip of wine. Then he slid her a look from the corner of his eye. "There was a woman."

"Oh." Willa glanced across the table at Alex. She didn't know why she did it; there was no cause to do so at that moment, and yet she did. He was watching her, and when their eyes met, she could no more look away than she could have stopped herself from kissing him in Italy. No, she could well believe Lunsford when he said that all the women became enamored of Alex.

"Yes, there was a woman, and she was in love with me."

Willa dragged her gaze back to Lunsford. "How could she not love you?"

He tipped his head toward her. "Thank you, Miss Stratton. That is a very good question. And yet we went to a dinner party one evening, she met Laurie, and though I managed to steal her back for one dance that night, I could tell that she was lost to me."

"Did you love her?"

One of Lunford's brows winged high. "Love her? No. Why do some women believe it is necessary for a man to love in order to want?" He sighed heavily, casting a glance up the table toward Thea, then returned his attention to Willa. "To shorten the story, Laurie made a bargain with me. He told me that if I would listen to him speak about his dyes and why I should invest in his company, he would return the woman to my arms."

Willa's fork clattered to the table—but not before it rang against the plate first and sent the eyes of those half the table away glancing in her direction.

She calmly picked the fork up again. "You bartered her?"

"Ah. I see you are dismayed, Miss Stratton. Perhaps if I told you how desperately I desired her it would help you feel better?"

"Not very."

"Surely there is something in your life that you've wanted beyond all reason."

Again, with no necessity for doing so, Willa glanced across the table at Alex—this time discreetly, at least, using the pretense of lifting her wineglass in order to covertly observe him. His head was tilted toward the lady at his side, and he was making her laugh.

She returned her attention to Lunsford without saying anything.

Lunsford cut a piece of veal and popped it into his mouth, moaning with delight as he chewed. The sound caught the attention of the lady on his opposite side. "Apologies," Lunsford said, then: "That veal is delicious!"

Turning back to her, he motioned to her plate. "Have you tried the veal?"

"I have, thank you."

"I'd heard Laurie was able to steal the Fenwicks' chef, but until now I didn't believe it was true." He then cut another piece and said, "I think you should marry Laurie."

Willa stared. "I beg your pardon?"

He inclined his head. "Of course, if you must marry at all, then I understand your first choice would be to marry a title, but I must tell you that even though I'm the son of an earl, I'm only the second son. No need to woo me."

"I have no desire to marry you, Mr. Lunsford." She grinned at his expression of feigned injury. "Although if you were the heir, I might change my mind."

"Ah, but he's to announce his betrothal soon to Lady Althea, so that will do you no good."

Surely she'd misheard. "Lady Althea?"

"Unfortunately for my brother, yes. Although I must say, I did try to warn him." Lunsford continued cutting into his veal, as if the subject bored him. "However," he continued a moment later, "I would like to bring your attention to the fact that you are currently in England hoping to make a match among the aristocracy, and my dear fellow Laurie purchased a house in Belgrave Square with an accompanying carriage that—" He shuddered. "Regardless, let us say that he has made great sacrifices with the hope of also marrying into the aristocracy. I assume your hope for marriage is the same as his: to expand his family's . . ." His voice trailed away as he looked across the table.

She didn't correct him about her reasons for being in England. She didn't say anything. Instead, Willa followed his gaze and found Alex giving Lunsford a questioning look. As he noticed Willa's stare, he shifted his focus to her, then looked away.

Lunsford sighed. "As I was saying, Miss Stratton, have you considered merging the two companies through marriage? You would be stronger together than apart, every investor helping the two of you instead of only one."

Willa lifted a brow. "And as a result investors would probably receive more, too."

He smiled. "This is true." Leaning forward, he turned his head and peered up the table. "Yes, there. Sitting three seats away from Lady Althea. Do you see the man with the black hair?"

Willa leaned forward and peered, too. The man sat straight and tall, his black hair thick, his shoulders broad. When he smiled, his teeth formed an even white row. He seemed to suck in the air of those around him, as if his mere presence commanded their attention and their every breath. Odd that she hadn't noticed him when she'd strolled through the drawing room beside Alex earlier.

"Yes, I see him," she said.

"That man is the Earl of Uxbridge, the heir to the Marquess of Byrne. He is the only unmarried lord here at the dinner party tonight. You could marry him and lead a life of dull monotony, plagued by people constantly deferring to your elevated status, with your children one day ruling over Society during their generation."

At the mention of the name Uxbridge, Willa's attention held. Apparently Lady Marianna wasn't the only reason Alex hadn't wanted her to come to the dinner party. She knew Uxbridge was Woolstone's brother, but she'd had no idea what he looked like before. If she were honest, she'd imagined him . . . differently. Middle-aged, paunchy perhaps, with crooked yellowing teeth. But Woolstone's brother was neither older nor ugly. He was actually quite . . . mesmerizing.

She found it suddenly advantageous to pose as the rich American heiress seeking to marry an English title. Turning back to Lunsford, she smiled as he continued.

"Or you could marry my friend the untitled but very debonair Mr. Laurie over there"—the tines of his fork arced through the air—"and live a life of excitement as you discuss potential investors together. And enjoy your mutual obsession with dyes. And . . ." He paused.

Willa shook her head. "You seem to have stalled in listing the reasons why we should marry, Mr. Lunsford. And after only two. This isn't very encouraging, I'm afraid."

He frowned. "No, it isn't. Not at all." He tilted his head, considering her. "But, of course, there remains the only reason why I mentioned it in the first place."

She fought against the urge to look down the table at Uxbridge, to catch his eye and begin the flirtation at once. "And what is that?" she asked.

A grin spread wide across his face. "Such a merger would make me very, very rich. Wealthier even than Lady Althea's family. She wouldn't be able to stand it."

*   *   *

Cigars were nasty things. Port was almost as bad. After a fair amount of time—half an hour seemed far too long, in Alex's opinion—he stood from the table and gestured toward the dining room doorway. "Shall we rejoin the ladies in the drawing room, gentlemen?"

As they walked back, Lord Dutton attached himself to Alex's side. "My wife has ordered me to leave Miss Stratton alone, Mr. Laurie, but I'm interested in hearing more about this dye business."

Alex tensed. "Would you like to hear of the Stratton dye business or the Laurie dye business, my lord?"

The older man's gaze was shrewd. "I imagine I'd like to hear more about the Laurie dye business. Specifically, I'd like to hear about why, if I decided to invest in such a business, I should invest in your company and not in Stratton's."

"That is a very good question, my lord."

As they entered the drawing room, Alex searched until he spotted Willa sitting near one of the windows, speaking to Jo, Lady Althea, and his mother. His mother was smiling—no, *laughing*—as Willa spoke, her hands shaping a box in the air.

Alex frowned, even though she had settled herself far away from Lady Marianna. He would far have preferred seeing her becoming good chums with Woolstone's sister.

Willa had no need to charm his family. And he didn't want them to *like* her. Of all the people, surely his mother understood why Willa Stratton could be nothing more than their enemy. At least Kat appeared to have gone off somewhere else, making friends with the other ladies as she was supposed to do. But he needed to separate Willa from Jo and his mother—

"And do you plan to expand to America, Mr. Laurie?"

Alex swung his head toward Lord Dutton. Damn it. He'd forgotten he was still there. This was more important than she was. Lord Dutton was an earl with much influence among the other gentlemen of the *ton*. And he even had a daughter . . .

"Indeed I do, my lord. Stratton might be the largest dye maker in America right now, but there's a new competitor he's dealing with. While they're dueling it out, I have plans to slip in and make Laurie and Sons the best-known and favorite dye maker among all Americans."

"Plans, you say?"

Alex glanced toward the window. "Yes, but I'm afraid I can't explain everything yet. As a shareholder, of course, you would be the first to hear of the news and the first to see any new invention."

Dutton was silent for a moment as he regarded him. "I'm interested in hearing more, Laurie. Will you be at the Massey ball?"

"I will, my lord."

"Then I look forward to seeing you there. And we shall talk some more." He clapped Alex on the shoulder. Alex bowed as Dutton turned and walked away.

Well. That couldn't possibly have gone any better

even if Willa had somehow shipped herself back to America. Alex straightened and squared his shoulders with a smile. Only a week into the Season, too. He'd made the right choice. Moving into Holcombe House, taking Lunsford's offer to help him become part of the *ton* circles. The rest of his family would soon see he was right.

At the window, it appeared his mother and Jo had moved on. Only Willa and Lady Althea remained to speak, and Alex had no qualms about leaving his nemesis with Lady Althea. He had two people he needed to speak with tonight. He'd failed in getting beyond formal parlor chatter when he visited Lady Marianna before, but he had every hope that either Woolstone's sister or brother would be able to point him in the right direction.

He had to find the Madonna dye before Willa did. Before it had been a simple matter of making the *ton* envious and arousing aristocratic investors' interest in Laurie & Sons. The possibility of increasing their wealth was nothing to be scoffed at, either. But now everything had changed; the Madonna dye meant more. Now it was a matter of pride.

Alex turned and let his gaze roam over the other guests in the drawing room. He found Lady Miranda, Lord Dutton's daughter, and cringed. She looked even younger than Kat's nineteen years. Fresh-faced debutante, indeed. He watched as she simpered and giggled, but it didn't take long for his attention to drift away. He would dance with her at the Massey ball, but at the moment he was not intent on the subject of his future bride.

Soon he located Lady Marianna, Woolstone's sister, as she stood among a group of other guests nearby.

Lunsford had all but salivated at the sight of her during the masquerade. With her mask off, she appeared even more beautiful. Glossy black curls were piled on top of her head and hung in tendrils at her neck and ears. Her eyes—doe-shaped and pale blue—watched everyone around her carefully. Observing. Considering. Measuring. She stood in a group mixed with both lords and ladies, but she didn't speak much. Her bearing spoke of nobility and breeding, she didn't giggle, and after bantering back and forth with Willa earlier in the evening, her quiet grace would be calm and refreshing—good God, Lady Marianna might actually be the perfect woman.

Alex strolled toward her and stopped at her side. "Good evening, Lady Marianna."

"Good evening, Mr. Laurie."

"My apologies," he said after a moment. "Is it often that men are struck nearly speechless by your beauty, or am I the only one to be afflicted in this manner?"

She hesitated. "You don't sound nearly speechless."

"How could I miss an opportunity to speak with you again?" he asked softly.

She pursed her lips, as if trying not to return his smile, but it didn't work. At last she turned her head toward him and offered her hand. "Congratulations, Mr. Laurie. You've now gained my attention."

He lifted her hand toward his lips. "Are congratulations necessary, Lady Marianna? Do you not give your attention to everyone who addresses you?"

"No, I don't." She let her hand rest in his. Through her gloves, he could feel that her fingers were cold.

Willa's hand was always warm.

Damnation. Would the woman *never* cease to bother him, even in his mind?

And then, as if standing before Lady Marianna while thinking of Willa was the perfect, magic combination he needed, his thoughts fixed on the idea. He'd planned to draw out the information of Woolstone's location from her, but of course he had no reason to believe she would comply. And especially with her aloof manner now, it seemed impossible that she would give up such a secret to a stranger. But if Lady Marianna was the woman he would pursue, if she were the one he would marry . . .

Not only would she be more likely to help him find Woolstone if he courted her, but she was also the daughter of a marquess, the sister of an earl. Her connections were impeccable, perfect to assist him in growing the company. And with her beauty and poise, she would also be the perfect wife upon his arm and as the hostess of future events such as this. She could even help to instruct his sisters on how to behave! He couldn't ask her about Woolstone at the mo-

ment, of course, because then she would think that he
only meant to use her when he also meant to marry
her, but the realization of the perfect circumstances—
perfect, yes, she was, in every single way—made Alex
want to crow with triumph.

Instead he *laughed* with triumph and shot a glance
toward the window—

Willa was gone.

Twisting, Alex found her after a moment in the
middle of the room . . . speaking and flirting with
Woolstone's brother, the Earl of Uxbridge.

Alex's laughter died as he watched them inter-
act. *No.*

"Mr. Laurie? Oh, have you met my brother the earl
yet?"

Alex shook his head.

Willa touched Uxbridge, placing her hand on his
arm, then laughed and retrieved it, clutching it to her
chest as she tilted her head back.

Alex switched his gaze to the earl.

The man was smiling outwardly, but the smile
didn't extend to his eyes. He watched Willa as if she
was a little canary and he'd suddenly developed an
insatiable hunger for birds.

Alex looked at Willa. "Bloody *hell*," he swore beneath his breath.

"Mr. Laurie?" Lady Marianna tugged her fingers
from his grasp.

Uxbridge wanted her, and she knew it. It was all
there, in the way she stroked her fingers along her

bodice, in the way she peered at him beneath her eyelashes, her gaze knowing and her lips curved in a seductive smile.

She had *never* smiled seductively at Alex.

"Mr. Laurie?" Lady Marianna said again, this time her voice bordered with impatience.

Alex's gaze remained glued to the other pair. His perfect plan no longer seemed so clever. Willa Stratton meant to use Woolstone's family to find the dye's creator, too.

Chapter 8

"Hurry, Ellen." Willa ran across her bedchamber at Mivart's Hotel and sat at the dressing table. "Something simple will do. We don't have time for anything else."

Blast.

Blast. Blast. Blast.

She'd told Ellen to wake her up at her usual time, and she had. But then—apparently, for she couldn't remember—Willa had told the maid it was fine if she slept for two more hours and to leave her alone until then. Her maid, obedient as always, had abided by her orders.

And now here they were with only an hour to spare before the time for callers. If they came; they might not.

Willa sighed as she peered at her reflection in the

mirror. They always did. Since the Earl of Uxbridge had begun showing her favor a week ago, the other gentlemen of the *ton* had decided she was not indeed another brash American heiress, but a woman of the greatest sophistication and grace.

Ellen scraped the brush through her hair, the bristles tangling in the waves that had become little knots during Willa's sleep. She winced.

"Sorry, miss," Ellen said, then hurried on.

As her head was jerked back and forth, Willa called into the adjoining sitting room of her suite. "Is everything in place, Sarah?"

"Flowers have arrived. Waiting for the tea service now," Sarah replied, her voice carrying, although she didn't shout as Willa did. Refined. Calm. Her companion's response reminded her to take a breath. It wouldn't do to ruin her newly gained reputation as a woman of the greatest poise.

Interesting to note that all the wealth and charm in the world did not matter to the snobbish English *ton* as much as the opinion of one man. If she *were* to marry into the aristocracy for the sake of her father's company, as Alex had once accused her, then the Earl of Uxbridge would no doubt be her first choice of suitors.

It also didn't hurt that in addition to being quite handsome and possessing a wicked wit, he also excelled at putting a glower on Alex Laurie's face whenever he touched her hand or bent his head near to hers.

She would have felt almost smug if not for the fact that when she'd ventured to ask Uxbridge about Woolstone—he seemed to prefer and be amused by her directness—he'd waved away her concern that he'd been taken by force and assured her that Woolstone was no doubt merely in hiding to thwart their father. He also said that he hadn't the slightest idea where his brother could be.

"But for you, my dearest Miss Stratton, I will endeavor to find out," he'd said. Unfortunately, he then went on to say that he suspected his sister knew of Woolstone's location, for they'd always been close companions since childhood.

That had been three days ago. It was also three days ago that Willa had begun stalking Alex Laurie as best she could, certain that Lady Marianna would surrender Woolstone's secret to her nauseatingly devoted suitor. It was *also* the reason why Willa had gone to bed so late the night before, having skulked around Holcombe House into the early hours of the morning, torn between the desire to sneak into Alex's study to see what information he had about the dye and the inclination to not turn herself into a common criminal.

If she could have called upon her father's resources to help her find the dye's creator, she would have. But she knew their loyalty lay with him, and she couldn't risk having letters sent back to America about Daniel Stratton's daughter searching for a man named Woolstone. Not when she was supposed to be charming Mr. Lunsford.

Ellen gathered her hair into her hands and coiled it tightly, then began with the pins. "I laid out the pink dress for today, miss."

"Pink is fine. Let's have the diamonds for necklace and earrings. The diamond clips when you're done with the pins." The rich American heiress had no qualms about dazzling England's lords with the splendor of her wealth. Besides, it was easier to hide behind diamonds without revealing her secret that her father had, in order to gain her compliance in marrying Eichel, stipulated that both her dowry and her inheritance would be forfeit if she didn't marry the groom he chose. Without the Madonna dye, any man who wished to marry her would do so for love alone.

Willa lowered her gaze to the miniature near the bottom of the mirror. It was the Madonna portrait of Queen Victoria and Princess Louise. The color of the Queen's gown in the painting was likely inaccurate; only the original was rumored to be painted with the same dye as the gown. But Willa didn't stare at the miniature as a reminder of Woolstone and his dye; she stared because of the tenderness in the Queen's eyes as she gazed down upon her infant daughter.

Oh, but Willa missed her mother. Twelve years had passed since her death, yet still she could remember the way she'd stroked her hair as a child, the mischief in her smile. Willa loved her father, but how she wished his ruthlessness might still be tempered by her mother's gentleness and good sense.

"Your hair is complete, miss. Are you ready for the dress?"

Willa blinked away the wetness from her eyes, tucked the memory of her mother away, and stood. A glance at the mirror as she turned away showed her hair drawn into a simple bun at the back, wisps pulled at her temples and ears to soften the severity of the style. It wasn't the most elegant or flattering coiffure, but it would have to do.

She held out her arms as Ellen wrapped the corset over her chemise and around her chest. Ellen pulled the laces tight. Willa looked at her figure in the mirror and sucked in her stomach. "Tighter."

Spreading her feet for balance, she held her breath and braced for each tug. A minute later: "Looser, Ellen, looser." Panting for breath, she sighed as the corset relaxed.

English food. It was a crime that such decadence resulted in added inches. She'd never eaten so well, not even in Greece or Paris. Where was the bread and cheese she remembered from her childhood? The gruel and oatmeal?

Must not indulge in biscuits when the men come. She took another breath, noting the ease with which her ribs expanded now that the laces were loosened. *Very well, perhaps just one.*

A knock came from the sitting room, then the sound of voices. Willa squeaked. "Surely they're not here yet? It's not even ten!"

Ellen paused to poke her head out the door and

returned with the crinoline. "Only the tea service, miss. And the servant's gone now. Lady Carlyle is arranging the cups."

"Oh, good. Still, let's hurry, Ellen, as fast as your fingers will go."

Normally calling hours weren't observed until much later in the day, but Willa had finally been forced to set ten o'clock in the morning as the earliest time she would receive her admirers. They had begun coming earlier and earlier, trying to speak with her privately before any of the others arrived. Of course, she did encourage their competition as well as their suspicions that a few favorites were allowed entrance before ten. Uxbridge, she believed, was a man who thrived on competition. And unless Alex led her to Woolstone first, she must continue with the earl and her hope that he would keep his promise to discover his brother's location.

Precisely twenty-seven minutes later, with only three minutes until ten o'clock, Ellen buttoned the last button on the pale pink morning dress. Willa jumped up and down five times, until the petticoats beneath lay flat, then rushed into the sitting room.

At least a dozen vases of flowers sat about the room, and two half-empty teacups and two plates had been placed to the side. Willa sat down in the chair at the head of the room—it was the chair where one could be seen best—tugged at her skirts until they lay gracefully around her hips and legs, then smiled and glanced over at Sarah.

The widow Carlyle nodded once. "Ready?"

Willa inhaled deeply, exhaled, then glanced toward the short, small hall which served as an antechamber to the sitting room. Ellen was now stationed at the entrance to act as the butler. "Let it begin."

To her left, the clock struck ten times.

At five past ten, Willa glanced over at Sarah. "Lovely flowers, by the way. Where did you get them?"

Sarah waved her hand. "Crutcher's hothouse. The hotel recommended them because they're very close. We didn't have much time for today to get out an order. I'll make sure that tomorrow's flowers are from Bellson's again."

Willa regarded three vases set on a table nearest her seat. One was a bouquet of red roses, the second white, and the third a dark pink. "Nevertheless, they're beautiful."

Sarah inclined her head. "Thank you. Did the Braithwaite dinner go well last—"

A knock came at the door.

Ellen disappeared into the antechamber, and Willa let out a peal of laughter. "It was quite remarkable, Lady Carlyle."

A murmur of male voices came from the antechamber.

Willa spied the teacup set before her and quickly reached forward and gulped half of its contents down. "I believe I've never seen anything quite like Lady Braithwaite's— Oh, good morning, my lords."

Willa and Sarah rose to their feet and curtsied as three men she recognized from the evening before entered the room: the Earl of Allesbury, Baron Spencer, and Viscount Lytton, heir to the Earl of Polwarth. The men returned their greeting with bows. "I was just telling Lady Carlyle—she had an awful megrim last night, unfortunately—about Lady Braithwaite's dinner party."

Baron Spencer stepped forward. "It was a splendid time, Lady Carlyle. I'm sorry you had to miss it and am glad to see you feeling well this morning. I must confess that my favorite moment of the evening was meeting Miss Stratton."

Willa laughed. "I shall never forget when Lady Arabella realized you were the same man who wore the bull's mask at the Winstead masquerade. Please, my lords, make yourselves comfortable. Tea?"

After they sat down and as Willa leaned forward to pour the tea, Lord Lytton gestured to the roses around the room and the two discarded sets of teacups and plates on the side table. "I see we aren't the first visitors this morning, Miss Stratton."

Willa sent him a flirtatious glance as she passed the first teacup to Lord Allesbury. "I find England to be a very welcoming place, my lord."

Alex tucked Lady Marianna's letter in his pocket once again and stared at the grand multistoried establishment on the corner of Brook and Davies and cursed.

Mivart's Hotel.

Willa bloody Stratton was staying at bloody Mivart's Hotel.

It wasn't enough that she came to England to pursue the Madonna dye. It wasn't enough that she had managed to capture the Earl of Uxbridge's favor and subsequently the entire *ton*'s attentions. She had to stay at Mivart's Hotel, the bloody best of the best.

She'd said she had no interest in marrying among the aristocracy, but either she'd been lying before or she'd changed her mind for the sake of the dye. Fortunately, if the lack of her gloating was any indication, it seemed Uxbridge hadn't confided Woolstone's location to her just yet. And once Alex called on Lady Marianna this afternoon to hear the news she had for him—there was no doubt in his mind her letter referred to Woolstone's location—then he'd have no need to worry about Willa finding the Madonna dye ever again.

Still, he was here now. Alex had never dreamed he would go to such lengths to best Willa Stratton, but he found as he climbed the steps to Mivart's Hotel that the idea of sabotage fit him rather well. At last he could understand Willa's actions in Italy; there was almost a heady sort of rush in planning the demise of one's rival. Or perhaps the excitement came only because his rival was Willa Stratton.

No matter. Although he doubted his actions today would result in Willa's immediate departure to America, he anticipated her realization that soon she would have no reason at all to remain in England. Indeed, it would be difficult for her to marry the earl or charm any investors if something should happen to make her appear less than desirable. . . .

Two of the hotel staff opened the double doors for him as he approached. "Good morning, my lord," they said in unison.

As if a man wearing fine clothes and entering such an establishment must be aristocratic in order to be deemed worthy of such entailments.

Sod off, he replied. In his thoughts, of course. On the outside he passed by with a short nod—which was much more than a real aristocrat would have given them.

As he climbed the steps to the second floor, Alex fully embraced the foul mood which had been lurking, ever present, since discovering Willa Stratton at the Winstead masquerade.

He despised the stair he ascended, with its plush, foot-sinking rug. He despised the walls on either side for their ornate panels and detailed moldings. He despised the chandeliers which greeted his sight at the turn of the landing from the first floor and then again when he reached the corridor on the second.

He despised the morning sun which streamed through the window behind him, blinding him as his head turned from side to side in search of the appropriate room number. It was too bloody early; his eyes ached for sleep—the same sleep which eluded him by necessity as he worked on the details of his invention every night—the same sleep that eluded him until after dawn every morning now, because memories of the kiss that he'd shared with Willa bloody Stratton in Italy assaulted his mind.

Alex glared at the numbers 215 as he stood outside her door. It galled him that her room number should be a nice, round number set in an increment of 5. If it had been 214 or 216, he might have felt a little better. She shouldn't have had a perfect, balanced number for her luxurious suite past sunlight, chandeliers, ornate molding, foot-sinking carpets, and staff who assumed everyone was nobility at bloody Mivart's *Hotel*.

Alex knocked.

He waited.

And waited.

And waited.

He knocked again—more forcefully this time. Very well, one might have described it as more of a bang.

There were voices inside. Many voices. And laughter. All ignoring him.

Alex took a step back, then two. He measured the distance to the door and squared his shoulders. If he ran—

The door opened to reveal a female servant, her demeanor as open and friendly as Willa bloody Stratton's had been when speaking to him at Jo's dinner party—in great contrast to the way she'd spoken to the Earl of Uxbridge, with her seductive smile and knowing gaze.

"My lord," the servant greeted.

"Alex Laurie," he corrected through clenched teeth. "*Mr*. Alex Laurie. I'm here to see Miss Stratton."

Her eyebrows rose a fraction before her expression smoothed once again—as though men without titles never called on her mistress—and she bobbed a curtsy. "If you'll follow me, Mr. Laurie . . ."

He entered a small antechamber choked with flowers and frowned. He thought flowers made her ill. The maid paused and glanced down at his hands. Alex gave her a small, tight smile. "Unfortunately, I didn't bring anything for Miss Stratton. I'll try to remember next time." The cacophony of noise coming from the next room nearly drowned out his words. He imagined he could hear Willa's voice over all the others—the sound of her laughter, mocking, the arrogance in her tone as she spoke. His anticipation at her downfall grew to much grander proportions.

The maid considered him for a moment, then turned aside to pluck a red rose out of one of the vases. She offered it to him. "If you do remember, sir, bring only roses."

One of the most expensive flowers—of course Willa would want only roses.

Alex's smile narrowed even further as he took the rose, his fingers pinching the stem. "If I remember." He hoped to never have another reason to return.

She nodded again. "This way, please, sir."

Alex followed, holding the rose before him like a weapon. The antechamber led to a sitting room larger than the house of his childhood. A pianoforte occupied one entire corner of the room, a corner which by itself would have held all of the Laurie personal belongings from twenty years ago. More chandeliers, more ornate moldings, more foot-sinking carpet. Alex glanced up at the ceiling. No banknotes drifting down? No fur insulating those inside from the poor dirty bastards in the London streets?

"Why, Mr. Laurie! What a pleasant surprise!"

Alex slowly shifted his gaze to the hostess seated at the front of the room, first scanning past all of the men lounging in half a dozen chairs and at least ten more who stood around the room. As expected, he found Uxbridge already present, although the earl seemed to possess an expansive amount of generosity in allowing other suitors to occupy the chairs on either side of Willa, while he spoke among another group of callers. Generous—or cocky, perhaps, to not feel threatened by any others. For some reason, Uxbridge's carelessness made Alex's mood blacken around the edges.

Either at the sound of Willa's raised voice or the call of a name which didn't begin with "Lord," all of the conversation in the room halted. Every head turned in his direction, and he could *feel* all eyes staring at him.

But Alex focused now on Willa—on her blue eyes and friendly, smiling mouth; on her pale pink dress and her darker pink lips; on the diamonds around her throat and the diamonds dangling from her ears.

She was beautiful—more beautiful than he remembered from their time together in Italy, more so even than the last time he'd seen her—and she wore her smile like a damned crown.

Alex felt his lips move. Slowly, wickedly, into a little smile of his own. He strolled forward, meandering past the other men, until he stood before her. He extended his arm. "I brought you a rose."

She looked at the rose suspiciously, as though if she tried to accept the gift, he would attack her with it. Alex bobbed his hand. "It's a rose, not a wild creature with fangs to bite you."

A few of the men nearby chuckled.

"Of course not." She reached out and took the flower. "Thank you, Mr. Laurie."

"My pleasure." Bowing, he moved to the side of the room.

Soon, conversation began again. The man to Willa's right leaned forward to speak to her and she echoed his movement. Alex watched, studying her as she interacted with her suitor. When the man laughed, she laughed. When he selected another biscuit from the tray, she did, too. She mimicked his motions and his gestures—from the way he leaned against his chair to the hand he laid on his knee. With dark amusement, Alex wondered whether she would continue the imitation if the man decided to belch.

After a moment he moved from his place near the wall to stand at the back of her chair. Leaning forward, he murmured near her ear, "You watched me."

She jerked, her hair brushing against his cheek as

she turned toward the sound of his voice. "What are you doing?"

Alex smiled and winked over her head at the man who now stared at them. "You watched me in Italy. That's how you know to mimic the way he moves. You saw it work for me, and you—"

"I have no idea what you're talking about." Her chin lifted as she angled her head, trying to see him.

"Miss Stratton?" her suitor said, sounding concerned or confused—probably both, though Alex didn't particularly care which.

He shifted to the side, still out of her line of vision, keeping his voice low enough that only she could hear. "When he drinks, you drink. When he laughs, you laugh. I even saw your skirts shift when he crossed his ankles. I assume your ankles crossed, too."

"I would prefer for you not to think about my ankles, Mr. Laurie," she said drily, then turned back to the man.

Alex moved to stand in front of their chairs. He might not win any investors today, but that wasn't the goal he intended to achieve. "Good morning," he said to the man. "I'm Alex Laurie, owner of Laurie and Sons."

The man paused, glanced at Willa, then looked at Alex. "A pleasure, I'm sure," he replied, then returned to speaking to Willa.

Alex glared at the top of his head. It was a reasonable response, as Alex had interrupted them more than once, but he didn't care. Though the suitor appeared to be in his early thirties—a few more years than Alex's own thirty—he could see from this position that the man was going bald toward the back of his head. Alex smiled.

Then he decided to begin listening to their conversation.

"—lives in Charleston. I've never met him, but we correspond regularly," the man was saying. "Have you visited Charleston, Miss Stratton?"

Alex bent at the waist and leaned in closer, looking at Willa. His nose was about a foot from her face.

She slid him a glance from the corner of her eye, then lifted her hand to block him from view, as if resting her head. "I haven't had the opportunity to visit Charleston yet, but I have—"

Alex tapped her shoulder.

She stilled, lowered her hand, and glared at him. "Yes?"

"I've been to Charleston."

"You have?" asked the man. "I say, do you know my cousin Mr. Reginald Archer?"

"No, I'm afraid I don't. How long has he lived there?"

"Since 'thirty-nine, I believe."

"Well, there you have it. Last I was in Charleston was in 'thirty-seven. You should visit. It's a beautiful city. Not like England at all, of course, but—"

"Ahem." A voice. Soft. Ladylike.

"—it's fair to say that no city in all the world could

compare to the cities and towns and lovely country-side here."

"My cousin says that Charleston is close to the ocean. I'm not sure why, but I always believed it was much farther inland."

"Hmm. You might be thinking of—"

"Ahem." A little louder.

"—Columbia. It's near Charleston, but—"

"Ahem." Persistent little thing, wasn't she?

Alex turned to Willa, his eyes wide. "Oh, Miss Stratton. I do apologize—I must admit I'd forgotten you were there." He smiled.

Her gaze held threats. Dangerous threats.

"Please excuse us for a moment, Lord Hadaway," she said to the man, rising.

"Of course, Miss Stratton." He stood, too, and Alex straightened. "Good to meet you, Mr. Laurie."

"The same, my lord."

Alex didn't follow her. He watched as Willa maneuvered through a space between chairs on the opposite side, then marched back toward him, her gaze filled with a martial light. Linking her arm with his, she tugged him away from the center of the room and toward the wall. Unable to help himself, he admired her hair and the curve of her neck as she led him, much as he'd done before he knew who she was at the Winstead ball.

I despise her hair, her neck, and everything about her.

When they reached the far wall she immediately

extricated her arm from his and whirled. "What do you think you're doing?"

Alex raised his brows. "Conversing with your guests?"

"You are irritating me."

He smirked. "Funny, that. I find the same thing happens to me when you're anywhere in the vicinity. Perhaps you should leave London. No, better yet, perhaps you should leave England. Then I won't irritate you, and you won't irritate me. I think that's an excellent idea."

Her chin lifted. "I could send for the hotel staff and have you removed from Mivart's."

Alex rested a shoulder against the wall. "You could."

Her eyes narrowed. "I believe I will."

He grabbed her wrist as she started to turn away. She wasn't wearing any gloves, and her skin was warm, silken beneath his touch. Some perverse part of him held on, knowing that this, too, would irritate her. "I did bring you a rose," he reminded her.

"Let go of my wrist." He'd been correct in thinking that it irritated her. Still, he didn't like how his thumb had started to twitch with the desire to smooth along the inside of her arm. He let her go.

"Your maid said to bring you only roses," he said. He glanced past her, to a row of vases lined up on the top of an escritoire. Yellow, white, red, pink—roses, one and all. "Is it that only certain types of flowers make you ill?"

Her shoulders stiffened and she hesitated, as if uncertain whether to answer him. "Yes. Most do," she said. "Roses don't seem to affect me as much."

"Oh?" He lifted his hand to the necklace encircling her throat. "Do all jewels but diamonds make you ill as well?"

She smacked his hand away and glanced toward her other guests. When she met his eyes again, she gave him a smug grin. "Pearls or diamonds. Either will do." She strolled away—he preferred to think of it as *running* away—toward a group of men on the opposite side of the room, cloistered near the pianoforte.

Alex considered the pianoforte for a long moment. He tried to contain his evil smile. It was difficult, however, and he failed. Following her across the room, he opened his arms and spun around, raising his voice to be heard above the rest. "Gentlemen, my lords . . . ," he called, waiting until they all quieted. Alex nodded at Lady Carlyle in the corner. He bowed. "And lady."

He could sense Willa's anxiety and displeasure at his back. His smile widened.

Sweeping his arm with a flourish, he turned and gestured toward her. "It is my great pleasure to announce that Miss Stratton has agreed to now grace us with a piece on the pianoforte. I admit it required some begging on my half to convince her—"

"Mr. Laurie—" Her voice was panicked, breathless, her ocean blue eyes nearly pleading. He hadn't expected such a quick surrender. It was a trick—a manipulation, surely. Next she would feign that her fingers were broken.

Alex quashed the faint pulse of doubt and wagged his finger at her. "I'm afraid you can't back out now, Miss Stratton. A promise is a promise, after all."

At the side of the room, someone began to clap. "Take pity on us and play a piece, Miss Stratton." He glanced toward the voice; it was Lord Hadaway, the man with the cousin in Charleston. Alex began clapping as well, and soon the entire room was clapping with enthusiasm—all of the suitors, including Uxbridge, Lady Carlyle, even the maid . . . all but Willa herself, who stood frozen at the center of attention. Her gaze drifted around the room, a bead of perspiration showing at her temple. Then her eyes locked on Alex and she smiled. All trace of panic and fear disappeared.

"I'd be delighted to play a piece for everyone, Mr. Laurie. However, I fear you neglected to tell them that you promised to play on the pianoforte with me." She tilted her head, matching smile for smile. "And as you said, a promise is a promise, isn't it?"

Alex held up his hands and started to back away. "Now, Miss Stratton, I would never—"

Strolling forward, she grabbed his hand. It was as if an iron manacle had clenched around his wrist. He hadn't even realized her hand was large enough to span around his wrist. But it probably wasn't; she crushed the bones well enough that her hand was just the right size, her fingers just long enough to keep him prisoner. Alex gave his wrist a little shake. Not even the slightest shift; she wouldn't budge.

"You will play with me, Mr. Laurie," she said in the same tone of voice in which he'd heard men issue death threats. "Now."

"But of course, Miss Stratton." With his free hand he waved toward the pianoforte, then when her gaze shifted he strode forward, tugging her along so he wouldn't be the one pulled by her. He sat down upon the bench and she released him. Alex grinned and patted the empty space when she hesitated to sit. "Come, Miss Stratton. I won't bite."

"I might," she muttered, and with all grace gone, plunked down on the seat.

The men's voices filled the room with a buzz as they watched Alex and Willa rifle through the music sheets the hotel staff had left at the pianoforte.

"How about this one?" he offered, handing her a sheet covered with what looked like a maze of dots and dashes.

"Tchaikovsky?" she hissed, slapping it aside. "I can barely manage 'Three Blind Mice.'"

Alex nodded solemnly and reached over to pluck the rest of the music sheets from her hand before she mangled them in her anxiety. "'Three Blind Mice' it will be, then," he said. "Are you ready? I'll signal for everyone to quiet."

Her ocean blue eyes flashed with scorn. "You realize this was a ridiculously childish thing for you to do. You will never succeed—"

"Have I embarrassed you yet?" he asked, looking down to examine his trimmed fingernails. Frowning, he rubbed his thumb over his index finger, then blew. At her silence, he slid a glance at her.

She appeared as if she'd like to slam his head against the keys. "Even if you do, I would never admit it. You, Mr. Laurie, are a bully."

"I told you I would win, Miss Stratton, and I mean to keep my promise. Now let us play."

She straightened her spine, then adjusted her skirts—a motion that amused Alex to no end, as it caused her entire torso to wriggle—and finally stared straight ahead, ignoring him. Alex stood. "We are ready to begin," he announced.

The room quieted at once.

Sinking to the bench, Alex placed his fingers on the keys—all but his middle fingers resting on the ivories; those he splayed lazily on the black bars at the back. He looked over at Willa. "You go first."

Willa didn't usually notate things about herself in the third person, but if she were to do so now, it would be: *Rage radiated from her every pore.*

"I could refuse to play," she whispered into the silence, conscious of the weight of her guests' stares on the top of her head. For heaven's sake, Uxbridge was there.

Alex didn't respond. Somehow, she knew that no matter what she chose to do, he wouldn't relent until he was satisfied in making a fool of her. Better to get it over with and laugh with her suitors afterward.

Willa banged out the first note, then the second and third.

Three blind mice.

Again.

Three blind mice.

Pausing, she studied the keys, trying to remember where to place her fingers next.

A deafening silence greeted her as the music stopped. *The rage built inside her like a pot brought to boil. She was going to boil over soon. She would kill him.*

See how they run.

Willa glanced over at Alex, who of all things was now whistling along as she played.

See how they run.

She lowered her hands to her lap and stared at him. He didn't move. "It's your turn," she whispered furiously. "Play the rest."

He shrugged. Then, drawing a breath, he lifted his wrists into the air and—

Played Beethoven.

No, he *was* Beethoven. He was the passion in the music, the emotion, instilling overwhelming awe into his audience.

After the first several bars of the Moonlight Sonata Willa gritted her teeth.

As it continued—on and on and *on*—she peeked

over the top of the pianoforte and peered around the room. Some of her suitors held teacups dangling from their fingertips; Uxbridge's brow was raised in salute.

No one spoke. They were hushed in reverence. For Alex.

But she had shocked them into silence, too. Horrified silence.

And then, at that very moment, at the decidedly unfulfilled age of six and twenty, Willa Stratton died.

Unfortunately, she didn't die as she hoped she would. She sat there for what seemed like an eternity and waited for the music to be over, staring ahead at the glossy black of the pianoforte—for she couldn't bear to look at him.

At last, it ended.

A yawning silence followed the echo of the last note and then, almost as one, his audience burst into applause.

Willa slowly rotated her head toward him. One degree at a time. *Slowly.*

Alex met her gaze with a grin.

"You might as well have played Tchaikovsky," she said icily.

He shrugged. "I can't read music."

"You can't—" She stopped. Narrowed her eyes. "You mean to say that you learned Beethoven's Moonlight Sonata *by memory*?" This last came out as a screech. Unfortunately. Fortunately, however, the applause continued and covered the moment when her voice reached the pitch of a bird's squawk.

"When we first moved into Holcombe House," he said. "It took me a few days, but I liked the piece and wanted to be able to play it for myself."

Willa studied him carefully, observing the triumph in his dark brown gaze, the smug curve of his lips. Attempting to ignore the heat of his thigh settled against hers on the bench. "I do not like repeating myself," she said slowly, "but it seems appropriate to say it again." She paused, attempting to summon the entirety of her disdain to resonate with each syllable. "I find you—"

"Delightful. Glorious. Amazingly talented."

"—trying. Extremely trying. God should have sent you to Pharaoh instead of frogs or locusts. It would have been much more effective."

"I shall refrain from pointing out the obvious fact that I wasn't born at the time and instead accept your statement as a compliment. One hopes that this means I have succeeded in driving you away?"

"No." She smiled sweetly. "It means I've decided to become your personal plague in return."

He truly was too close. She could feel not only his leg against hers, but his hip as well, and his shoulder, too. His face was angled toward hers, near enough that she could see the distinction between the black of his pupil and the dark mahogany of his irises. She imagined she could even feel the warmth of his breath on her cheek as they stared at each other, and she was quite aware of the short distance between his lips and hers. If they had been any other man and woman sitting side by side quietly while her callers waited for them to stand, Willa was certain they would have been suspected of hiding amorous touches behind the pianoforte.

As if he read her thoughts, he murmured in a dark, contemplative voice, "Do you suppose this would make Uxbridge jealous?" And then he placed his hand upon her thigh.

Chapter 9

Willa lurched from the bench, jostling the keys in a discordant chorus as she went. Everyone stared. She cleared her throat. "Thank you very much, gentlemen, for calling on me today. I apologize, but I will have to leave very shortly for a previous appointment."

"Who is the fortunate man, Miss Stratton?" asked a bright, curious voice beside her.

Willa ignored Alex and continued. "I must retire to my chamber now to prepare, but I look forward to seeing each of you soon." She was flustered, her composure ruined. She, who had told herself she would never run from Alex Laurie, was in full-fledged retreat.

Lord Uxbridge strolled forward and took both of Willa's hands in his. "Your company, as always, Miss

Stratton, is a pleasure." She noticed he didn't say anything about her ability to play the pianoforte. "I look forward to seeing you at the Pattersons' tonight."

"I do, too, my lord." She forced a smile. She would need to wear her best gown to make him forget this visit. When he turned away, she made straight for Sarah, who appeared serene and unruffled in the middle of the sitting room—whereas Willa felt like a ship that might capsize at any moment.

"Don't let Mr. Laurie leave," she whispered to Sarah, then strode into the adjoining bedchamber and closed the door. She went to her bed, sank down upon the mattress, and inhaled deeply.

She wanted to cry.

But instead, she made herself think of the pianoforte and laugh.

The mirth began like tiny hiccups at first, then grew to unbelieving chuckles that she fought to contain lest the departing guests hear her on the other side of the door. Dear God. She'd just played "Three Blind Mice" for a roomful of lords and heirs to lords. Not even the entire piece!

But as easily as she encouraged it, her amusement faded as his image returned to her mind once again.

Alex Laurie.

He of the cheerful grin that hid a wicked heart—of course, not quite so wicked as hers—and of a persistent charm that carefully concealed his deviousness. He'd finally mounted his attack, but little did he know that his touch to her thigh was much more di-

sastrous than the embarrassing trick with the pianoforte.

A few minutes later a knock came at the door; then
Ellen appeared. "Lady Carlyle sent me to tell you all
of the gentlemen are gone but for Mr. Laurie." A
pause. "Miss, are you all right?"

Willa sat up and tucked the hair that had strayed
from her bun behind her ears. "Yes, I'm fine. Thank
you, Ellen."

"Your—" Ellen tapped her head. "One of the clasps
is falling out."

"Oh." Willa reached up and patted her hair until
she found the dangling clasp. She took it out, then
used it to pin back the hair that had come undone. "It
doesn't have to be perfect," she said as she peered
into the mirror nearby. Not for him, at least. "As long
as I'm presentable."

"You look beautiful as always, miss."

Willa grinned as she strolled past her maid. "I do
believe it's impossible to like you any more than I already do, Ellen." She opened the door and stepped
into the sitting room. Alex and Sarah were sitting on
a sofa together, their heads bent close as they both
stared down at her palm, held between them in the
brace of his hand.

"Do not tell me you are a palmist as well as a grand
pianist."

Sarah jerked her hand to her lap, blushing. Alex
stood and strolled toward Willa, squaring off a pace

away. "I'm not accustomed to being ordered about, Miss Stratton, but I confess to being curious. You asked me to remain?"

Willa looked at her companion. "Sarah, would you mind—"

"No, of course not." Rising to her feet, she disappeared into her chamber through the other door leading off the sitting room. And Ellen had remained in Willa's bedchamber.

They were alone. She inhaled. Exhaled. Nearly bit her lip through.

If she wasn't assured of how much he despised her, she might have been afraid of exposing herself and risking her vulnerability. But it was precisely *because* he despised her that she could say it, knowing he would never look further than the surface of her words.

"It wasn't very nice of you to send her away," he said.

"I would appreciate it if you didn't touch me like that again," she said at the same time. "I find it offensive and improper."

He raised a brow. "We're concerned about propriety's sake now?"

Willa regretted saying it, after all. She'd meant him to accept her request, not to explore it in depth. Instead, she latched onto his other comment for rescue. "Lady Carlyle is my friend. She understood my intentions to speak privately. On the contrary, she knows I am nice—*everyone* believes I am nice except for you."

"Oh, I believe you're nice." There was something in his voice . . . The mistake wasn't what they spoke about, but in asking for him to stay behind, in being left alone with him for the first time since Italy. "You're very nice," he continued. "Beautiful, intelligent, charming. You're everything a man could want, Miss Stratton."

Willa's breath caught; her heart stopped beating and hung suspended midpulse in her chest.

He raised his hand to her cheek, stroked his thumb over her skin, entirely ignoring her request for him not to touch her. Willa stared into his eyes—caught like a butterfly, feeling fragile, knowing to remain was dangerous, yet unable to escape. "You're beautiful, with your golden hair and ocean eyes and slender grace. A man would be proud to have you on his arm, as the hostess at his table."

His hand trailed upward, his thumb massaging lightly against her temple. "You're intelligent—knowledgeable and witty enough to carry on an amusing conversation. You know the things a man likes to hear and how to engage him on the appropriate subjects. Always careful to let him carry the conversation lest he realize that your mind is quicker than his and that you're already bored with the topic you introduced two minutes ago."

Willa's legs trembled as he lowered his hand but leaned forward—why wouldn't her feet *move*?—and his mouth brushed against her ear as he spoke. "And you're charming, with your mesmerizing smiles and your open laughter. You make a man feel good about himself when you're near, as if he's the most important person in the room because you've deigned to spend time with *him* rather than with anyone else."

Abruptly he stepped back, his mouth unsmiling, his gaze flat. "That is the Willa Stratton you present to the world. That is the Willa Stratton that everyone adores. But that woman is a deception, isn't she?" He backed away farther, as if he couldn't stand to be near her. "If you want to know what I think, Miss Stratton—"

Willa lifted her chin. His cravat wavered before her eyes. She raised her gaze to his. "I don't."

"I think you've used that Willa as your identity for so long that you can't even remember who the other one is. And there must be more to you, somehow, but I can't see it." He paused, then softly added, "A pity, that."

She swallowed and stared at him for a long moment, unable to speak. She could feel the heat on her cheeks, the errant rhythm of her heartbeat. Words warred within her, all fighting at once to get out—to refute his claims, to recount all of his false attributes as deftly as he had hers.

He turned. Finally, as he neared the antechamber and the door leading to the corridor outside, Willa called out, "Mr. Laurie!"

He continued without looking back. Dismissing

her quite easily. As she spun toward her bedchamber, she caught a glimpse of her reflection in the mirror on the wall. Alex had been mistaken, after all, for the woman staring back her did not appear beautiful, charming, or intelligent.

All she appeared was lost.

Chapter 10

*L*ater that week, Willa heard a dog's bark, the low voice of a man given in response. Taking a deep breath, she straightened from searching for her mother's pendant among the rosebushes and carefully peered around the corner of Holcombe House.

She sighed. It was only a footman, carrying the new cocker spaniel puppy as they returned from their nightly outing to the park. The puppy had just recently made its appearance. Previously there had been no cocker spaniel puppy, and then two nights ago she'd heard it yipping for the first time. It was an adorable, wriggly thing, its ears hanging over the footman's sleeve. As if it sensed her presence, the puppy cocked its head toward her and barked again.

Willa ducked back into the shadows, slamming her body against the wall. The stuccoed exterior was rough beneath her palms, even through her black gloves.

When a minute passed and no puppy or footman intent on capture approached her location, she sighed again, then slid down the wall to sit. Drawing her knees up, she reached to pluck a blade of grass. The loss of her mother's pendant—the only keepsake she wore on her person at all times—seemed appropriate as only the latest sign that she was utterly inept as a spy. No matter that her instincts said that this was for the best; stealth and patience were plainly not her strengths.

This was why she'd been born to a man who became a businessman and not the criminal sort; the night held nothing but darkness and waiting, and she wasn't particularly fond of either. During the day at least she could keep an eye on Alex openly, as she pretended to be part of the passersby in Hyde Park, or watched him from the shops across the street as he accompanied his sisters and mother shopping. He continued to make regular calls upon Lady Marianna, which, after hearing from Uxbridge how Woolstone favored his sister, was a concern in and of itself. But so far he'd made no move to hold any secret meetings. She could only hope that if he did receive word to meet with Woolstone, her attention to his every move would give her the advantage of this knowledge.

Would it be tonight? Perhaps. That possibility was the only reason she stayed when she'd much rather be ensconced in her suite at Mivart's, wrapped in her robes and sipping chocolate as she read. Just one night away from the social whirl and Uxbridge and the fear that Alex Laurie would steal her freedom away: it didn't seem too much to ask. Of course, the black ensemble of boys' trousers, shirt, and coat which Sarah had found did make her feel rather dashing. She blended in with the shadows well, moved freely without the restriction of a corset and voluminous skirts.

She was Willa Stratton, mistress of intrigue.

Willa Stratton, American heiress by day and watcher of the night by . . . night.

Perhaps she *was* supposed to have been born to someone of the criminal sort. A thief, perhaps. Her parents would have trained her how to sneak into houses, how to pick locks and break windows without making a sound.

She'd always been curious about how to do that, anyway.

Rising to her feet, she assumed an offensive position, as if she might be attacked on all sides: arms raised to protect her face, right foot planted forward with knee bent. She turned her head from left to right, right to left. No one would be able to sneak up on her. She was invisible. She was *invincible*. She was . . .

Willa sighed again and leaned back against the wall.

. . . bored beyond reason and, even worse, irritated by her own company.

It was better to focus on why she was here, better to dwell on her future: freedom from an arranged marriage, personal wealth to do as she wished, wherever she wished. Alex had called her beautiful, intelligent, and charming the other night, condemning her for such qualities with all the censure of a man certain of his victory. But she would defeat him, and the next time he accused her of having no substance, she would be prepared. She would laugh instead of hurt, accept his words for what they truly were: the scorn of a man who still nursed his wounded pride.

And she would make him add to her catalogue of traits. She would build his vocabulary of her one word at a time. Tonight she would begin with this one: resilient. Let him mock her as he wished; she would not be discouraged.

Willa tensed as she heard voices. There, they came again. Oh, but only above her.

Glancing up, she saw two women's silhouettes framed by the window. A maid and his mother? Two sisters?

She scanned the exterior of her wall. Yes, *her* wall— she'd become very possessive of it these last few days. Quite a few of the windows above were lit brightly from within, but on the lowest floor, which she stood just outside of now, only two windows glowed with a friendly welcome.

"I suppose I should be grateful you haven't decided to burglarize the house yet."

Willa whirled. A man's silhouette stood a few feet

away, leaning negligently against the wall. She couldn't see his eyes or mouth, but only the breadth of his shoulders and the leanness of his hips stroked in shadows.

Her eyes narrowed. She didn't fancy being snuck up on. She certainly didn't appreciate being snuck up on and then observed in secret by Alex Laurie. It had set her heart to racing, her pulse to thrumming, and she refused to give him control over her body's impulses. She breathed deeply, willing to the surface the apathy which she'd much prefer to feel when around him.

He lifted his arm in an expansive gesture toward the windows. "Unless, of course, thievery was what you were planning to do tonight? How fortuitous, then, that the footman saw you sneaking about first."

Willa sniffed and folded her arms. "I had no intentions of burglarizing your house." Although she had, admittedly, considered breaking inside and searching for any information he had on the Madonna dye. But that was neither here nor there. "And I was not sneaking about." She paused. "I was waiting. Patiently." The addition of the word "patiently" was the result of nothing less than a moment of brilliance. It implied a certain amount of virtuousness to the action of waiting.

Waiting. Stalking. They were nearly the same.

He tilted his head and was silent, as if he could somehow see more of her in the darkness than she could see of him. Idly, Willa wondered whether he had any cause to call for a constable. She wouldn't put it past him; *she* certainly would have called for a constable if he'd been found stalking around her house— if for no other reason than so she could be assured he was unable to meet with Woolstone and get the dye.

He turned around and began walking toward the front of the house. "You should come inside." It was almost a friendly sort of invitation.

"Why?"

"I have something to show you."

Willa's stomach lurched. There could be only one reason he treated her so courteously, as if he had no cares at all where she was concerned. "You have it, don't you?"

He paused but didn't look back. "I do. Follow me."

She went—not because she had any desire to obey him, not because she wanted to see the physical evidence that he had the information about the dye. No, she went simply because she could think of nothing else to do. Her thoughts spun as she followed him around the corner, her feet dragging with each step. How could he have the dye? Of course, she hadn't been able to keep up with him every minute of every day, but he'd had obligations to meet, too.

He waited for her on the steps before the front door, the light from the lamps nearby casting his features in grooves and hollows. His expression would have been inscrutable if not for the tiniest curl of his lips—more of an impression of a smile than an actual curve.

She fisted her hands at her sides as she climbed the steps to stand in front of him. "You don't have it."

He laughed, a low sound that pulled at her anger and hopelessness. "I've wondered for a long time how your face would appear in this moment, when you've finally realized that you are the one defeated, Miss Stratton." He rocked back on his heels. Moments passed, and yet he said not another word. She watched that impression of a smile slowly transform into a satisfied grin, and she forced an answering smile to her lips. *No defeat here, you bloody bas—*

"Ah, yes." His lashes lowered, then rose again. "How I do treasure this moment."

"Are we going inside or not?" While they remained on the steps, Willa's good sense returned and swept away the helplessness. He was delaying, but for what reason? Only to torment her? Perhaps as a distraction?

"Of course. It's in the desk in my study. If you'll follow me."

Any other man would have offered her his arm, but not Alex. He nodded to the footman at the open door—the same one, Willa saw, who had taken the puppy out and must have seen her; she lifted her chin—and strolled on.

When they reached the room she assumed to be his study, he walked inside instead of waiting for her to pass before him.

"I see that even a gentleman's clothes and a gentleman's house does not the gentleman make," she murmured as she followed. She frowned, looking toward the desk, then toward the hearth on the opposite side of the room.

The sound of the door closing came behind her, and she turned. Alex stood against the door. He inclined his head toward the desk. "Top drawer. Right side."

She hesitated. He seemed so . . . unconcerned. If she were the one in possession of the dye's secrets, she would have acted with much more caution. Why, the fire poker could easily incapacitate him—

"I have no fear that you'll take anything, Miss Stratton. I would catch you before you could escape through the windows, and you only wish to see it, don't you, to prove to yourself that I have finally won?"

She startled at the similar train of his thoughts. But she didn't reply. Truly, if he had indeed gained the dye information, then the only good thing about his victory was that she would never have reason to see him again. Pivoting sharply, she marched toward the desk.

"I do wonder, Miss Stratton . . ." His voice trailed away.

Willa ignored him and rounded the desk.

"What did you hope to accomplish by spying outside of Holcombe House? Surely you couldn't have believed you would win the dye that way."

She shrugged as she rounded the desk's corner. "Perhaps." She would have followed him and somehow taken the dye for herself. Possibly even have stolen inside Holcombe House to retrieve it if necessary. Her conscience could have been subdued.

"Yet obviously your plan didn't work."

Willa tugged at the drawer.

Locked.

She opened her mouth to tell him exactly what she thought of his little game, but when she glanced up she found his hand stretched toward her, a key lying across his palm. Again, soundlessly, he'd crept toward her without her realization. As she reached out to snatch the key away, his fingers closed, trapping hers inside his fist.

Damn him—her breath shook. He stood so close she could feel the heat of his body. She wanted to back away but forced her legs to lock and her feet to remain in place. His every piece of clothing was intact, but he might have been wearing nothing at all for the images that flashed across her vision. Daydreams from the past. Merely another inconvenience she must dismiss to get what she wanted.

"Mr. Laurie," she said, yanking her fingers from his grip. "I refuse to play along. Either unlock the drawer and show me that you have the dye papers, or do not and I will be glad to leave. Might I remind you, however, that you were the one to invite me inside?"

He didn't say anything for several moments, and finally Willa lifted her gaze to meet his. She sucked in a sharp breath, the movement causing a physical ache at the back of her throat.

"You lied," he said.

Willa swallowed at the look in his eyes—as if he'd suddenly seen through that outer shell of charm, intelligence, and beauty to everything she kept hidden beneath. "Very well." She nodded. "I'm leaving, then."

She turned, but he caught her wrist.

"You lied about that kiss in Italy, didn't you, Miss Stratton?"

His fingers burned into her flesh despite the long sleeve of her shirt and her gloves. Willa forced another sigh. "I already admitted that I did it deliberately to distract—"

"Have you ever kissed a potential investor?"

"Of course not!" As soon as the words escaped, she knew she'd made a mistake. She should have confessed that every strategy included giving away a night in her bed. That would make him no different from all the others. He *wasn't* any different from any other man.

"You have other rivals, I believe. We're not the only dye makers. What about that company in America? Have you ever kissed another rival to distract him from winning an investor you wanted?"

But somehow the words she knew she should speak became tangled in her throat. She frowned and tugged at her wrist, but he wouldn't let go. She reached with her other hand for his, the one that held the key. "I—"

"I can't believe I never saw it before." Suddenly he released her and laughed.

She willed the heated flush on her face to disappear, but it only worsened, scouring her cheeks and throat and ears. "I don't know what you think you've seen, and I don't particularly care. Now *give* me the damned key, or I'll—"

"Or you'll what?" he jeered softly. "Find another excuse to kiss me? For that's what it was, wasn't it? You didn't kiss me to distract me. You didn't even know I would be distracted. You kissed me because you wanted to kiss me. Is that not the truth, Willa?"

She stilled. Each of her senses was on alert, though it was pointless now. Somehow, her body had already betrayed her. The flush hadn't come until afterward. He'd seen it in her eyes, perhaps, or in the way her pulse hammered at her throat—she could feel that now, as if being so close to him caused her cells, sinews, bones, muscles, and even her blood to leap with joy. Perhaps if she loved him, she could have understood it, but she didn't even know him very well. All she felt was lust—this mad longing to surrender her flesh to his and let him do as he wished with it . . . and, even more, the desire for him to surrender his body to her, for her to do whatever *she* wished with his.

But, oh, how cocky and arrogant he was, to stand there with that smug grin on his face, his eyes dark and knowing, to act superior to her now when they had both been born in the East End of London, when the fact was that he, too, had enjoyed their kiss.

This was exactly what she had feared: with his knowledge of her desire, no longer were they equal rivals. Every time he looked at her now, he wouldn't see her strength or determination. Her features would compose an essay on her weaknesses; he would notice how her gaze lingered on the lines at the corners of his eyes, on the creases around his mouth, on the sharp planes and hollows of his stubbled cheek; he would find ways to explain the trebled pulse at her throat when he was near, or the press of her lips together, perhaps wondering if she did it to ease the ache of that first kiss's memory. He would pause at the slight flutter of her eyelashes when their gazes met, take note of the stillness of her breath when he came too close.

He would see every betrayal of her body and claim it for himself, tempting her only because he knew he could.

Willa stepped toward him, girding herself with her armor—a smile. If there was to be any hope at all, she prayed that she would find him just as weak. "Yes, that's the truth," she murmured. She clasped her hands about his shoulders and tilted her face up to his. "I wanted to kiss you, Alex." She dragged her hands down his arms, pausing only momentarily at the bulge of his biceps, then again at the corded muscles of his forearms, which she could feel beneath his sleeves. "But you did want to kiss me, too, did you not? I wasn't the only one who wanted, was I?"

His hand was still clasped around the key. Her fingers wrapped around his wrists, then guided his hands to bracket her waist. He could trap her so easily like this, one short step sideways toward the desk. But she counted on the wary hunger she glimpsed in his eyes, the quickening of his breath . . . the way his hands tightened on her of their own accord, his fingers loosening about the key . . .

Beyond the roar of the silence in the room as their gazes held, Willa heard the soft thump of the key as it fell to the ground. Perhaps they were both weak together. An even more frightening thought.

She bent and scooped up the key, his fingers grasping at her as she moved, but as she turned and inserted the key inside the drawer's lock, they fell away. She fumbled inside the drawer, down the length of it, to the very back. There was nothing . . . She heard the rustling of paper as she scraped against the far right corner and drew out her prize.

It was paper wrapping, not any sort of paper which would reveal the secrets of the dye. A thrill of hope flared—until that same hope died as she realized he could have the dye information somewhere else. He wouldn't truly wish for her to know its location, after all.

Still, she unwrapped the paper—its weight light enough for her to suspect nothing was actually held inside. Then she smiled: a reluctant curve of her lips. "Thank you."

She slipped her mother's pendant deep inside her pocket.

"We found it after the first night you were caught."

Her head snapped up. "You knew I was here before?"

Alex had moved around to the other side of the desk and taken a seat in one of the chairs. He leaned back, his chin propped on the heel of his palm as he watched her. "Of course. And yes, I also know that you've been following me everywhere else, too. Truly, Miss Stratton, you might find a more clever way of hiding yourself." His gaze trailed down the length of her body. The heat in his eyes made her feel naked, though not an inch of skin below her neck was bare.

For a moment she almost wished she hadn't moved out of his arms to retrieve the key. "Do you have the dye information?"

He continued as if she hadn't spoken. "Although I do appreciate the shirt and trousers you've donned for your nocturnal activities. I have no complaint about those."

"Enough. I don't care about three years ago. I don't care about the kiss, and I don't care about what you think about my clothes. All I want to know is whether you have the dye. Tell me."

His dark gaze made a lazy ascent up the path of her body, an accompanying fire simmering beneath her skin wherever it touched. He met her eyes and smiled. "Of course."

And that was when she knew: Alex Laurie was a far more terrible liar than she had ever been.

More than an hour later, Willa watched from a different spot outside Holcombe House. She saw the messenger arrive. She spied Alex's shadow move about the windows that she now knew belonged to his study. After twenty-odd minutes had passed, Alex called for his carriage. When the coachman pulled it from the mews to the front and waited for Alex to emerge, Willa was inside. Curled up on the rear-facing seat, her knees to her chest as she pressed herself into the shadows.

She held her breath as the door opened and Alex climbed inside. She sent a silent prayer of thanks heavenward when he didn't request that either of the lamps be lit. Her fingers dug into her forearms and became numb as she counted each second that passed before the carriage shifted with the groom's weight and the horses pulled the vehicle forward.

All the while, Alex never once looked in her direction.

She wasn't sure how much time had passed, but it must have been at least ten minutes more when her legs became heavy with numbness also. Still, she didn't move. She didn't make a sound. She wasn't fooling herself in thinking that they would travel all the way to their destination without him noticing her, of course, but the greater the distance from Holcombe House, the more likely it seemed that at least *some* part of her plan for getting the Madonna dye would work.

She no longer cared that desperation had become part of that strategy; the end result was all that mattered.

After probably another ten minutes, Willa relaxed. She let her head rest against the wall as she stared at Alex, who meanwhile stared out the carriage window into the night. Every so often they would pass a lamppost which would reveal a glimpse of his features. They felt like secrets—the full curve of his bottom lip, the cliff of his chin—secrets offered in the dark, for her and her alone.

"What I do not understand," he mused aloud, turning his gaze toward her corner to pierce through her protective shadows, "is how well I seem to know you and how you don't seem to know me at all."

For a moment she considered pretending that she remained hidden; she liked him much more when he didn't speak. "You didn't know I would be here," she protested, then gave a small groan as she extended her legs across her seat.

"You're right; I didn't know. Not until I climbed inside. Good God, you are the most stubborn woman I've ever met."

"You lied about the Madonna dye."

"Of course I lied. I wanted you to think I already had it, just so you would stop doing such foolish things like this. I am *weary* of your presence, Miss Stratton."

Willa straightened. "Then we're going to meet him? I was right?" She gave a little laugh of delight.

His response cut through her laughter. "No, Miss Stratton, *I* am going to meet with him."

When, exactly, Alex wondered, had he begun to *feel* Willa Stratton's presence?

He'd felt it earlier tonight, before Thomas the footman ever came inside to report on a suspicious person lurking outside the house. He hadn't even needed the carriage door open to know that she would be inside. He could have demanded at that point that she get out and he would have gone alone to meet with Woolstone, and he knew that's what he should have done, but somehow he found the anger and frustration at her presence across the carriage from him . . . satisfying.

Letting her remain also meant that she would soon see him take possession of the dye information and then leave him alone, but in the meantime he felt rather . . . enlivened . . . to know she was there, across the carriage, still plotting how she would best him and take the Madonna dye for herself.

Her hands spread wide. "We could both meet with him. He's agreed to give it to you in any matter, hasn't he? What harm would it do to allow me to accompany you?"

Alex bit back a grin. "Trying to lull me into a false

sense of security, are you? You will smile and flutter your eyelashes at him. You'll no doubt try to convince him to surrender the information to you instead."

In truth, the only way he could keep her from meeting Woolstone once they arrived was to have the groom and coachman guard the door and keep her locked safely inside. A consideration he hadn't yet dismissed.

She hesitated. Then: "Of course I will," she acknowledged, and he could see the flash of her teeth in the darkness as she smiled. "You're not afraid I'll succeed, are you?"

"No." He laughed disbelievingly, as she probably expected. Humor appeared to be the new rule in the game they played; any currents of animosity remained cloaked among the shadows, and a tacit agreement had been made to ignore anything else that lay between them.

In keeping with this, Alex decided to pretend to ignore her and looked out the window on the carriage door again. Soon afterward Willa pried the blinds on her side away from the window and peered at the dark facades of the buildings passing by.

Then she sniffed.

A few minutes later, she sniffed again.

"You're not crying because I'm going to win and get the dye, are you?" he asked warily.

"No!"

"Good."

Another minute passed. "What is that horrid smell

in here? It smells like a rat's carcass." Her voice was nasal, as if she held her nose.

"What lovely words do flow from your lips, Willa." He caught his breath at the inadvertent use of her given name.

"And my apologies," he added, though his regret had nothing to do with saying her name. It had sounded like a foreign territory on his tongue, strange and exotic; somehow, just the thought of saying it again caused his heart to beat faster. He cursed. "We've scrubbed the damned thing from top to bottom and at least half a dozen times, but the smell remains. I've been meaning to purchase a new carriage. Kat believes Lord Holcombe died in this one."

"What?" she screeched, scrambling off her seat and stooping in the middle of the swaying carriage.

"Sit down," he said, tugging at her hand. "You're going to get hurt, and I don't want to have to send for a physician and be late for the appointment. Besides, I hardly think he died on your side, if that's what worries you."

"No, what worries me is that he died in here at all, and that smell— How did he die?" She sounded suspicious. Nauseated, too, but still suspicious.

"He . . ." Alex cleared his throat. Solemnly. "It is believed Lord Holcombe had too much to drink."

"And that killed him?"

"It was most likely the inciting factor. The groom found him facedown in his own vomit and excrement upon arrival at Holcombe House."

Willa gagged. *"Blehhhh—"*

Alex flinched, immediately contrite. "I'm just teasing you. The physician said he died from an issue with his heart. There was no vomit or excrement in the carriage."

He eyed her with concern but was relieved to find her more focused on glaring at him than casting up her accounts. He grinned. "I'm sorry."

Her mouth pursed. "Then what is the smell?"

"We don't know."

And it didn't matter, not right now. His hand was still holding hers, tugging her gently, insistently. His fingers remembered the shape of her hips beneath her boys' clothes, the daze he'd felt when she'd suddenly disappeared to retrieve the fallen key. "Sit down before you fall, Willa."

At that moment the carriage took a sharp turn and she pitched to the side. She would have crashed into the door if not for Alex's strong grasp. He growled and leaned forward to wrap his arms around her waist, hauling her back and onto his lap. "How can you become even more infuriating and obstinate the longer I know you? I didn't think it possible."

"I can sit on the seat, Mr. Laurie," she said stiffly. "There's no need for you to hold me."

He chuckled and placed his lips at the curve in her neck, near the top of her spine. "But I find I always have a need to annoy you, Willa." He couldn't resist saying her name. Over and over.

She froze.

A moment later, Alex went still, then eased his mouth away.

"You kissed me," she said calmly.

He sucked in a slow breath. "I did."

"You don't like me."

"No, I don't."

He'd spoken the truth before: she was beautiful, intelligent, and charming. And sometimes she could be amusing. But he still didn't like her. He tolerated her—quite a bit.

And he wanted her; he couldn't deny that.

Neither of them mentioned their conversation in the study.

"I'm fairly certain I don't like you very much, either," she said.

"Oh, I think you're wrong." Alex breathed across her shoulder and angled his head to study her, watching for any reaction: a shudder, perhaps, or a quick breath. He smiled when, in the faint light, he saw the slight ripple of her throat as she swallowed. "I think that deep down inside of your little black heart, there's an infinitesimal, tiny little part of you that wanted me to kiss you."

Willa turned her head. She was so close that they nearly bumped noses. "And what if you're correct? What if I did want you to kiss me?" Her voice was low, sounding like more of a confession than a curiosity.

He smiled and brought his mouth to her ear—a whisper away. "Then I have even more of an advantage over you than I thought."

She lurched off his lap and tucked herself into the opposite corner of the carriage again. "I should have stolen one of your horses to follow you."

"Is that an admission regarding the kiss, then?"

She reached down and threw her shoe at him.

It hit his chest and he caught it as it fell, laughing. "It'll be our little secret, Willa. I promise not to tell anyone."

"Might I remind you that *you* are the one who kissed *me* just now, Mr. Laurie?"

He waved her shoe, then lowered it to the floor of the carriage and sent it sliding toward her. "A momentary lapse. Won't happen again."

"Hmph." Willa put her shoe back on and crossed her arms. "See that it doesn't."

Italy and the memory of *that* kiss—of everything he now knew it meant—echoed between them.

She peeked behind the blinds. "We're traveling through the countryside. The meeting's not in London?"

Alex smiled. "Hence the carriage."

She didn't respond but continued staring out the window, and Alex turned his head slightly to once again pretend he was staring out *his* window. He watched her out of the corner of his eye, and it seemed as if the entire world had suddenly become a most glorious, wondrous place and he had been named king.

Willa Stratton had kissed him in Italy not because of strategy, but because she desired him. The truth had been present tonight when he came too close in the study, at the slight stutter of her breath and the quick aversion of her gaze. It was true that she had hidden it for a long time and had hidden it well.

And it was a shame that he wasn't a nicer man, for a nicer man would surely have allowed such things to remain in the past. But Alex decided the role of the scoundrel suited him just fine; her secret was his now, and he intended to never let her forget it.

Chapter 11

*I*t was a small cottage in the country, surrounded
by trees in all directions. As they walked toward
the front door, Willa breathed in the faint scents of
foxglove and lavender, roses and honeysuckle. She
sneezed.

Oh, no. No matter—she would breathe through her
mouth. She *must* find a way to convince Woolstone to
give her the dye instead.

"God bless you," Alex said, then knocked on the
door.

A man whose head came higher than the doorway
stood on the opposite side. He stooped to see them,
and when he did his eyes narrowed at her. "Who is
she?" he asked Alex.

"Mr. Woolstone, may I present Miss Willa Stratton?

She is the daughter of the American dye maker who is also interested in your dye."

Woolstone, not a servant? True, he had the black hair and pale eyes of the Earl of Uxbridge and Lady Marianna, but he was much thicker, much larger. As he turned and led them into the cottage without saying anything else, she saw that he easily topped Alex by at least six inches. The man was a giant!

How was she to charm a giant who didn't even acknowledge her presence beyond a "ho-hum"?

Willa glanced around the inner room of the cottage— for it was a true cottage, very small and simple, with one main room and only two doors leading elsewhere. A bedchamber, perhaps? A kitchen?

But worse—much, much worse than the fact that the giant didn't seem to like females—was the fact that nearly every surface of the room was covered with plants. Flowers, ferns, potted trees, small bushes, ivies. They crept along the floor so that Willa and Alex had to hop from open space to open space to avoid crushing them underfoot; they climbed up to the furniture, entwining their leaves and branches to create a domestic forest; they stood on thrones and pedestals from one corner to the next: on chairs, on tables, on a small ladder and a very old, very worn gardener's workbench.

She was in hell. God had tired of all her lies and manipulations and now he was doling out his judgment.

"Ahhhhhhhh-CHOO!"

Apparently breathing through one's mouth didn't help.

Both Woolstone and Alex whirled toward her, the first wearing a scowl and the second an expression of surprise. It *had* been an especially loud sneeze.

"Are you all right?" Alex asked. Woolstone had already turned around and continued stomping his way—careful of his precious plants, of course—to a haphazard group of chairs.

Willa nodded, then sighed as he, too, turned around.

She hated sneezing. She hated sneezing worse than she hated snakes, or spiders, or playing the pianoforte, or even—yes—*even more* than she hated blood pudding. She hated the tickling feeling that started at the top of one's nose that made one aware that the sneeze was impending. She hated the inevitability of it, and that no matter how hard she tried *not* to sneeze, it was doomed to happen. She hated the awful squealing sound she made when she sneezed, the occasions when she didn't have a kerchief to put over her nose before it actually happened—and it seemed she *always* sneezed when there wasn't a kerchief nearby, such as now.

She hated sneezing more than anything else in the world, but the swelling in her throat was much scarier.

"Ah, Alex. I mean, Mr. Laurie." She sneezed again. *Three* times.

He'd already sat down across from Woolstone, and

this time his expression was one of growing annoyance as he looked up at her.

"Yes, Miss Stratton?" Then he stared, his mouth open in horror, and Willa tried to surreptitiously put her hand to her nose to make sure it was clean. It was. Then she looked down, to make sure there weren't any—blemishes—on the front of her clothes. There weren't.

"What is it?" she asked. "Why are you looking at me like that?"

"Miss Stratton," Woolstone said, because of course he had to look at her, *too*. He stood abruptly from his stool. "It appears you are having a reaction to something. Your face is swelling."

"It is?" She put her palms to her cheeks, then to her forehead. Her eyes felt small and dry. She tried to swallow and winced. Her throat was worse.

"I need to leave," she said, then whirled and ran out the door, most likely killing some of his vicious little plants on the way.

She stopped in the drive, the ribs of the corset pressing against her own as she tried to breathe. Wait, no—she wasn't wearing a corset. "Dear God," she said, planting her hands on her waist and panting up at the sky. "If you let me live, I promise to—"

What could she promise? Alex wanted her to return to America and leave him be so he could have his precious dye. Her father wanted her to marry Eichel and help him expand the company through their alliance. She didn't have anything to give up, nothing except her dreams for her own independence and happiness. And it appeared that she wouldn't even have those since Woolstone was most likely handing Alex the dye information right now.

She started crying. She couldn't breathe—whether from running or because she was about to die from the plants inside—she was still sneezing even as tears rolled down her face, and she was fairly certain the squishy substance beneath her foot was a small part of a rather large pile of horse manure.

Then suddenly Alex was there, his hand on her shoulder, his face blurred before her eyes. "Willa, are you all right? Why are you crying?"

She cried harder, gasping for breath.

"Willa?" Both of his hands were on her shoulders now. He shook her. "Willa, answer me." He cursed and left her there, and she heard voices shouting, felt a cool cloth on her face, turned her head and glimpsed the statue-shadow of a tulip a few feet away, rising to the sky above . . .

She heard whispers. The not-so-very-hushed, loud-trying-to-be-quiet whispers of children.

Willa opened her eyes, frowned at the yellow canopy above her head, and sat up.

Upon sitting, she became aware of three odd and equally disturbing things: first, her head seemed to want to collapse upon her neck every direction she tried to turn and ached like someone had taken a wooden plank to it; second, the walls were also yellow, which meant that unless the Woolstone giant had a very cheerful conscience inside his gruff exterior, she now lay in someone else's bedchamber entirely since she was most certainly not in her suite at Mivart's; and third, the two girls and one boy whispering back and forth from one side of the bed to the other looked remarkably like Alex. At least, the younger girl and boy did. The older girl was blond with blue eyes.

Willa watched as the girls whispered. "She's awake," the younger one said. Willa turned her head slowly to the other side of the bed as the boy whispered in response.

"I know she's awake, don't I? I can see her sitting up, can't I?"

"What does she look like?"

At the eager question from the older girl, Willa searched her gaze. Sightless eyes stared back at her.

The boy looked up at Willa, squinting. "She has—"

"I have blond hair that is very similar in shade to yours. Though mine is wavy and your hair is very nicely curled. Blue eyes like yours, although mine have some green in them, too, whereas yours are the clear, shining color of the sky. My nose is a trifle blunt, my lips too wide, and my forehead high."

The girl had started grinning when Willa complimented her in comparisons of their hair and eyes, but now she frowned at the latter description, her brows puckered. Then she looked in the direction of her younger sister and whispered, "The first part sounded nice, but I'm not sure about the rest. Is she pretty, Tor?"

The girl named Tor grinned up at her, proudly displaying her missing two front teeth. "She forgot to mention her face is all puffy," she said. "Sorry about your face, Miss Stratton. Alex said that flowers attacked you. Is that true?"

"He did not!" said the boy, squinting at her again. Did he have spectacles he'd misplaced? "He said that she attacked the fl—fl—flow—"

"Flowers," Willa finished for him, smiling at Alex's version of the story. Of course he'd painted her as the villain. The smile disappeared when the boy scowled at her.

"He doesn't like it when people try to correct him," the blind girl said. "You have to wait and let him finish it. Even if it does take hours."

"Oh, I apologize," she directed to the boy. "I didn't realize . . ." She'd thought he just couldn't remember the word, not that he had a stutter.

He turned his scowl toward his sister. "You don't have to go about telling everyone and the whole world, P—P—P—"

The blind girl shook her head, then turned toward Willa and made a small curtsy. "It's nice to meet you, Miss Stratton. My name is Miss Philippa Laurie. You may call me Pippa, though. I like how you described my hair and eyes." She paused. "But is the rest of my face all right, too?"

Willa swallowed a laugh and realized her throat felt amazingly better, almost normal again. "You are quite beautiful, Pippa."

The girl's open expression turned suddenly shy for a moment as she ducked her head.

"And me, Miss Stratton?" asked the younger girl, Tor, bouncing up and down. "Am I beautiful?"

"You are also quite beautiful," Willa said, smiling again. And she was. She had curls like Pippa's, but hers were dark brown instead of blond, her eyes also brown like Alex's and incredibly large in her small, delicate face. In truth, she was far more beautiful than Pippa, but Willa would never have said such a thing aloud.

"Do you think *David* is beautiful, Miss Stratton?" Pippa asked, and both girls giggled.

"Boys aren't beautiful," their brother said, scowling again. "And I don't care what she thinks."

Willa considered the boy, a little older than Pippa with the same dark coloring as Tor. If he didn't have spectacles, then he should, for his squint looked very uncomfortable. Without the squint, though, she was very confident that he would grow up to be nearly as handsome as his older brother. "You're correct, Mr. Laurie," she said, pressing her lips together as he stood a little straighter at being addressed so formally. "You are most *handsome*. In fact, I fear that if you were any more handsome, I would be in grave danger of losing my heart to you."

The girls giggled again.

"Oh," said David, squirming a little. "I'm sorry."

Willa couldn't help laughing, then groaned as her head throbbed in response. She might have lain down for a moment, but as she lifted her gaze from the three siblings she found Alex leaning against the doorframe, a half smile playing across his lips. "You can't resist trying to charm every male you see, can you, Miss Stratton?"

An older girl, probably of fifteen or sixteen years, skidded to a stop beside Alex, panting. Shoving past him, she hurried to the bed and executed one of the deepest, most extravagantly perfect curtsies Willa had ever seen. Willa stretched her arm, hesitant to tell her she needn't act as if Willa were the Queen of England. "I . . ."

The girl slowly straightened, clasping her hands in front of her waist and inclining her head toward Willa as if *she* were the Queen. "Good day, Miss Stratton," she said in perfectly crisp, aristocratic tones. "I am Miss Anne Laurie. It is a pleasure to meet you."

Willa's mouth was agape; she was certain of it. "I— I—"

"David, Miss Stratton has a stutter, too!" Tor whispered across the bed.

Helpless, Willa looked beyond Anne to Alex, whose half smile had turned into a full grin.

"Anne is our reigning champion of all things fine," he explained. "Elocution, pronunciation, grand curtsies—"

"Don't forget the stare," Anne said, glancing over her shoulder and breaking the act.

"Ah, yes. The stare." Alex winked at Willa.

"What stare?"

"Show her, Anne," he said.

The girls giggled again. "Wait till you see the stare, Miss Stratton," Tor said. Willa watched Pippa, who giggled along and turned toward Anne as though she could see her with perfect clarity.

"You're missing it, Miss Stratton," David said.

Willa angled her gaze toward Anne, who was ever so slowly turning her head back toward the bed. Willa saw her eyebrow first, arched and frozen high. Then her eyes, lowered to half-mast and looking through Willa rather than *at* her. Her nose—how had she altered her nose? It appeared thin and pinched, as if she were trying not to breathe the same foul air as Willa. Her mouth formed a flat, aloof line except at the corners, which turned up, though it was obvious her small smile was false and made only for the benefit of those around her, whom she was required to endure. In whole, it was the stare of ennui, of a woman wealthy and bored with herself and everyone else beneath her.

Willa arched her own brows, then slowly began to clap. "I think I'd like to crawl under the covers now," she said, and Anne's face split into a grin as the younger siblings clapped enthusiastically with Willa. Once again, she appeared lovely, friendly, and—thank goodness—rather *normal*.

"I believe it's time for Miss Ross' daily lesson," Alex said, strolling in from the doorway. "Go, everyone, before you're late. I need to speak with Miss Stratton."

The younger girls waved and hurried out the door, holding hands, and David followed shortly after them, then reappeared, offered her a wide, little-boy smile with, "Nice to meet you, Miss Stratton," and disappeared again.

Alex looked at his remaining sister. "Anne?"

She gave him the *stare*.

"I need to speak with Miss Stratton. Alone. And you need to go to Miss Ross' lesson."

"But you said my elocution and pronunciation were perfect," she protested.

Apparently Willa was correct to have already made the assumption that the Laurie family was learning how to speak properly from *someone*. Their aristocratic English was actually better than hers, and her father had always claimed there was no one more talented at picking up accents and dialects than she.

"Besides," Anne added, "Mama said you couldn't speak to Miss Stratton by yourself. You have to have a chaperone at all times, she said."

Alex heaved a sigh. "I am not about to ravish Miss Stratton, Anne. Look at her." He pointed toward her face.

"Well!" Willa said, all charitable feeling aroused in her breast by his lovely siblings now entirely erased.

Worse, Anne sighed when she looked at Willa, her

shoulders slumping, and she turned toward the doorway. "Very well." She started to close the door, then poked her head inside. "But I'm leaving it partially open, so the servants can hear if she screams."

Alex smiled at Willa after they heard Anne's footsteps recede down the hall. "I've only had women scream a very certain way when I've been in their bedchambers, and it wasn't because they were terrified."

His guest shook her head, dismissing his halfhearted attempt at flirtation, but Alex barely noticed. He couldn't stop staring at her, and his feet refused to retreat from the room, no matter how much he tried to convince himself he had no reason to be here. There was something about seeing her swallowed in the center of the large bed in *his* guest chamber in *his* house . . . It was the only explanation he could find for this sudden rush of possessiveness that made him want to stay here and watch her instead of doing a hundred other things that required his attention. His business, for one. He'd been neglecting several issues that needed to be resolved while he courted Lady Marianna and chased after the Madonna dye.

"I need a mirror," Willa said, glancing about the room. Her gaze fixed on the dressing table at the left side of the room, and she began to pull the coverlet away.

Alex didn't say a word. If she was too distracted to notice that she was about to let him see her clothed in only her chemise—well, then, who was he to point it out?

But she had to look down, as her legs were tangled in the blanket, and she promptly gasped as she finally realized her lack of dress.

He sighed. "I knew it was too much to hope for."

Willa gave him the stare. It wasn't very bad, but it wasn't nearly as terrifying as Anne's. He burst out laughing when she tried again and again to lift only one brow, but succeeded only in waggling both.

"Bring me a hand mirror, Alex."

"Oh, am I a servant now? Let you ride in my fancy carriage, pay for a physician's visit with my own coin, let you sleep in my fine guest chamber, and this is how you repay me?" Alex strolled over to open a drawer at the dressing table. No mirror. He checked the second. "I even carried you up the stairs," he said. Third drawer. Ah. Hand mirror found.

"You didn't," she said as he returned and gave it to her. Their fingertips brushed. Neither was wearing gloves. Somehow nothing had ever seemed as intimate as this briefest of touches. Though he immediately tucked his hands behind his back, she didn't seem to be bothered in the least.

"I did. I also undressed you, even out of your chemise, and bathed your fevered, naked flesh loyally all through the night." He pasted a leer on his face, dropping his gaze to her breasts.

Willa snatched the coverlet to her chest. "You did

not!" She paused. "I had a fever? I don't usually have a fever—"

"You didn't have a fever," Alex admitted, feeling the tiniest bit guilty.

"So you didn't bathe me?"

"No. Don't sound so disappointed, Willa." He winked.

She scowled. "And you didn't undress me, either."

"Oh, I did undress you."

She waited, as if she *knew*.

"And, yes, my mother and Jo helped. In fact, they were truly the ones who undressed you. I only stood in a corner, trying to catch glimpses of things I shouldn't." It had been from the hallway where he'd been expelled, not the corner. But he'd left the door open a crack and peeked in from time to time. She didn't need to know how worried he'd been.

"You are an awful, awful man, Alex Laurie."

"True," he said, grinning. "Now, look at your face, as I know you've been dying to do for the last several minutes."

She lifted the hand mirror and was silent. Alex forced his eyes to the coverlet, his fingers aching to trace over her swollen skin. But he was still angry and scared from the helplessness during her reaction at Woolstone's cottage, and he didn't trust himself not to grab ahold of her shoulders and shake her until her teeth rattled in her head.

After a moment, she said, "I suppose you're happy

now because you have the secrets of the dye. I never had a chance with Woolstone and his vicious little plants."

"Do I seem happy?"

She lowered the mirror slowly and studied him. "Yes."

"Odd, that is. Because in fact I did not get the secrets of the dye. Instead I, being the noble and self-sacrificing man I am, whisked you into my carriage and made my coachman treat the poor horses terribly to make it into London quickly enough that you might still live. And you did." He paused, then leaned over and kissed her cheek. She smelled clean and womanly and *Willa*. "Perhaps that is why I'm happy."

She'd stilled when he kissed her, and she eyed him cautiously as he backed away.

He gestured wide with a flourish of his hands. "Now you may proceed to fall at my feet in gratitude."

"Thank you, Mr. Laurie."

"Laurie, is it now? What happened to your moans in the carriage last night on the way back to London? *Alex*, you cried, over and over again." He swallowed, disguising the motion with a smile. God, he'd thought she would truly die. He'd held her in his arms as she lay still and quaking, little gasps of breath shuddering through her swollen lips. He'd felt almost as helpless as when Pippa went blind.

He breathed in, then exhaled, again and again, the rage continuing to build deep inside him. She'd nearly died. From *flowers*.

Perhaps it was because she was still weak and partially sedated from the laudanum the doctor had given her last night, or perhaps it was because she lay in his house disoriented and her defenses weren't properly maintained, but instead of giving a scathing retort, she blushed when he spoke of her moaning his name. Turning her face away, she laid the hand mirror aside.

"Thank you, Alex," she murmured, so softly he could only read the words from her lips.

"You're welcome." He clenched his fists and his jaw, embracing the anger now.

Flowers, for God's sake.

He should have stayed and assured her that she looked beautiful, that the swelling was really much better than it had been previously, and to let her know the physician said that as long as she didn't experience any further problems breathing, she could leave the bed anytime she wanted. But he spun on his heel and left the room because he didn't want to tell her she could leave. And he might say something harsh and undeserved, blaming her for almost dying, in keeping with their usual animosity, when all he really wanted to do was hug her to his chest and kiss her until they both needed the physician to help revive them.

*   *   *

When he returned later in the day after seeing Lady Marianna and attending to a myriad of business affairs, Willa's door was closed. He knocked. Voices paused in the room, then began again. Jo opened the door.

"Oh, it's you." Turning, she strode away.

Alex pushed the door open and walked inside. "A pleasant greeting, as always, dear sister."

Willa sat at the dressing table, a deep purple dressing gown covering her chemise to the froths of lace at her wrists. It extended to her ankles and below, where only the very tips of her toes were visible. But her hair—sweet God, her hair . . .

Alex stared at the unbound mass of it, golden and thick, pouring down her back. His mother—who had obviously loaned Willa the dressing gown Alex had bought for her—brushed her hair, one long stroke at a time. The lady's maid, who should have been performing such work, stood in the background, hands folded at her waist, a frown at her brow.

Willa met his gaze in the mirror. He'd been wrong before; he'd never felt so helpless as *now*, staring into her ocean blue eyes, unable by any force of willpower to look away.

"Where have you been?" Jo whispered beside him. "Mama refused to allow her to leave until you returned."

"She tried to leave?" he asked. He meant it to sound skeptical, but instead he feared his sister would hear the dismay in his voice. He forced his gaze away from Willa's and returned it to the dressing gown. If she hadn't managed to put anything else on in his absence, it appeared she might need another day entirely in order to return to the hotel.

"Yes, as soon as you left. One of the maids came and told me, or she probably would have walked out the door without anyone knowing."

Strength, he reminded himself. How many times would he forget the strength that lay beneath her smile?

"Why is our mother brushing her hair?"

"I suspect because she thought Hodgkins was doing a poor job of it," Jo said, then moved to Willa's side.

Willa looked up and smiled at Jo when she began talking.

His family adored her. Not only the little ones, who didn't understand what it had been like before they were born and the Lauries went a day or more without food, when they'd never stepped inside a school and no such thing as separate bedrooms or a nanny had existed; the older ones liked her, too. Anne, Kat, Jo, his mother—they knew who she was, and yet they allowed her to disarm them with her smile and her charming manner. Jude probably would have liked her, too, had he not been away at Eton.

It had been nearly two decades ago, but Alex could still remember her father, Daniel Stratton. As a boy Alex had passed many nights underfoot while Stratton and Joseph Laurie plotted out calculations and strategies for their new business as dye makers. Both had lived in poverty for most of their lives, and both had little schooling. But what his father lacked in learning he made up for in ambition and determination, and once he had a purpose in mind, he found people to teach him what he needed to know. The first investment for their new company had been a nice sum from a middle-class merchant, who then went on to influence other tradesmen to invest, too. The company had just begun to take shape beyond that of a dream when Stratton's American wife had fallen ill and they moved across the ocean so she could be with her family.

Alex remembered the anger and bitterness and resignation between the two men those last few weeks. They'd worked so hard to try to build something worthwhile—and God knew most members of the working class didn't often have a chance to become their own masters—only to see it slip away due to fate's circumstance. But though they were forced to give up their shared dream, neither would give up their hope for it entirely. Instead of remaining partners, once the Strattons left England for America, they became rivals.

Perhaps Alex's family didn't care that Willa was Daniel Stratton's daughter. But that wasn't their burden to shoulder: it was his.

She was Alex's enemy, and his only thought of her should be in regards to the Madonna dye and any other potential investors. There shouldn't be anything more—not a desire to protect her and certainly not this damned possessiveness, which he noticed hadn't abated even though she was no longer in the bed.

He knew she was beautiful and that he desired her, yet any man would have also—this wasn't a weakness. And if he studied her closely, it was because he needed to understand the workings of her mind to try to discover her motives—he could use this knowledge against her. But he wasn't supposed to care about who she was beneath the exquisite surface. She was never supposed to play any other part in his life but that of rival. Even in Italy, even when he'd been drawn to her and kissed her then, this had been clear. Willa Stratton did not fit into his plans for either his family or his business. He could not trust her loyalty. She could not gain him the connections he desired among the aristocracy.

"She cannot be anything more." He murmured it to himself as Willa turned in her seat as she spoke and looked up at Jo and his mother. The three of them laughed together.

If he had any regrets, they were for bringing her back to Holcombe House instead of returning her to Mivart's Hotel.

He would send a note to Woolstone to arrange for a new meeting—one he hoped would take place before Willa was well enough again to follow him to the appointment. As he'd told her before, he intended to win this time. And if he had to use her recovery to his advantage, he would do so.

Alex's gaze caught on her smile, on the golden hair streaming down her back, on the picture of her in his house engaged in laughter and conversation with his family. With Jo and his mother, two people who he knew didn't surrender their affections easily.

Then he turned and quietly slipped out of the room.

She was his rival. She would never be anything more.

Chapter 12

Alex nodded to Thomas, the second footman, as he slipped outside into the cool April drizzle. Tucking the brim of his hat lower over his head and turning up the collar of his overcoat, he slipped his hands into his pockets and made his way through the shadows of Belgrave Square.

Woolstone had chosen a different location this time: a meetinghouse where the Grand Botany Society convened to discuss, presumably, plants. And Alex knew from the first traumatic visit with Willa that Woolstone had an extreme fondness for any item with fronds, leaves, or petals.

Alex shivered as rain slipped inside his collar, trickling cold and wet down his neck. He could have taken a carriage, of course, but the short distance to the meetinghouse meant that he was saved the awful stench of the vehicle. He would rather be drenched than sit inside the carriage for even one more minute. Once the Madonna dye was secured, his next item of business would be the immediate procurement of a new enclosed vehicle.

A smile trespassed on his face as he remembered Willa's reaction to the theories for the smell in the carriage and how Lord Holcombe had died. It fell, however, when Alex realized he was being followed.

It was easy enough to pause and wait for a coach to pass, watching out of the corner of his eye as the familiar figure in black trousers and black coat ducked into the shadows created by the eaves of the nearest house.

Alex gave a small sigh and crossed the street to the meetinghouse. The black, she executed well again. The men's clothes cloaked her womanly form as they had before, though this time he found it more difficult to keep his imagination from straying to the curves hidden beneath. But her hair?

Even tucked inside the little hat she wore, her golden hair stood out like the sun in the darkness, catching the reflection of the lamps and the wetness of the rain.

But her presence didn't matter. Yes, he was annoyed that she must have been sneaking about the house and spying on him *again*, but if Woolstone's reaction at their first introduction was any indication, he was the first man Willa had met whom she wouldn't be able to charm.

Indeed, the only thing Alex had to worry about was the mysterious warning at the end of Woolstone's answering note.

I wish I'd never created it. I wish someone else the greatest of successes. Meet me on Tuesday, following the 9 o'clock conclusion of the Grand Botany Society's meeting. But beware: they will come after you next once they realize you also know the secret.

Who pursued Woolstone, and what danger did they pose that they had made him go into hiding? Were they other botanists, perhaps, who wished to claim the same fame that had come upon Woolstone when the public discovered the Madonna portrait? Were they painters obsessed with the portrait who wished to use the dye for their own works? Were they possibly other dye makers—perhaps Stratton's American competitor?

Scowling, Alex waited deep in the corner by the side door of the meetinghouse where Woolstone had indicated. If the man felt the need to leave through other than the front door, then he must not feel he was safe.

Suddenly Alex wished he had a knife. He was fairly certain the person following him had been Willa; even now he could see her tucked against a statue ten feet away, her blond hair still shouting her presence to the world. But what if she wasn't the only one there? What if someone had been following Woolstone and now they would start following *him*?

Alex glanced at Willa again. They might think she was with him, too, might consider her their rival. That thought disturbed him even more. Tensing, he flicked his hand. *Come here.*

She didn't move, pretending he couldn't see her.

Silently cursing, he removed his hat and pointed at her, then beckoned toward his chest. Shaking the hat, he pretended he was trying to remove the raindrops collected on the brim. He returned the hat to his head.

And still she didn't come, although she did shift, her face accidentally leaving the shadow of the statue. He could see her eyes, dark and wide as she watched him.

"*Pssst!*"

Her shoulders jerked.

"Yes, I can see you there," he whispered furiously. "Come here."

She frowned and shook her head, then sank back into the statue's shadow.

"Obstinate *plague* of a woman," he muttered to himself as he ran the ten or so feet toward her and ducked down beside her. "What are you doing?" he asked—or, rather, shouted in a whisper, if one could very well shout in a whisper.

"I'm watching you," she said calmly, in a normal level of voice, as if danger weren't lurking *everywhere*. She crossed her arms. "When Woolstone comes out, I'd like to speak to him before he gives you anything. If you'll recall, I didn't get a chance to do so before."

"He doesn't want to speak to you! And you're

supposed to still be recovering!" He wanted to hail a hansom cab and have her whisked away to safety. No, he wanted to bundle her up and escort her himself, see to it that she was securely ensconced in her guest chamber back at Holcombe House. Or, better yet, at her hotel. But now was not the time to have this argument. Besides, he knew she was too stubborn; he would never convince her to leave until *one* of them received the Madonna dye from Woolstone. "I think someone is watching us. Do you have a weapon?"

She stared at him as if he'd spent too much time with his head in a vat of dye. "No, Alex," she said slowly, "I don't have a weapon." Her head turned as she peered around him, then from side to side. "And what do you mean, someone's watching us? Who?"

"I don't know," he said irritably, then paused. She glistened with raindrops: her lashes, lips, and skin. The moisture was beginning to soak into her clothes, the material clinging to her curves. An odd desire to nuzzle the side of her neck and lick the wetness from her throat suddenly consumed him. "I thought it would be better if you stayed close by me, just in case something happens."

She looked up at him, only the slightest hint of blue showing in her dark eyes. Her lips curved, a small half-wondering, half-mocking smile brightening the shadows. "You intend to protect me. From the thief or murderer or drunkard, whoever he might be?"

"Against my better judgment, yes." He wrapped

his hand around her arm. "Now, let's go. Back to the door."

Thankfully, when he rose from the crouch she followed, and together they scurried the few feet back to the deep corner beside the side door.

Though it had been only a very small distance, they both panted as if they'd crawled a hundred yards. "What now?" she asked, gasping.

"We wait for Woolstone." Woolstone was a Goliath. What need had they of weapons when they had him?

"And if he doesn't come?"

Alex fumbled as he tried to retrieve his pocket watch from his coat. An unsatisfactory endeavor, of course—it was impossible to read the time in the darkness. He snapped it shut. "He'll come. But if he doesn't, then we'll return to Holcombe House and I'll send you to Mivart's in my carriage."

She wrinkled her nose. "No, thank you. I'll hire a cab."

Alex nearly laughed. "As you wish."

They peered out into the night together, the steady April drizzle blurring the shadows. Minutes passed as they waited, tense and wary of the unknown. The longer she stood beside him, the greater his awareness of the woman huddled against him became. His attention strayed. Though they were out of the rain, droplets continued trickling from her hat into her hair and down her neck. From her temple down the smooth curve of her cheek. He watched one particular raindrop trail to the corner of her mouth, then hover there for a moment before sliding along the edge of her lower lip.

Alex's breath shuddered as he inhaled. "You should have stayed at Holcombe House."

"He's not coming," Willa whispered.

The door swung open with a loud shriek of its hinges, and Willa screamed. Alex jumped and raised the hand holding his pocket watch—because a pocket watch would surely incapacitate any would-be attacker.

But of course it was Woolstone. He frowned down at them, then leaned forward and peered in both directions. "You brought her again? Very well. Come."

Alex gestured for Willa to precede him. Even while she walked, she tortured him with possibilities: the elegant line of her spine offered the perfect path for his hands to follow; he imagined plucking off her hat and spinning her around, tucking his fingers deep inside the waist of her trousers—

She stumbled and pitched forward. Alex lunged to catch her.

"I'm all right," she said, breathing heavily. She smiled up at him, and something pierced Alex's lungs.

Woolstone half turned to see why they were delayed. He frowned. "Are you coming?"

Alex waited until Willa straightened, then released her. His hands acted oddly, though. As soon as he stopped touching her, they lifted again, stretching out toward her.

She's not the one.

They dropped to his side.

"Mr. Woolstone," Willa said, hurrying after their host, "who is following you?"

He stopped and whirled. "You saw someone following me?"

"No," Alex answered, "but I assumed from your note—"

Woolstone slashed his hand through the air. "Once they learn I no longer have it, they will leave me alone. Dear God, I pray they leave me alone."

"But who are *they*?" Willa demanded.

Woolstone's Adam's apple bobbed as he swallowed and leaned forward, his thick brows lowering. "The women," he whispered.

The women.

For the first time since Alex told her someone was watching them outside, Willa's muscles relaxed, and she breathed a sigh.

"The women" didn't sound very dangerous. After all, she was a woman and the best she could do was jab someone with a hairpin or knee someone in the groin. "The women" didn't have quite the ring to it that "the Black Raven" or "One-Eyed Georgie" did at all . . .

"They're everywhere I go," Woolstone muttered darkly. "Accosting me in the street, knocking at my door in the middle of the night. One crawled through my window and offered herself to me if I would help her dressmaker create a gown for her."

Willa laughed. "You can't mean women in general? Because they're interested in wearing the same color as the Queen?"

Woolstone glared at her, obviously categorizing her as one of them. No wonder he'd taken an immediate dislike to her; he never would have been susceptible to her charms if every woman in England was trying to charm him out of the dye. "It is like a plague."

Willa turned to Alex and grinned. "Still think someone was watching us tonight, Mr. Laurie?" He'd tried to protect her, even if the monsters had been imaginary. She wouldn't forget it.

His lips thinned and he ignored her, instead addressing Woolstone. "Thank you for being willing to meet with me again. You have the dye information?"

Woolstone folded his arms and shifted—looking, to Willa's mind, distinctly uncomfortable. Hope soared within her breast. "My apologies, Mr. Laurie, but I could not keep my word. She needed my help."

Alex flinched at the same time Willa's breath hitched.

"You gave it to someone else?" he asked.

She stepped forward. "Who? Who did you give it to?"

"My sister now has the dye information, to do with as she pleases."

Willa's shoulders tried to slump, but she wouldn't allow it. Simply because Lady Marianna had the dye didn't mean that she would give it to Alex. They weren't yet betrothed, either. It might never be his. But she also couldn't see a reason why Lady Marianna would give it to her.

"Ah." Beside her, Alex sounded relieved.

Woolstone cleared his throat. "I know you are courting my sister, Mr. Laurie, but you should know that I gave her the dye so she would have the freedom to marry or to not marry as she wishes. If she chooses you, she will need the dye as her dowry, because I know my father won't approve of the marriage."

"I don't need her dowry. And I intended to marry her regardless." Alex ran his hand through his hair, then down his face, as if he could wipe Woolstone's words away.

It was difficult to find any pity for him. Though it was possible he wouldn't succeed in convincing Lady Marianna to marry him, from everything Willa had seen, it appeared he had a very good chance.

Willa, on the other hand, did not. In a way it could have been amusing that both she and Lady Marianna regarded the Madonna dye as their means to freedom, to choose to live their lives as they wished. Only Willa was fairly certain what Lady Marianna would choose; she could practically hear the wedding bells for Alex and the marquess's daughter now.

"I'd like to return to the hotel," she said.

Alex nodded and they bid good-bye to Woolstone.

Once outside again, they discovered that the drizzle had softened to a fine mist. It blanketed her skin like dew, and Willa turned her face to the heavens. As soon as she returned to the hotel, she would decide what to do next.

Willa pursed her lips, lowering her head. For the moment she didn't want to think about Alex marrying Lady Marianna.

"We will return to Holcombe House first," he said as they walked along. "I would prefer to take a hansom cab, but I fear it's too late for many to be about, and I don't want to wait. My apologies for the state of the carriage."

Willa swallowed. "How goes your courtship of the Lady Marianna?"

He stiffened, then narrowed his eyes. "What are you planning?"

"Nothing." It was the truth; she hadn't even considered sabotaging their relationship until now.

He gave a bitter chuckle. "Well, thank you. I suppose it's a good thing I like her so well already, isn't it? If you marry Uxbridge we will again be competing for investors, won't we?"

Would she still consider marrying the earl? It had become a possibility, if only as a last resort so she wouldn't have to marry Eichel. And she was fond of Uxbridge. "If I married the earl, I would no longer work for my father. You would have the investors to yourself. And the Madonna dye."

"Perhaps I could convince her to sell the dye to you, so you could have your freedom. As I said, I meant to marry her, anyway."

Willa stared at him. "I know you want the dye. Why would you—"

He stopped walking and swung around in front of her, taking her shoulders in his hands.

"Alex—"

He kissed her. It was not at all the slow, exploring kiss of Italy, but an angry, sweeping, passionate kiss that had her bringing her hands up to his chest, uncertain whether he meant to maul her to death.

It turned out that being mauled to death by kissing might not be such a bad thing.

Wrapping an arm about her waist, he backed her against the wall, pressing his body against hers in every place she'd yearned for him for the past three years. But Willa fought just as well as he did; she lifted her hands to his face, scraping her fingernails along his jaw as their lips clashed in sensuous battle. She didn't give him quarter by opening her mouth to him, but sought to invade his with her lips and tongue, wrapping her leg around his calf to take everything he was willing to give her.

Unlike in Italy, no moans escaped from her throat. Moans were for pleasure, and this kiss wasn't a kiss of pleasure, but of greed. His hand slid from her waist to her backside, groping as he rocked hard against her pelvis. She dug her fingers into his damp hair, knocking his hat aside, wriggling against him to get closer.

More, more, more.

Their lips parted, clung, moving together and against each other. Neither gave but took, and only when the hot brand of his palm cupped between her thighs did Willa jerk to her senses.

She wrenched her mouth from his.

His hands immediately retreated and he stepped away. In the mist of rain his heavy breathing created gusts of fog, but otherwise he appeared calm. Unmoved. In complete control as he studied her through dark, alert eyes. Whereas Willa's body pulsed in places it shouldn't, her skin sensitive and throbbing from his touch. Perspiration gathered on her chest, below her breasts. A piercing ache lay between her thighs; a wetness gathered that made her wish if only for a moment that they hadn't stopped. She collapsed against the building, resting her head on the wall.

They watched each other not as predator and prey, but as equal combatants.

He waited for her breathing to slow, for her chest to cease heaving, before he spoke. She hadn't known he carried such patience around in his arsenal of weapons; how much more generous it would have been for him to take her arm and hurry her along to the future, where she could forget these past few precious moments had occurred.

"I suppose you intend to tell me that kiss was disgusting as well."

She understood then: this kiss was all of the regret she would receive for the choices he would make. There would be no words to express what might have been.

Willa straightened and stepped toward him. She

lifted her hand. He flinched. Adjusting the lay of his cravat, she said, "It was adequate." She patted his chest and began walking again. "Come, Mr. Laurie. Take me to my hotel and then you can continue practicing the improvement of your kisses on Lady Marianna."

Not only did Alex have to endure another carriage ride; he had to sit in the carriage across from Willa. Even though he abhorred facing backward, he did so; it was either that or sit beside her, and then he'd have to worry about things. Such as whether or not he'd be able to keep his hands off of her before they reached her hotel. He'd refused to even consider letting her go alone—not because he feared for her safety without him, but because he knew he would be jealous of the minutes he could have spent in her presence.

He sank into the corner shadows of his seat, beyond the dim light of the lamp which swung gently to and fro with the sway of the carriage. He studied her—the proud tilt of her chin, the current aloof curve to the perpetual smile she seemed to wear, the profound interest she exhibited in the night occupations of London street rats as they traveled from Belgrave Square.

Across the carriage, Willa gave a small sigh, soft enough that he might have mistaken it for his own breath if he hadn't seen her lips part and her chest fall.

He shifted, his fingers clenching the seat's edge. Even if he gave up the Madonna dye, even if he refused to marry Lady Marianna, he could not have her. Not if he intended to legitimize his family and business with aristocratic connections. Not if he wished for more aristocratic investors to smooth the way for future expansions, for the acclaim of his invention once it succeeded.

"Do you mean to marry Uxbridge if he proposes?" he asked casually, the first words either had spoken since entering the carriage.

Her shoulders jerked, but she didn't look at him. "I haven't decided."

"What will you do if he doesn't propose? Will you return to America to marry Mr. Eichel? Or will you stay here to encourage another suitor?"

Finally she looked at him, her eyes searching for him in the shadows. "Truly, Mr. Laurie. Simply because you kissed me a little while ago doesn't mean you must be privy to all of my thoughts and plans now."

He gave a short nod and jerked his gaze away, his hands clenching into fists on his thighs. She was correct. She was not his family, not his wife. They weren't lovers; they weren't even friends. And it didn't matter if she didn't marry Uxbridge or Eichel. It didn't matter if she never married at all. She wouldn't be his.

"I fantasize about you, Willa," he murmured in a low voice.

She stilled, and he wondered whether she would pretend to have not heard him.

He went on, not giving her the chance to pretend.

"I've dreamed about kissing you like that a hundred times, a thousand times in the past three years. Perhaps I shouldn't tell you—"

"You're right. You shouldn't." He heard her take a long, shaky breath, then whisper: "Please, don't."

He cursed beneath his breath, but he didn't say anything further. Everything he wanted to tell her was too late. And none of it was enough. Even if he could have, he couldn't speak to her of love.

He could speak of want, and desire, of lust not only for her body but also for her soul: to claim her and possess her wholly. But love? No, he could not speak to her of such. Even if he felt it, it wasn't his right. And she deserved much more than torrid words spewed out of desperation.

They arrived at Mivart's shortly after. The footman opened the door and unfolded the steps. As Willa rose to descend to the street, Alex tugged at her hand.

Her head turned, her gaze meeting his. He forced a smile at the wariness he found there. But all he said was, simply, "Good night, Miss Stratton."

Chapter 13

As far as strategies went, Willa had decided not to leave her fate in the hands of others.

She had learned a few things while stalking Alex and Holcombe House. First, the more one was able to blend into the night, the better.

Tonight, she wore black trousers, a black shirt and coat, black boots, and a short black wig to cover her hair. Nothing would hide the fact that she was a woman; her face would always give her away. But she would keep to the shadows and avoid allowing her face to be seen.

Second, one mustn't leave evidence behind.

Tonight, she'd left her mother's pendant at the hotel.

Third, one must know one's objective.

While at Holcombe House her intention was al-

ways to follow Alex and hope he led her to Woolstone, tonight she waited for the Marquess of Byrne,
the Marchioness of Byrne, and Lady Marianna to leave
for the Athertons' garden party she knew they would
attend.

Once they did, Willa crept to the low garden wall,
hoisted herself over, and covered her nose and mouth
with a kerchief to avoid any reaction to the flowers as
she ran to the terrace doors.

Oh, yes: and one must learn how to pick a lock.
She'd practiced that for hours and hours in her hotel
suite with a hairpin until she'd become quite the ex-
pert.

A quiet click sounded as the lock released, and Willa
eased the door open quietly, her breath frozen in her
lungs. She waited a few moments, her ears listening for
any movement outside the corridors of the Byrne ballroom that would indicate the servants somehow had
discovered her intrusion. No one came; all was well.

Slipping inside, she closed the door and pocketed
her handkerchief, giving her eyes time to adjust to the
darkness before making her way to one of the interior
doors leading away from the ballroom.

Lowering herself to the floor, she searched beneath
the crack of the door for the movement of shoes. All
was quiet, still. A footman or the butler might be at
the front door awaiting the family's return, but the
other servants were most likely in their quarters, resting or enjoying the family's absence.

It was all too easy.

Releasing a shuddering breath, Willa opened the door. She crept quietly through the corridors, slinking from wall to corner to alcove.

She was nearly caught at the main staircase—she didn't dare try to sneak up the servants' stairs—when a maid turned a corner in front of her just as Willa stepped forward out of the shadows.

She froze, her heart beating at her throat, but the maid continued on, unaware.

Willa scurried backward into the shadows again.

The possibility of being discovered had occurred to her many times. After all, she knew it could happen. She'd been discovered at Holcombe House. And there was no feasible explanation for her being here now, not when the family was gone, not when she was dressed as a person who appeared inclined to burglarize the house. She could confess that she meant to sneak in to meet with Richard for an assignation, pretending ignorance regarding the fact that he lived alone somewhere else.

It was the best she had, and even that would thoroughly ruin her reputation. But she was desperate, and if she wasn't discovered and she escaped back to Mivart's in possession of the dye papers, then that would be a very, very good thing, indeed.

A full half hour passed before Willa found the courage to continue, her breath hitching at every small noise emanating from the depths of the house. Only one other servant—the butler—passed by during that time.

If she were going to go, then it must be now. Otherwise she should turn around and leave the house as she'd come in. She'd run up the stairs at the count of three.

One. Two. Three.

She didn't move.

Perhaps after ten.

No. *Now.*

Blood beat at her ears as she rushed from her hiding place and surged up the stairs. She tripped on the last step, tumbling face forward on the landing. Her elbows caught the brunt of her weight.

She heard voices, then footsteps.

Oh, God.

Pushing herself to her hands and knees, Willa scrambled up, then ran down the hallway and inside the first room she found. She shut the door and slammed herself against the wall behind it, her lungs bellowing and her entire body pulsing with terror.

Dear God. Could she possibly be a *worse* criminal?

Although more shadows hugged the room she'd entered, there were shapes strewn throughout the long rectangular room she could identify. A pianoforte. A harp. A viola on its stand.

A music room.

Shouts echoed outside the door, and Willa's gaze darted to the window on the opposite side of the room. Of course she couldn't jump from the window. It was at least fifteen feet to the ground, if not more. She would break bones; she might die.

The floor beneath her feet shook. Willa tensed. Someone ran past the music room. Seconds later, a thunder of noise—more people running—past the music room. These were the voices she'd heard.

"Stop, thief!"

"Get him!"

Him? Someone *else* had snuck into the house?

A hysterical giggle caught at the back of her throat, but Willa swallowed it. She mustn't make a sound.

She heard a door slam far in the distance, then another. And another. Closer this time.

They were searching the rooms!

She should hide, quickly. Beneath the pianoforte. No, they would see her. Behind the harp. No, not there, either.

Her breath came faster and faster as she glanced about the room, from corner to corner, from chair to instrument, from instrument to chair. There was nowhere to go.

Then the door opened, and she forgot to breathe at all.

A man's form appeared—another shadow in the darkness—and he quickly turned, shutting the door quietly.

The other intruder!

She watched, frozen, as he, too, scanned the music room for a place to hide. They'd called him a thief. A true criminal. Did he carry a weapon? A knife, perhaps? If he discovered her there inside the room with him, would he think her a threat and stab her?

A silent scream built low, starting all the way from her toes. It coursed up her legs, through her stomach, into her chest.

Voices. The next room—the door slammed there. They were coming!

The man's head jerked toward the corridor; then he lunged behind the music room door and against her.

Willa's head bounced against the wall. Making claws of her hands, she attacked everywhere she could reach. His neck, his shoulders, his jaw. The scream reached the back of her throat, and she opened her mouth.

"What the bloody—" He pushed his body into hers, clapping a hand over her mouth as he pinned hers arms to her chest with his weight.

She sank her teeth into his palm.

He gave another low curse, then shoved his mouth against her ear. "Stop, Willa. It's me. Alex."

"*Alex?*" she mumbled against his hand. "You—"

The door to the music room opened.

Willa watched it swing toward them, stilling an inch away from Alex's back. A flicker of light shone on the wall to her left. Through the crack between the door and its frame she could see three male servants enter the music room. The last one paused at the door, his sleeve still in her vision.

She swallowed the scream. She scarcely dared to breathe, lest the stirring of air from her nostrils or the movement of her chest against Alex's alert the servants to their presence. Alex must have thought to do the same, because his warm breath at her ear came slowly, softly—almost a caress.

The light reflected on the left wall dimmed.

"Look behind the curtains."

A snap of cloth, as if the servant had been prepared to catch the intruder with an "Aha!"

"He's not here."

"Could he have gone out one of the windows?"

"No, I've been checking them in all the rooms."

"C'mon!" The man by the door spoke. "He must've gone down the other way when we weren't looking. Sam, you go upstairs. Tim, you go downstairs. I'll search the other rooms again."

They filed out, taking the light and slamming the music room door behind them.

Thirty seconds might have passed, at least no more than a minute. All at once sensation returned to her body, and right along behind it, awareness of the man who still stood against her, pinning her to the wall with his strong, hard, heavy body. His nose pressing into her hair, his mouth at the top of her ear.

Neither of them spoke and neither moved for several minutes.

Finally Alex sniffed. "Your hair. That's where the cinnamon comes from."

"Please move."

"I think we should stay like this. They might come back at any moment."

"Alex . . ." She paused. It was a tempting suggestion.

"I suppose you want to know what I'm doing here. I followed you."

"Obviously. But why?"

"It's what I would have done in your circumstances."

"Wonderful. You might have been stealthier in the following. Now we'll both get caught."

Down the hall in the opposite direction, they heard another door close.

They froze, not saying anything until minutes later when the echo of yet another door, farther away, slammed.

"Please move," she whispered. "I—I don't want you near me." Any longer and she feared the places her hands would travel, the hollows her mouth would seek.

He lurched backward. Moonlight streamed in from the curtains the servant had left opened, framing his silhouette. She couldn't see his face, but she could hear the frown in his voice when he mumbled, "I'm sorry. I was only thinking— Of course . . ."

Running footsteps overhead. Sam was very enthusiastic and probably thorough in his search. The whole house was probably crawling with servants. They would be back this way. They would probably search the music room again.

Willa stepped to the left and tried to edge around Alex toward the window. It was the only way.

He caught her wrist and pulled her toward him. "No, the next room. There's a tree."

Loosening his grip, he slid his fingers down to hold her hand, then led her toward the door. "Follow me," he whispered.

He opened the door and Willa blinked against the light. The servants had set all the wall sconces blazing. Turning his head in both directions, Alex said, "We'll wait until he comes out and goes into another room. When I say go, we go. Understand?"

Voices shouted nearby, a brighter light flickering against the wall. More servants coming up the staircase.

Alex cursed. "We don't have time. Go!"

He ran out the door, then ran back and grabbed her hand. "I said go!"

"I know, I know," she said, gratitude and pleasure flooding her that he'd come back for her. She'd stood frozen, her feet unable to move—not because she didn't want to follow him on principle, but because of fear.

They ran into the next room, a salon, and to the window nearest the fireplace, where the sturdy branches of a large tree stretched toward the house.

Alex threw open the window. "I'll go first," he said, swinging his legs over the sill. "Then I'll pull you with me."

Willa considered the branch nearest the window— quite medium-sized, it was—then looked past Alex to the ground below. "All right." She might break an arm and a leg tonight, after all.

Alex placed one foot on the branch, bouncing a

little to test his weight. He grinned back at her. "God loves us, Willa." He climbed out onto the branch, then turned around to face her, straddling the branch as he held out his hands.

The door crashed open behind her.

"There he is!"

"There are two of them!"

Willa glanced over her shoulder. "Now!" Alex shouted. With the scream finally tearing loose from her throat, she hurried onto the sill and took his hands.

Someone caught the back of her coat. They tugged.

She screamed again, unbalanced. Her gaze flew from Alex's face and his dark wide eyes to the branch now wobbling with his weight, to the ground far below.

His hands tightened around hers. "Jump! I'll catch you, I promise."

She didn't question him. Jerking forward to escape the fingers clutching her coat, she fell against his chest. Her legs dangled in air. "Alex," she gasped.

"Don't worry. I have you."

The faces of Byrne's servants crowded the window.

"Tim, go get under that tree. Quickly! Sam, go find the magistrate."

Alex pulled her against his chest. She swung her leg over the branch. He took her chin and forced her gaze to his. "We have to go now."

"Yes!"

He turned and crawled toward the tree's trunk, then lowered himself to the next branch. She followed and slid down. He caught her around the waist. They did the same for the next branch, then the next. She never hesitated. Probably she should have. But she didn't. She trusted him to help them escape.

At one point she caught a glimpse of his face as he turned away for the next branch. He looked back, grinning, then winked at her. "One would think you're enjoying this," she said.

"I am. Aren't you?"

"No." But she was. Now that they were closer to the ground, now that the servants were far above them. Every time he put his hands on her, her heart beat a little faster, and it was already racing so quickly she thought it might stop from exhaustion at any moment.

"I believe I deserve a kiss," he said as he lowered her to the last branch.

The servant Tim came running around from the back of the house, his lamp swinging.

They jumped together, and Alex pulled her up from the ground when she landed on her hands and knees. "Hurry," he said.

They ran to the front of the house, Tim fast behind them.

A carriage slowed to a stop on the street, the crest of the marquess on its side. The family had returned. A groom climbed down from the top and unfolded the steps.

"We can't make it," she panted. Her side ached; her lungs burned.

"Have a little faith, Willa." The bloody man didn't even sound like he was sprinting beside her. "To the right."

The groom opened the carriage door and held out his hand.

Behind them, Tim shouted, "Paul! Catch them!"

The groom Paul looked at them just as they hit the sidewalk and turned right.

"Please tell me your carriage is somewhere nearby," she said between gasps for breath.

"No, followed you on foot."

Then he took her hand, ducked into the shadows clinging to the next town house, and pulled her with him up into another tree.

"Don't breathe."

His arms wrapped around her as he leaned against the trunk, standing and holding her back tightly to his front.

Tim, Paul, and two others appeared through the branches, running along the street.

"They'll come back."

"How do you know?"

"*Shh.*"

And there were Tim and another servant again, holding up the lamp and peering toward them. Willa held absolutely still. She could feel Alex's chest rise and fall against her back. One strong arm wrapped around her waist, the other beneath her breasts. This time his breath shuddered behind her ear. She closed her eyes.

She couldn't hear anything but Alex's breathing and the hard, rapid beat of her own pulse in her ears.

"They're gone."

Her spine collapsed and she sank against him, opening her eyes again.

He pressed a quick kiss to her ear. "We'll wait a little while," he said in a hushed voice. "Not too long. I'm sure they'll try to search again. Just a few minutes."

She nodded, afraid to speak lest they somehow hear her.

His arms relaxed around her. "I still believe I deserve a kiss for that."

Tilting her head up, she turned her neck toward him. He kissed her before she could speak her refusal, a short, warm brush over her lips that liquefied the muscles in her thighs.

"One more minute," he said.

Willa lowered her head. She could feel his heartbeat at her back, nearly as fast as her own.

Chapter 14

The next evening, Willa spied Alex immediately after entering the Byrne box with Richard. It would have been difficult to miss him since he was sitting in the first row of seats in the box, beside Lady Marianna, who presently laughed at something he said.

"Are you all right, Willa?" Richard whispered near her ear. "You look rather pale all of a sudden. Shall I take you back to the hotel?"

Willa smiled brightly up at the earl. "Thank you for your thoughtfulness, but I feel perfectly fine."

Richard inclined his head and met her eyes—something lurked there, something deep and meaningful and altogether terrifying. Still smiling, Willa turned and gestured toward the empty seats. "Where shall we sit, my lord?"

"Anywhere you wish, Miss Stratton."

Willa swallowed at the note of disappointment she heard in his voice—presumably at her continued formality. Once he escorted her to two seats behind Alex and Lady Marianna, she said, "Did you receive my note for the flowers? They are beautiful."

Richard chuckled. "Yes, but you don't need to send a note every day. I want you to take time to enjoy them, not feel obligated that you have to write me your thanks every time you receive more."

Alex looked over his shoulder. "Flowers make her ill," he said, then returned to his conversation with Lady Marianna.

Willa stared at the back of his head.

"Is that true?" Richard asked.

"Yes. No. That is, yes, I do have a reaction to flowers, but I do not react badly to all of them. I'm sorry. I should have told you."

"No, I apologize for sending you something that could have harmed your health. How does Mr. Laurie—"

Willa dismissed Alex with a wave. "I met Mr. Laurie three years ago on a business trip in Italy. I'm certain he remembers from that time."

"I see."

Although his expression never changed from one of content amiability, she could tell Richard wasn't happy. "But I do keep the roses," she said cheerfully. "Please don't stop sending those. Even if the others didn't make me ill, they are still my favorite flower."

Richard sent her a seductive smile and lifted her hand to his lips. "Then I will send you a hundred roses," he murmured low, his voice suggestive and meant only for her ears. "Perhaps one day I can surprise you with a thousand, Willa, spread throughout your bedchamber."

The lights dimmed and the opera began.

"My lord," she replied, her tongue thick. She didn't need to pretend to blush; she could tell by the way Alex's shoulders tensed and his head turned slightly toward them that he'd heard every word.

His shoulders tensed. . . .

Tightening her fingers around Richard's, she glanced at him through her lashes. "That is a day I look forward to very much, my lord," she said, a little more loudly than the quiet murmur he had used. "But I hope you would be in my bedchamber also."

"Oh, dear," a woman's voice said behind them.

Willa froze. Richard's *mother's* voice—the *Marchioness of Byrne.*

"No," she whispered.

Richard chuckled against her knuckles and winked at her, then lowered her hand to his arm. "Perhaps we can continue our conversation at a later time, Miss Stratton."

"Yes, I think that would be wise." Her voice came out like a mouse's squeak. She stared straight ahead, toward the stage over Alex's head. Of course *he* made no indication he'd heard her response. *He* appeared much engrossed in the buxom singer wearing little more than a scrap of sackcloth. Or at least he appeared engrossed in the singer when he wasn't turning his head to whisper in the buxom Lady Marianna's ear, his lips grazing her lobe from time to time.

Willa drank her champagne and alternated between watching the opera, watching Alex continue to whisper in Lady Marianna's ear, and pretending to pay attention to the sweet little nothings that Richard continued to whisper in *her* ear.

By the time the first intermission arrived she was ready to return to Mivart's, but she allowed Richard to take her arm as they mingled among the crowd in the lobby. She couldn't remember whom she met or what she said, though.

"And how are you enjoying the opera tonight, Miss Stratton?"

At the sound of her name, Willa jerked to attention. She tried to find the person who'd spoken to her in their current circle, but no hint appeared on anyone's face. She couldn't even remember if the voice had been male or female. With a great smile, Willa met the gaze of the other four people in their group. "It's quite wonderful." She looked up at Richard. "Although I must admit the company tonight is even more enjoyable. Lord Uxbridge has been marvelous at translating all of the songs for me from the Italian."

And, for the most part, translating them incorrectly. She was fairly certain the hero of the opera had not been singing a mourning song about his dog dying.

But it was nice. There were far worse things a man could do to offend her than speak poor Italian.

Richard asked a question of someone else, and Willa's gaze narrowed over the shoulder of one of the guests. Alex stood beside Lady Marianna, and he was trying to catch Willa's attention, motioning her to the far right side of the lobby.

She shook her head.

He smiled at an older couple nearby, then nodded in her direction. "Please," he mouthed, then turned back to respond to something Lady Marianna said.

Rising to her toes, she made her excuses to Richard regarding an issue with her gown, then turned and threaded her way through the crush of the crowd toward the far right side of the lobby.

Five minutes later, tapping her toes, Willa pretended not to notice Alex as he finally made his way toward her.

He took her elbow. "Come." He tried to lead her away, but she rocked backward and locked her knees.

"Please say what you must, Mr. Laurie. I wish to return to my host before the intermission ends."

Alex turned and searched Willa's face, noting the sharp little lines at the corners of her eyes, the stubborn cast of her chin. Unfortunately, he wasn't in a very fine mood at the moment, either. In fact, his mood could have been described as something most foul, a sour disposition that had had time only to deteriorate for the better part of the first act.

A thousand roses in her bedchamber, indeed.

"The intermission will be over soon," he told her, his fingers gripping her elbow and tugging her toward him. "I'd like to speak to you while I escort you back to the box." He paused, noted the rebellious glint in her eye, then added through clenched teeth, "If you please, Miss Stratton."

When he tugged again she hesitated only a moment, then allowed him to lead her up the staircase and down the corridor, which was empty of all except for passing attendants. After the fourth attendant they were alone in the corridor. He heard Willa open her mouth with an indrawn breath, but he didn't give her a chance to speak. Pulling her into a dark alcove opposite the boxes, he turned her against the wall and kissed her.

God, this was all he'd wanted.

Her lips were soft and warm, her body pliable with surprise, and she smelled like what he imagined heaven must smell like: cinnamon and Willa. Before she could stiffen and push him away, Alex drew back.

She blinked at him, lips still parted and dewy, a small indentation lined between her brows. She was adorable.

"Willa Stratton, speechless?" Alex chuckled and drew a finger down her cheek. "Oh, happy day. I never thought it could happen."

She tried to shove past him, but he captured her shoulders and pushed her back against the wall, then bent his head to hers. He nuzzled the shell of her ear, then pulled the velvet soft lobe gently between his lips.

"I truly wish you wouldn't do that," she said, all stiff and icy and lying through her teeth. Alex touched his tongue to her ear. "I d-don't like it when you touch me."

"I don't like it when you touch me, either," he replied. "You should put your hand on my chest. I would absolutely *abhor* it."

She did, though the first impact was more of a punch. "Like this?" she whispered, a moan edging the end of "this" as he sucked and played with her ear.

"Exactly so. Oh, that's horrible. Willa Stratton, touching me. I can't bear it." Alex shuddered, then whispered, "It would be much worse if your hand were to go a little lower."

Her fingers slid down his waistcoat ever so slowly, then paused in the center of his stomach. "Here?"

"That's frighteningly dreadful, but if you truly wish to offend me, I suggest you go even lower."

"V-very well."

She tilted her head. Alex closed his eyes and sank his lips against her throat, intoxicated by the hot satin of her skin, the delicate pressure of her fingers flattened against him as they skimmed downward over his abdomen.

Her fingers paused as she reached the tip, and her breath caught on a gasp. "There?" It was a wholly flattering sound, as if she'd expected having to go much lower to find him.

"Yes. *There.*" Alex rewarded her by catching the delicate tendon of her neck between his teeth, then soothing it with his tongue.

"Oh, Willa," he murmured against her throat. "I've never been so disgusted in my—"

She snatched her hand away and gave him a tight smile, her cheeks flaming even in the dim light. "Perhaps you should have asked Lady Marianna to touch you," she said, then lifted her chin and ducked out of the alcove.

Chapter 15

Willa spent the entire second act of the opera thinking about touching Alex.

Richard kept leaning over to her every few minutes and asking if she was all right, because her cheeks *refused* to return to their normal color—she could feel their blistering heat just as much as she was aware of the dampness between her thighs.

When the attendants lit the lamps again for the second intermission, Willa was the first to stand in their box. "I'll meet you in the lobby," she told Richard, then whirled and hurried to the ladies' retiring room.

In the retiring room lay a basin and a pitcher of water upon a stand, and Willa poured water into the basin with shaking hands, then dipped a cloth into the water and patted her cheeks, her forehead, her throat.

Oh, God.

She'd touched him. *There.*

She'd been quite honest when she told Alex that she didn't like it when he touched her. He made her feel . . . uncontrolled. Helpless.

Lost.

Which might be all well and good if he were a man she could find herself with, but he would one day marry a woman of the English aristocracy, and she would one day marry someone else. And she wanted intimacy with a man she could love, with someone who could love her in return.

And that man wasn't Alex Laurie.

Willa turned and looked into the mirror on the wall. Her cheeks were still rosy but no longer felt like they were on fire. Soon she would need to speak to Richard. He deserved to court someone who could marry him and *not* think about another man's private parts while Richard was sitting beside her, trying to make her laugh with ironic observations of the singers onstage.

Willa left the retiring room as a trio of other women entered.

When she neared the Byrne box, she found Alex standing there, leaning against the wall with his arms and ankles crossed.

Watching her, he drew back the curtain to the opera

box and gestured inside. She walked past him and sat in the empty box, in the seat she'd taken before, beside Richard. Alex sat in front of her again, though he twisted in the seat halfway to look at her. Those who remained in boxes nearby would see them talking, nothing more. No more dark alcoves, no more inappropriate touches or kisses.

Alex cleared his throat. "What is the number one complaint about your father's dye, Miss Stratton?"

Willa hesitated. It was not at all what she'd expected him to say. "I don't understand. Do you truly believe that I would expose such a weakness to his rival?"

"Allow me to phrase it another way, then. What is your favorite color?"

"Pink," she answered immediately, then narrowed her gaze. "Why do you want to know my favorite color, Mr. Laurie?"

He shook his head as if clearing it. "For an example. If you were to wear a pink gown, what would happen to your chemise and petticoats and corset that touched the gown?"

"They would turn pink as well, of course . . ."

"And if you were to wear a pink chemise, what would happen to your skin?"

Willa pursed her lips. "I don't think I like this question. You're not now imagining me dressed only in a pink chemise, are you?"

Alex grinned at her. "Perhaps. But answer the question, please."

"If I were to wear a pink chemise, then I imagine my skin would turn pink."

"Aha! Yes, that is the correct answer. Congratulations, Miss Stratton."

"And this is important because—"

Alex leaned in, beckoning her to come close. She did—only out of curiosity, not because she was drawn to the way his eyes shone or the creases at the corners of his mouth when he smiled.

"Because, Miss Stratton," he whispered, "at a certain mill in a certain town there is a new process being tested, one which I have invented wherein dye on one cloth will no longer stain another cloth or the skin it lies against."

Willa drew back. She knew her eyes went wide, saw how pleased he was at her astonished expression. She couldn't help it. If his invention truly worked, he would be fabulously wealthy, ten times more so than her father. "No . . ."

"Yes, very much so." His smile faded. "I'm leaving in a few days for another visit to the mill. I'd like for you to go with me."

"With Lady Carlyle?"

"No. Alone."

They stared at each other. Willa nodded. "I would be delighted to visit your mill."

She stood from the seat. She'd promised to meet Richard in the lobby again, and the intermission was already halfway over. Something urged her to hold out her hand again, although she shouldn't have. His hand was always too large, too strong. It made her wish he'd wrap his arms around her and never let go. "I look forward to it, Alex."

He took her hand, and it was everything she feared. She wanted more.

Chapter 16

$f$our days later, the owner of Alex's mill, Ronald MacFadden, scratched his chin.

And no wonder, Willa thought, focusing on the thick blond beard covering the man's chin instead of on Alex, who stood right beside her. The beard was a monster, bristling and wiry. It probably tried to kill him in his sleep.

"Is it all right if we look around?" Alex asked.

"Look around all you like. Let me know if you want to change something. Just don't get in the way of the girls."

"Thank you. Good to see you again, Mr. MacFadden."

The mill owner tipped his hat. "Mr. Laurie. Miss Laurie."

Alex stood still until he walked away, then turned to Willa. "Don't say a word until we go outside."

He took her elbow and guided her down the narrow stairs to the lower floor, away from the offices that overlooked the manufacturing lines.

He led her out the side doors, to the small, barren courtyard in between the main mill and the factory on the other side.

"I'd prefer if you didn't touch me, Mr. Laurie. I believe I told you that earlier at the inn."

Alex opened the door to the factory, then waited for her to step inside. "You're supposed to be my sister," he said behind her. "Try not to act so hostile."

"I'm fairly certain Jo would act even worse," she retorted, smiling at the women and girls who glanced quickly away from their stations as they walked past.

He caught up beside her. "Perhaps, but MacFadden has met Jo. He hasn't met Kat, and Kat is much more amiable. Kat *adores* me."

Willa looked up.

He shrugged. "It's true."

"Kat *tolerates* you better than most, Mr. Laurie. Besides, I'm too old to be Kat. Perhaps we can pretend I'm another older sister they never met."

"Impossible," he said, shaking his head. "You clearly look too young to be my older sister. In fact, you look closer to Kat in age than you do to Jo. You're beautiful. No wrinkles, no bitter skepticism showing in your eyes, no blemishes on your skin."

Willa peered at him. She was usually quite good at

reading him, but she couldn't tell now if he was flirting with her or if he'd actually misunderstood. "Not your older sister, Mr. Laurie. A sister who's older than Kat. I wouldn't need to be older than you are. I could still be six and twenty."

"Ah." He'd misunderstood. "Very well, then. But you should still act nice toward me. Pretend you are Jo on a very, very good day."

He'd misunderstood, and still he'd called her beautiful. Willa lifted her face without wrinkles, blemishes, or bitter skepticism and presented him with a bright, sunny smile. "Does Jo ever have a very, very good day? I must admit to being quite impressed with only her good days. Although I'm certain she acts much better around me than she does around you."

Alex chuckled and came to a halt, his hand grasping her elbow again and turning her to the right.

"The door in front of you. It's through there."

A few minutes later, after they strode across the wide expanse of the open factory, where women and girls—some appeared as old as sixty or as young as twelve—sorted through the fabric spit out on the belts, Willa pushed through the far door he'd indicated.

A thick, pungent odor immediately assaulted her nostrils. Willa took a deep breath, a sense of peace for the first time since she'd come to England filling her. This she knew; with this she felt at home. The chemicals, the colors, the vats of boiling water.

Dye.

She could have stayed in this particular room for hours, strolling around each station and studying the processes of MacFadden's workers. She could have observed what they did differently, how their stations were set up compared to those of her father's workers. She could have reported back to him—

"This way, dear sister." Alex blocked her vision. He didn't touch her, but stood before her and angled his body toward the left, where he wanted her to go.

Willa turned toward the left, then followed him a short distance. Finally, they'd arrived at the stations testing his nonsaturation process.

Alex chatted and smiled with the women working there, charming them in less time than it took him to pick up a piece of dyed cloth and turn around to hand it to Willa. "Look at this," he said. "What do you see that's different?"

She held the cloth—a dark blue wool—and turned it over in her hands. "Nothing. I don't see a difference from what it would usually look like."

He grinned at her. "Precisely. Thus far that is the achievement I'm proudest of. It's taken at least six months to figure out how add the glaze so thinly it wouldn't leave any residue or crystals behind."

"Are you only testing wool now?" she asked, glancing down the line. She noticed that the women watched her more closely than they did before, the young girls staring at her day dress and the others—the ones old enough to understand Alex's flirtation—sending her little daggers with their eyes when they thought she didn't see. She repeated herself loudly. "Are you only testing wool now, brother?"

Though his profile was now to her, she saw the twitch of his lips before he turned back with a new cloth in his hands. This one was purple and shimmered even in the dull light.

"Here you are, sister. Satin. The very first time I've seen the product after it's been tested."

Willa studied the cloth, rubbed it between her fingertips. Alex had insisted she wear gloves before they left the inn, had said she needed to appear like a lady. After hearing him speak of MacFadden and after meeting the manager, she now knew why. She started to roll her glove from her elbow, but he stayed her with a hand on her arm.

"No need to do that. It doesn't work yet."

When their eyes met he frowned and immediately removed his hand, as if he thought she wished him to do so but couldn't in front of the other women. This time, however, she hadn't tensed. She hadn't noticed. And now that he'd removed his touch from her without her request, like the contrary creature she was she wished it was there again, his fingers warm even through the glove.

Willa gave the satin back to him. "Why doesn't it work? It looks clean, and if it's run through your glaze, or whatever you call it—"

He shrugged and turned away to hand both the wool and the satin to one of the women workers. "I don't know." He lifted his other hand and showed her the blue and purple stains on his fingers. "I'll figure it out soon enough."

His eyes lit with frustration, but still he smiled again. Always smiling, no matter how he truly felt. Just like she did. They were both charmers, she and Alex. Smiling and charming the world, one person at a time. She wondered if he ever tired of it, too. Or, if they both laid down their facades for one day, what they would each find behind the smiles of the other.

"Thank you, ladies," he said, bowing to the workers. They smiled and nodded—some giggled and curtsied back—and then he gestured for Willa to precede him out of the factory. "Come, sister, I believe it's well past noon and time to eat, and I'd very much like to try the mutton pie at the Boar's Head."

Though the Boar's Head inn was only a short distance away from the Three Crowns on the opposite side of the small village of Abysmount, the structure was far less hospitable and welcoming. And much more disgusting. The owner snatched a toothpick out of his mouth, then inserted it into a piece of mutton pie to see if it was done.

"Er, thank you," Alex said, then carefully cut around the center of the pie with his fork and moved the acceptable pieces to one side.

He glanced at Willa, who just sat gaping at her piece, so he reached over and did the same for her pie, too. Alex smiled at the keeper, chef, and owner of the face which in fact resembled a boar's head—a *remark-*

able resemblance. Helped one to remember the inn, too. "I'm sure it's delicious," he said, and ate his first bite.

When Willa only stared at him, he gestured with his fork for her to eat, then turned his gaze back to the innkeeper. Merriman, the man's name was—though at least in this there appeared no correlation between his name and his nature. That would simply have been cruel.

No, he was a mean, ugly, boar's head of a man, and Alex ate another piece of pie to show him how much he liked it before speaking again. "Mmm. A better piece of mutton pie I've yet to taste. Don't you agree, Alexandra?"

She'd insisted that they be twins on the return to the village. Even though he'd pointed out that her fair coloring contrasted with his dark coloring to such a degree that everyone would question it. Still, her newly assumed role seemed to make her happy.

Alexandra née Willa agreed, nodding as she ate another forkful. Her eyes told him she felt differently. Perhaps he should have scooped her toothpick piece onto his plate.

The innkeeper stared down at them. He didn't polish the counter with his apron—of course, the state of the counter beneath their plates attested to the fact that this wasn't surprising. He didn't answer to another visitor's request for an ale. He didn't fawn over them because Willa wore the dress of a lady and Alex had changed into a fresh set of clothes before going to the mill this morning. He just stared down at them. "Glowered" might have been a better description.

Next to Alex, Willa cleared her throat delicately, then tilted her head and fluttered her eyelashes at Merriman.

That seemed to get his attention, the biased bastard. Not that Alex had ever tried to flutter his eyelashes, but he was fairly certain that even if he could achieve the exact same eyelash-fluttering frequency, it still wouldn't have resulted in the same effect Willa seemed to have on the man.

Tipping his mug of ale back, Alex drank and watched the mistress of charm flaunt her assets. He also drew his legs up close to his chair, prepared to reach down for the knife tucked in his boot in case he needed to protect those assets.

"Mr. Merriman," she began, stretching forward and leaning until the surface of the table pushed her breasts up to mouthwatering proportions. She touched the innkeeper's arm—a light fluttering of a touch as quick and harmless as her eyelashes, no more substantial than the brush of a hummingbird's wings. The innkeeper's posture shifted, becoming taller and broader as he brought his legs together from his wide stance, straightened his spine, then squared his shoulders.

Oh, she was good. *Very* good.

Alex took another drink and let his other hand rest on his thigh, closer to his knife.

She and Mr. Boar's Head Merriman had some sort of connection. They stared at each other, a little smile tucked into the corners of her mouth while the fist-sized indent centered in his chin softened to the size of a shilling.

She extended her gloved hand, palm down, like a lady's. "Miss Alexandra Laurie."

The innkeeper stared at the hand, his mouth parted, then shook his head. "Thank you, Miss Laurie, but I wouldn't want to sully your gloves with these big old washbasins here." He tucked his own hands—and the polishing apron, unfortunately—out of sight behind the counter.

"Well it's a pleasure to meet you all the same, Mr. Merriman. I must confess I've never liked mutton pie much before now, but you have a special recipe, don't you?"

Alex smiled into his mug. *Yes, it's called saliva on a stick.*

Her foot kicked his shin beneath the table. He jerked his gaze toward hers, saw her eyes cut back to Merriman's as she smiled. Alex set his ale down and picked up another forkful. "I agree, Mr. Merriman. Although I would never tell my mother. I'm sure you understand, don't you?" Alex winked.

Merriman beady little boar's eyes twitched. "I'm sure I don't, Mr. Laurie, as I don't have a mother anymore to tell."

Damn.

Willa kicked him again.

Very well. He'd just leave the talking to her and nod or shake his head as needed.

She reached forward to touch Merriman's arm again—this time, for twice as long. Alex's eyes narrowed. "How terrible. Mr. Merriman, I'm so sorry. We're both sorry, aren't we, Alex?"

Alex nodded.

"I'm sure you don't want to talk about it, but you must know—"

The innkeeper placed his hand over hers. His big washbasin of a hand that swallowed up hers and half her forearm as well. Alex's fingers twitched for his knife.

"She was a good woman, Miss Laurie. A truly good woman."

Willa nodded. For good measure's sake, Alex did, too.

"Would you like to hear about her?"

"Oh, only if you have time, Mr. Merriman. I don't want to disrupt your business."

Merriman swung his heavy jowls toward the other customers in the inn, scowling. Those watching the exchange between Beauty and the Boar's Head flinched and stared down at their tables. "I have time." Trundling around the bar, the innkeeper pulled out a stool and sat down beside her with a groan. "As I was saying, Miss Laurie, my mother was a good woman, one of the finest women I've ever known—present company included, of course."

Willa smiled shyly and twisted her back away from Alex, setting her chin on her folded hands. "I wish I'd had the chance to meet her."

Alex gave an inward sigh, ate the rest of his mutton pie, then reached over for Willa's plate.

Four and a half hours later, Alex and Willa strolled side by side back to the Three Crowns on the opposite side of the village. Her pace was much livelier than his. Alex was tempted to fall facedown in the dirt and sleep.

"You shouldn't have dismissed the carriage," she told him, her eyes sparkling a brighter blue than the sky above her head.

He waved his hand with a flourish, bowing slightly at the waist. "I suppose you're right. But I thought that at least the coachman and groom could enjoy the rest of the day and I could live vicariously through them. Four *hours*, Willa. No, nearly *five* hours, Willa."

He'd surreptitiously checked his pocket watch every time Willa had leaned forward and asked the innkeeper to tell her more. The first hour he'd listened to Merriman recount the number of times his mother had taken care of the blind, lame, sick, and poor until Alex started picturing her as a resurrected female Jesus ingrained into the table's scarred wooden surface. After the second hour, he tested to see whether his legs would still work and went outside to dismiss the carriage. After the third hour, Alex had given up and hung his head over his empty mug of ale—because Merriman couldn't be troubled to fill it again, oh no— and contemplated the meaning of life as well as the ways in which a man could undress a woman from the back without her realizing it.

He couldn't remember what he'd done or thought after that. He was pretty sure he'd found some sort of alternate plane of existence where one's body could remain in an inn, one's head nodding and shaking on command, while one's soul drifted in limbo, called back only by the gentle then forceful nudging of a beautiful woman's hand on one's shoulder.

"He might have killed you, you know," she said after a minute. "He didn't like you very much."

Alex whirled her toward him and kissed her fast and hard, then broke away. He started walking again.

"You shouldn't have kissed me. I'm supposed to be your sister. What if someone had seen?"

Alex laughed and reached over, tucking her hand into the crook of his elbow. He liked the way she fit against his side: comfortable, like she was supposed to belong there. "To tell you the truth, I honestly don't care. All I want to do is get to our inn, eat my supper, go to my room, and sleep until noon tomorrow."

A few minutes later—or it could have been ten or fifteen minutes later, as he'd lost all track of time and was too tired to pull out his pocket watch again— Willa said, "Did you want me to walk beside you so you could lean on me for support?"

"Perhaps."

"That's what I thought."

Chapter 17

Willa startled awake, breathless, heart pounding. She searched the darkness of the small bed-chamber at the Three Crowns. Nothing there. No one. Nothing to wake her.

Sighing deeply, she lay back and turned over, hugging her pillow to her chest. She closed her eyes.

"Willa!" Alex's voice. A banging on the door. "Willa, wake up!"

Throwing back the coverlet, Willa scooted to the edge of the bed and lit the oil lamp nearby. She grabbed her dressing gown and wrapped it tightly around her waist, then ran to the door.

As soon as it opened Alex rushed her, picking her up and spinning her around. "It works, it works!"

Willa gave a shriek, clutching tightly to his shoulders. It made him laugh as he spun her again, and she smiled at the joy in his eyes. He set her down. "Alex—"

He picked her up and spun her around again. Three times, the dark wood of the walls and the light from the lamp blurring beyond his face. When he put her down, Willa lifted her eyebrows, waiting.

He grinned. "I'm done, I promise."

"Alex—"

"Look at my hands, Willa." He held up his hands, palms forward. "No dye!"

Over the span of several seconds the pieces finally clicked together. "Your new process works?"

"Yes!" He moved behind her and shut her door, then took her by the hand and led her to the bed.

She understood that it was a matter to celebrate, and she *had* just been having a terrific dream that involved her, Alex, and a bed—one much larger than this one, though—but still . . . this was rather sudden. She was still half asleep.

"Ah . . . Alex—"

"Sit down."

She sat, then stood and opened her mouth to speak again, but he'd already whirled away, pacing the floor. "Oh," she murmured to herself as she sat on the bed. He wasn't thinking about romance, after all.

"I have you to thank, Willa," he said, pointing at her and smiling as he paced.

"You do?"

"Yes. I was lying in bed after supper, trying to go to sleep, but I couldn't stop thinking about all the things that bloody innkeeper went on and on about this afternoon."

"Merriman, you mean."

"Yes, him. He was talking about his mother, and how she used to create the most fabulous blackberry cobbler—"

"Berry."

He stopped, staring at her with his brows slammed together. "What?"

Willa shifted on the bed. "There were blackberries, but blueberries and raspberries, too. It was a wild berry cobbler, not just a blackberry cobbler."

He stared at her harder, then shook his head and continued pacing. "Regardless, I remember how he spoke about her complaints with it. The juice always got on her hands and clothes, staining them."

He looked back at her. Willa nodded.

"No matter what she tried, she couldn't remove the stains from her clothes. I was lying in bed, thinking about this, cursing the innkeeper and his mother and her blackberry cobblers—"

"Berry cobblers," Willa interjected. Merriman's mother had sounded like a truly wonderful woman; she deserved for her memory to be preserved correctly. And it made Willa feel like she was contributing something.

"Yes, yes, berry cobblers, whatever they were. I was furious that I couldn't go to sleep because I was so tired—you saw me earlier."

She nodded again, hoping he was going to get to

the end soon. She'd just realized that her hair was unbound, and her feet were bare, and although he didn't
seem to notice, *she* was now very aware of her state of
undress.

He smacked his hands together. "And then it came
to me! The reason why it never worked isn't because
the process was wrong; it's because the dye has to be
sealed."

Truly. She had no idea what he was talking about.
But he looked delicious standing there, his dark hair
wild and his shirt unbuttoned so that she could see
the deep V of his chest. He wore no waistcoat or
jacket, no cravat either, and now that Willa was fully
aware of her own state of undress, she was even *more*
fully aware of his state of undress. And they were
alone together. In her bedchamber. With her door
closed. She was sitting on the bed. And he wasn't ravishing her.

Willa gave a small sigh. "I see." Of course she knew
that he wouldn't be interested in ravishing her in the
least. He was excited about the fact that his new process that would make him thousands upon thousands
of pounds finally worked, and that was important. He
also didn't like her very much even though he could
lust after her—as evidenced by the carriage incident—
and that might have been a reason to influence his
decision in not ravishing her.

Even knowing all this, it was still a tad disappoint-
ing to stare at the man she wanted to be ravishing her,
wishing that she could ravish him, while he con-

tinued to talk incessantly for ten more minutes about *dye* and *sealing* and *chemicals* and *heat* and whatnot.

Actually, he went on for twenty more minutes. Then he suddenly stopped and stared at her.

He stepped forward with a frown and took her hand. He looked at their two hands joined together, then up at her face. "Thank you, Willa." He paused, then cursed. "I left lamps burning in the factory. I must go before the disastrous occurs and a fire starts. MacFadden would have my head if his mill were destroyed—"

He smiled at her and caught her up in his arms, spinning her around once more, then laughing as he set her down. "No, it will be my mill soon."

Willa braced her hand against the bed pilaster. "If it's not destroyed by fire."

"Right." He opened the door. "Thank you, Willa. Thank you for everything."

She smiled again; his joy was infectious, even if she hardly felt like what she'd done merited his praise. Well, except for the Merriman bit. That had been pure genius. "You're welcome."

Their eyes met, and his smile faded as he stared at her. "Good night."

"Good night."

He left the room, closing the door behind him, and Willa flopped back upon the bed with a shuddering sigh.

Alex Laurie had succeeded in creating a process for nonsaturation that would change the world for dye makers—and, more specifically, for him. He would be rich beyond measure and successful.

He was happy, she *should* have been happy, and . . .

It was a horrible time to realize that she was in love.

Willa was dreaming.

Even in the dream she knew it was a dream, and somehow this made the dream even more pleasant. She could choose not to wake up. She could stay in this dream with Alex forever if she wished.

"Willa."

She loved the way he said her name. As though it were a secret shared between only the two of them, something precious and cherished.

She walked toward his outstretched arms, freely moving, without hesitation. She didn't have to pretend that she'd rather be somewhere else. She didn't have to protect her heart any longer. They would finally be together.

"Alex."

She said his name even though her lips didn't move.

Then they were at Woolstone's cottage again, except that in her dream she didn't sneeze. She told him this, and he smiled at her while holding her hand.

They walked through the garden and he picked flowers for her—roses, yes, but lilies and orchids and daisies, too. He tucked one behind each of her ears, then more in her hair.

The Willa that knew it was a dream became impatient. She wanted him to kiss her.

And so he did.

Plucking out one of the flowers he'd just placed in her hair, he brushed the petals beneath her chin, tickling her, as his head bent. His lips—

Willa's eyes flew open. The black void of the small inn's bedchamber greeted her.

She groaned. The dream had disappeared.

Huffing, she turned restlessly onto her back and stared into the dark above. It wasn't fair. He'd been just about to kiss her. If she closed her eyes, she could almost *feel* his lips on hers—

"Willa!" Alex's voice. He was knocking on her door again.

This time Willa didn't move as quickly. She didn't want him to *know* she was thrilled to see him, after all. She stretched her arms toward the ceiling, stretched her toes toward the end of the bed. Arched her back and rolled her head from side to side.

She sighed, pleased with her own apparent nonchalance regarding Alex's reappearance. She might be in love, but that didn't mean she *needed* him. It didn't mean she would run to him with excitement every time he was near.

"Willa!"

Oh, God. What if the factory truly had *been on fire?*

Willa tore the covers away and rushed to the door, not bothering with the lamp or her dressing gown or anything else. She flung the door open, her heart hammering wildly in her chest, and stared at Alex.

He didn't smell like smoke. His face wasn't

streaked with soot or ash. No signs of burns on his skin or clothes.

Willa exhaled a shaky breath and sagged against the door. "Are you all right?"

"Yes," he said, stepping toward her. "I forgot this."

And then he kissed her.

Kissing Willa was one of the smartest things Alex had ever done; in fact, he should have done it earlier that evening. Yesterday. Every minute of every day since the last time he'd kissed her.

Cupping the delicate bones of her jaw between his palms, he walked her backward into the darkened bedchamber and closed the door with a kick of his foot. The darkness of the room seemed to ease the tension from her body; she melted into him as if his kiss, his touch, everything he wanted to do to her in the inky black nothingness surrounding them, would forever be a pleasant little secret between them.

Alex drew back. He didn't want to be dismissed so easily in the future.

"I'm going to turn the lamp on," he said, laughing low when she made a mewling sound of frustration. The light flared in the glass, a steady but dim flame. Still, it was enough to see her, and that was all he needed.

Alex didn't ask her to come to him, because he couldn't be certain that she would obey him. Instead he went to her, drawing her between his arms as his hands sifted through her long, gloriously golden hair. He'd never seen another woman's hair like it; he wanted to wrap himself in her hair, to use it to keep her always within his reach. He thought of telling her that he would never let her go, but it sounded like a lie, something to be said when a man held a woman in his arms.

No lies. No words, if he could help it. Nothing to make her break away or doubt him.

Her lips were restless, seeking his over and over though he tried to settle against her, to assure her that this time he wouldn't dismiss her. He'd been a fool to think he could protect them both so easily.

"Willa," he whispered against her lips.

Very well. One word. But only her name. That was all he needed. He pressed it against her mouth again, then on her cheek, the underside of her jaw . . . lower, to the side of her throat. Her hands pulled and tangled in his hair, clutching him toward her. She didn't speak, either, not even his name. Only her small staccato whimpers and breathy little sighs floated through the air, urging him on when he pushed her against the edge of the bed like a hasty lover, when his hand cupped and squeezed her breast like a young, inexperienced boy.

"Willa." He kissed the name to her shoulder, then laid his forehead in the crook of her neck.

He felt the subtle movement at her throat as she swallowed. "Alex? I'm not sure— Are we—?"

He breathed in the scent of her, wrapped his arms tightly around her waist. She felt so slender and fragile to hold. How had he never noticed before?

Lifting his head, he caught her gaze and moved them until he could see her eyes in the lamplight. He knew what he wished to do. It was the same thing he'd wished ever since he'd first met her and saw her smile. He wanted her for himself. He desperately wanted to keep her, as his and his alone.

But their lives weren't where they were three years ago, when he might have been able to promise her the next day, or the next day after that. All he could offer was this: one reality inside of a dream that could never be.

"I want to give you every day for the rest of our lives, but I can only give you tonight." He looked into her eyes, their color the same as when he'd first complimented her, the bluest blue of the Mediterranean ocean he'd sailed upon before arriving in Italy. "Tell me to go and I'll go. Ask me to stay and I'll stay." He bent his head to kiss her once more, then drew his arms back and stepped away. "Tell me what *you* want, Willa."

Tell me what you *want, Willa.*

"That's a dangerous opening, Mr. Laurie," she said, smiling.

"Not Mr. Laurie," he corrected her. "I'm Alex right now."

She nodded, suddenly uncertain of him. Of herself, most of all. "Yes. Alex."

He waited for her to speak when she would have preferred for him to kiss her again. She, who desired control of her life most of all, wanted him to take it away at the moment when it was offered to her.

He offered her options. Alex Laurie was a gentleman, despite the fact that he tried to disguise himself as a self-seeking commoner most days. "Do you want me to leave?"

"No." Her answer was immediate, without hesitation. Of everything she *did* want, she knew it wasn't for him to go.

He smiled and stepped toward her again. "Then you want me to stay."

"Yes." Her heart added, *Always*, but she didn't say it.

"What do you want me to do next, Willa?"

She tilted her head, studying the steady flicker of shadows the lamplight created across his face. Shadows hid in the corners of his mouth as he smiled, sank into his eyes as he watched her, waiting. She remembered different shadows in his eyes before, earlier in the day, at the factory, when he realized the nonsaturation process had failed again. She recalled his smile then, too, the facade she'd realized they both employed.

"I suppose you expect me to ask you to kiss me again," she said.

He spread his arms wide, palms outward. Nonthreatening. Always protecting, this man she loved. "If that is what you wish, then I'll do it. But only if you ask."

"Perhaps I would like for you to touch me instead."

"Just tell me where, when, and how long," he quipped, smiling again. Fleeting, that smile, but the shadows remained.

"I want you to tell me what's behind your smile," she said. She stepped toward him, meeting him toe to toe as the smile she named disappeared. She reached up, placed her finger at the corner of his mouth, traced the seam of his lips. Swallowed as she met his eyes. "We are the same, Alexander Laurie. We use truth and flattery alike to get our way, though only we realize that we are the ones trapped, unable to escape our own manipulations. I know you see me as someone more than the person that I present to the world, someone more than I make myself for the sake of my father's company."

She let her hand fall, away from his lips, on his chest and sliding down to still between them. Over his heart. "Tell me, Alexander Laurie," she whispered. "When you're not trying to charm someone, who are you?"

He watched her, his eyes traveling back and forth as he searched hers.

She discovered that he was silent. An observer. A seeker.

His hand lifted. He placed it against her cheek, and she rested her head as they stared at each other.

He was a protector.

She'd known that from the beginning.

He was a nurturer; he tried to soothe her with his touch.

He was a man she could love. He was a man she already loved.

"I am but a man," he said, his voice low and hoarse. "I am a man with dreams and ambition, a man who needs to assuage his guilt for his failures, who believes he can only do such by proving his success. I am a man with flaws too many to count, and a hope that one day I'll be as great a man as my father was."

He paused, his breath abruptly silent. As if he'd meant to say something else but stifled his words.

"Yes?" she whispered, and felt his heartbeat speed beneath her fingers.

"I am a man who wants you."

She looked into the shadows of his eyes, and she saw the words he left silent. Or perhaps they were words she hoped for, other words she feared to be true.

I want you more than anything else.

I need you.

Don't ask more of me than I can give.

Willa pressed her lips together and lowered her lashes, deliberately shuttering her eyes from his gaze. Then she reached over toward the lamp and extinguished the flame. She slid her hands up his chest, over his shoulders. Wrapping her arms around his neck, she lifted to her toes and pressed her lips against his.

"I want you, too."

Her teeth scraped against his bottom lip, and he let her lead their kiss as he scooped her into his arms and walked forward until his knees bumped against the bed. He laid her down, then stripped off his clothes and crawled over her, his elbows and knees braced on either side of her body.

"You're naked," she said, her laughter filled with a sort of delighted wonder as he bent his head to nip at her lips.

"You should be, too. I laid you down and gave you time to undress while I removed my clothes, yet here you are."

She ran the flats of her palms up and down over his back. "It's only my shift. And I had a thought that you might want to help me get rid of it."

Alex kissed from the corner of her lips across her cheek. He placed a quick kiss below her ear. "I love the way you think."

Rolling onto his side, he drew his hand down the length of her body, his mouth pressing smiles into her shoulder as he felt her shiver beneath his touch. He bunched the cotton shift in his fist at midthigh, then ran his finger back and forth along the hem, teasing her.

"Are you sure you want to take this off?"

Her breath fanned cool across his face as she turned her head toward him. "I've fantasized about being naked against you, your skin against my skin. My breasts against your chest, stomach to stomach, thighs to thighs. I want to feel you against me, Alex."

"All right. We'll take it off." He exhaled a long breath, his cock equally enticed by the image she painted. He pulled the hem up.

"Lift your hips."

She did, wriggling as his fingers skimmed over her skin, tickling the sensitive flesh between thigh and pelvis.

"Sit up, please." She started to obey, and he put a hand to her chest to halt her. "No, wait." Fumbling in the darkness, he gripped the thin material of her shift with both hands, then ripped the garment apart from neck to hemline.

"Impressive," she said drily.

He grinned and helped her shrug out of the remnants. "That was from one of my fantasies."

As were the soft, rounded hills of her breasts, the firm but pliant silken flesh hot against his palms. Her nipples were silken as well between his fingers, but velvet in his mouth, against his tongue.

Willa cried out, her feet finding the backs of his calves as she rolled toward him in the darkness. Alex steadied her with his hand to her hip, gliding it along her back to fist in her hair. She lifted a leg over his thigh, nudging closer and closer, and Alex released her breast from his mouth as she brushed against his cock.

"*God*, Willa." He pulled her head back and sank his teeth against her throat—nipping, then soothing, biting and kissing. She arched her hips and breasts against him, her body undulating beneath his caresses. Impatient, greedy. Exactly the way he felt.

He pushed her to her back, kissing across her breasts and sucking at her nipples again as he moved over her and in between her thighs.

She jerked when he touched her the first time. When he put his mouth on her, she cried out, lifting her hips off the bed. Then he used both his mouth and hands to drive her higher and higher, not relenting until she came for him.

When her body continued to quiver, he soothed her with his tongue, not stopping until she stilled and said his name.

"Alex."

He couldn't help but smile at the sound, for she said it as she stretched, obviously pleased with herself. Pulling himself up, he hovered over her.

"Alex," she whispered in his ear, hugging her arms around his neck. "I want you inside me, all of you. *Now*, please."

It was the only permission he needed. She pushed against him, and he slammed forward, catching her gasp in his mouth. Again and again he pushed inside, then pulled back. Pushing and pulling, groaning at the velvet friction.

She arched against only him twice more, begging his name with another *Please, Alex*, and *Now, Alex*, and he had to tear himself away, spilling himself on the bed near her hip.

Afterward he apologized and pulled the blanket off. It was awkward then. Not knowing what to say. Having too much he wanted to say but couldn't. He lit the lamp, and it was as if the low circle of light brought both their doubts back in the room to hover at their shoulders.

"I should leave," he said. Hoping she would ask him to stay.

When she didn't say anything, he moved to stand, but she stilled him with a hand on his arm. "Remember when you asked me what I wanted, Alex?"

"Yes, of course. What do you want now?"

She tugged at him, smiling as he returned to her arms. "I want you to hold me," she whispered.

And he did.

Chapter 18

*F*or the third time that night, Willa awoke with a start before dawn could break over the sky.

Something was crawling up her arm. Plodding, as if it had premeditated calculations on what it would do when it reached its next destination. Willa stiffened, then opened her eyes.

Alex's face was above hers, smiling. He'd lit the lamp, and Willa's stomach flopped at the sight of him: dark hair hanging over his brow, dark stubble peppering his jaw and disappearing into the creases on either side of his mouth. Golden light from the lamp washed over the muscled contours of his shoulders, arms, and chest. His eyes were lazy as he watched her, making a study of the texture of her skin, the leap of her pulse, as if she were the most intriguing puzzle to be solved or a wild, untamed land to be explored, and he meant to be the first man to claim such territory as his.

"You shouldn't smile in such a way," she murmured, her voice low and drowsy.

"Oh?" One eyebrow arched, and his fingers paused for a moment before continuing their strategic ascent up her arm.

His smile ... that smile ... it suggested things to her mind. Images of future mornings before dawn, waking up at his side. Of laughter and shared secrets and surprise kisses. That smile punctuated their past with new possibilities: arguments completed with lovemaking, tempers broken by understanding, rivalry erased by admissions of love.

Love? Willa turned her head aside, a chuckle lifting from her throat. Even if he could love her, love wasn't in Alex Laurie's plans.

"If I can't smile," he said, his fingers rounding her shoulder and trailing the sensitive path of her collarbone, "then I hardly think it fair that you should be allowed to laugh."

"I thought this was about what I wanted," she said. "I clearly remember you asking me, 'Willa, what do you want? I'll do whatever you ask. Anything for you, Willa.'"

His smile gradually faded to nothing more than a quirk of his lips. His touch became bolder, marching over the swells and valleys of her breasts. "Yes, but that was then. Now it's my turn."

"I can't even have an entire night? Honestly,

Alex—" Her breath caught as the movement of his hand changed, gentling, becoming a butterfly's caress skimming around and around her nipple.

"Afraid not." He didn't sound regretful in the least. On the contrary, he sounded extraordinarily pleased. "There are too many things I want to do to you. For example, there are things like this . . ."

His head dipped, his hair falling against her chest and throat now as his lips covered her nipple. He pulled her into his mouth, hot and leisurely, as if he meant to take nights—no, *years*—before he would give her control again. He tasted her, teased her, rolled his tongue over her nipple as if trying to answer a hypothesis regarding the varied lengths of her sighs, the loudness of her moans, the staggering of her gasps.

"Alex—"

"*Shh.*" He lifted his head and kissed her lips. "Don't say anything, Willa. Not a word. Don't think, not about what I'm doing or what you'd like me to be doing instead or even what you'll tell me to do next time. Just feel."

He kissed her again, touching his tongue to hers, capturing her lips between his, waiting long seconds to move again and again, until it was no longer a kiss but something much more. Their lips held a knowledge of each other that even their minds hadn't before: a restful, peaceful intimacy that her soul had long hungered for. She'd never known she'd wanted it or needed it. Now she knew, and even as he broke their kiss to press his mouth along her cheek and throat, a new, overwhelming ache of loss built in her chest.

"Let me pleasure you," he whispered as his mouth trailed away farther below, coasting past her breasts, then pausing to linger at each rib. "Shall I tell you how long I've wanted to touch you like this? There's never been a moment since I met you when I haven't dreamed of it, even after I realized who you were. Perhaps I'm mad to admit such a thing aloud. Promise not to hold it against me tomorrow."

She could feel his smile shaped in the hollow of her abdomen. Though her hands had fisted in the sheet at her sides, she raised one now and placed it over his head.

Yes. I am the same. Though I am too cowardly to say it. I love you.

He chuckled, his breath warm against her skin. There, too, was intimacy. Many men she'd graced with her smiles. Only this man had hidden his smile against her naked flesh.

"I see you wish for me to stop talking. Where shall I go now? I wonder. Do you mean for your hand to send me below again? I fear you are too greedy, Willa. You must learn to be patient. I want everything, you see—starting with this."

His tongue found her belly button, and Willa shivered at the unexpected decadence of such a kiss. He nibbled along the line of her pelvis, then smoothed his palms along each leg from upper thigh to ankle, a procession for what he intended to do with his mouth.

Willa squirmed the closer he came to the juncture of her thighs—her quim.

Please. Her hand did tug at his hair this time in an attempt to guide him. He ignored her.

"Patience, darling."

She sighed loudly, her protest to his puritanical lecture of virtues. He laughed and tortured her with his mouth, scattering kisses along the insides of her thighs. She moaned. "Alex—"

"Don't think. Just feel. Feel what it's like when I kiss the back of your knee. The front."

She felt vulnerable—more vulnerable even than when he kissed her in the most intimate place of all. Knees were not for kisses, and yet he seduced her into believing hers would never be useful for walking again.

"The curve of your calf."

Sensitive. How sensitive her skin was there. She'd never known. She'd always remember the slow slide of his fingers and mouth over her calf, her shin, the skin in between.

"The delicate bones of your ankle. God, how fragile you are. And how easily you disguise it."

She didn't feel fragile. She felt a mistress of pleasure, given to complete abandon as her lover knelt between her legs, her ankle lifted high to his chest as he bent his head with the greatest attentiveness. Willa's hands had fallen from his head the lower he descended, and she raised her arms above her head, exposing herself from the tips of her fingers to the soles of her feet. Her cheeks were heated, flushed, as she watched him place a final kiss on her foot, then slide up again to start with the other leg.

As he performed the same attentions to that leg, the flush in her cheeks began to travel downward. It burned her chest and left her breasts even fuller, her nipples even harder. The flush heated her belly, pulling low in her abdomen. She knew it slicked the flesh between her thighs. She could feel herself aching, wanting, there. It ran down her legs like twin streaks of flame, causing her thighs to quiver, the ankle he held to jerk in his hands.

His gaze flew to hers, and she wondered if he felt the same flush. His eyes were hot, his brows lowered as he lowered her leg, as though he'd been so consumed in touching her that he'd forgotten she watched. "Turn over," he rasped.

Willa obeyed, and she was more graceful in that one fluid motion than she'd ever been in her life. She was powerful, confident, invincible, seductive. She was everything he believed her to be.

She held herself on her hands and knees, and he groaned behind her. "No. Lie flat on your stomach."

Willa slid up the bed, like a cat stretching, the simple cotton fabric of the sheet beneath her suddenly like a silk or satin caress. Air surrounded her where the bed did not; she was fully naked, fully exposed, and fully unashamed. She was wanted.

He wanted her.

There was a long, silent moment once she lay down on her stomach. He didn't stir or make a sound, but she could feel his regard on her skin, like the prickling, heart-stuttering awareness from a lion's stare.

She swallowed. "Alex?"

Willa trembled. She could hear him breathing behind her, hard and fast, and she closed her eyes. Endlessly needing, endlessly aching.

"Please," she said, even though it wasn't allowed. "Please take me, Alex."

Only the slightest pause came before: "On your hands and knees again."

She quickly complied, no longer worrying with grace when she burned so hotly. The blood hummed in her veins, and her heart felt like it might burst from her chest at any moment. The waiting, the *patience*, would kill her.

His hand moved to her back, resting upon her hair before sweeping it to the side. It fell in a curtain past her shoulder, obscuring half her vision. Willa looked up; she had been looking down before, at the mattress. Before her was nothing more than a headboard—a plain, dark wooden headboard. It held no ornamentation, no scrolls or fancy work. It would lay smooth and cool beneath one's palms . . . hard and unforgiving against one's head.

His hand—hot against her spine, callused and large—smoothed down her back. Both hands settled at her hips and pulled her backward, urging her toward him and away from the headboard.

His cock brushed against her buttocks, then was gone, replaced by the firm muscles of his chest as he leaned over her and pressed his mouth to the vulnerable skin right below her spine and above her buttocks. Willa nearly cried out—both from the disappearance of his cock and the sensual touch of his kiss.

She hissed with pleasure when his fingers stroked between her thighs.

He hissed, too. "You're so wet. So fucking wet."

His finger plunged deep inside her and she screamed, pushing against him and arching her back. He must have lost all patience then, too, for after this reaction he pulled his hand away to settle on her hips once more and she felt his cock at her lips.

Her arms shook beneath her. There was a silent, unspoken question.

"*Now*, Alex."

She'd taken over control again; she suspected it had been when he asked her to roll over. At her command, he drove his cock inside.

"Oh, God. Oh, please," she begged, gasping.

He reached around her thighs and stroked her again, and the flush which had been building since he'd kissed down her body exploded from the inside out, sending heat shuddering through every nerve and vein. Willa's head hung limp between her shoulders as her muscles clenched and trembled, as Alex pounded against her again and again, building more ecstasy upon an already peaked crescendo.

His fingers dug into the flesh at her hips, holding her tight and steady for his own pleasure as he drove in and out, groaning, every few seconds moaning her name.

Don't leave me.

It was a foolish thing to think, an even more foolish thing to say. So she didn't.

And when he suddenly thrust away from her, leaving her naked and alone on her hands and knees as he poured himself on the bed behind her, she simply collapsed to her stomach and stared at the lamp.

A wetness slid down her cheek, and she reached to quickly swipe the tear away, before he could see.

Soon he was beside her on the bed, his arm wrapping around her as he tried to pull her against him. He nuzzled her neck. "Everything and more than I dreamed." His arm tightened around her waist. "Shall I hold you again?"

Willa nodded, then tried to get up. "Let me extinguish the lamp."

"No, let me look at you."

"All right." Settling back against him, she listened to the sound of his breathing near her ear, concentrated on the circles he traced beneath her breasts with the pads of his fingers.

And in that moment as he held her, Willa realized she had never felt so happy. Or so immensely desolate.

Miss Willa Stratton: Greedy. Impatient. Very, very hopeless.

Chapter 19

Alex sat in the main room of the Three Crowns the next morning, waiting for Willa to descend from her chamber. He'd watched her fall asleep, then rose quietly so he wouldn't wake her as he returned to his own room. It was difficult to leave her. It shouldn't have been.

The pair of men at the table beside him stopped discussing the various issues with their sheep's dung—thankfully—and began whispering. "Well, look'ee there."

"Now, that's a sunrise I wouldn't mind waking up to each morning."

Alex's gaze jerked toward the staircase. Willa walked down the last few steps, her hand gracefully sliding along the banister, her back straight like a queen's, and her chin held high. She was as common as any street rat, as common as he, and yet with her bearing and confidence it was no wonder she mingled among the aristocracy well. She appeared born to marry a lord, to breed an heir and multiple other ladies and honorables.

God, he'd made a mistake. He should never have kissed her again, never written those letters, never gone to her bedchamber, not even if he'd discovered the secret of alchemy. If he'd simply forgotten and ignored her as best he could, it was possible he wouldn't now be burning for her again or desperately desiring to maim and mutilate her future unnamed, faceless husband.

She is not for me.

She had money but not the connections or influence needed to grow the business of Laurie & Sons. Even with the nonsaturation process working, he needed the aristocracy to fulfill his vision of its success. She couldn't give his family legitimacy and help his other siblings make aristocratic marriages. Not to mention the fact that she was her father's daughter, his greatest rival. She'd proven her loyalty three years ago when she'd stolen his secrets in Italy. That truth, if nothing else, removed her as a choice for anything beyond one night in a bed at an inn in a small village in Northamptonshire.

He'd been her lover, but he couldn't marry her. He couldn't even be her friend.

At that moment Willa turned toward him, the most beautiful, open, lovely smile upon her face. The men at the table beside him stared, speechless, and for a moment Alex did the same, his chest tightening, every pore soaking in that smile as if she truly were the sun and her smile the sun's rays.

He couldn't blame himself for wanting her; any man with breath in his body would. But he should have stayed away despite the temptation. She might be his rival, but she deserved better. She deserved a man who would throw everything at her feet and desert all just to make her happy.

Sprawling back, Alex hooked an arm over the back of his chair. "Good morning, dear sister." He couldn't be charming—she might think he was encouraging a relationship. He couldn't banter with her as before— the heat between them turned to fire too quickly. But he could be negligent. He could pretend like she meant nothing at all.

"Good morning, Alex," she replied, her smile still as bright.

"Did you eat breakfast?"

"Yes, thank you for having it sent up. That was very thoughtful."

He'd done it deliberately. More time for them to spend apart. The question now, of course, was why he'd waited for her at the inn instead of going to the factory to work more on the nonsaturation.

They stared at each other, memories of the previous evening exchanged in their gazes. Knowing they couldn't return to where they'd been before, but also knowing they had no future together. It should have been a relief that she understood the role she would play, and yet he was inexplicably disappointed that she didn't ask for more, that she didn't even hint at marriage. As if he meant nothing to her, either.

"Well." Alex planted his hands on the table. "Shall we go?"

He helped her inside the carriage he'd had waiting for their short journey to the mill, then climbed inside after her. If he sat beside her rather than on the opposite side as he should have, it was only because he truly did despise riding backward—not because he took any pleasure from her nearness.

As soon as the groom closed the door behind him, Alex turned his head to stare out the window on the carriage door.

"You're very quiet," she said.

Alex tensed. He didn't reply. He barely breathed. But he did begin to hum.

"Is this how it's meant to be, then? A couple of romps and then we ignore each other?" Her voice wasn't harsh; it wasn't even judgmental. Hell, he wished it had been. Instead, she was quite, quite cheerful.

She laughed, a merry, pleased sound—as if he'd done something greatly amusing. Alex shifted his gaze toward her, wary.

"Come, Alex, do not believe me to be one of the young debutantes. I am six and twenty, an old, wise woman. We had our fun, didn't we? There's no need to act as if I mean to throw myself at your feet at any moment, begging for a pledge from you. Although, if you were so inclined to beg at my feet, that should be something I'd like to see."

She grinned at him, teasing him for his fears, his anxiety. She wouldn't ask for more from him; she didn't want to give him anything, either. With her jaunty yellow hat perched at an angle on her head, a smart yellow-and-white pinstriped walking dress showcasing the tiny circumference of her waist and the creamy-white skin at her throat, she was happy sophistication, optimistic and without a care in the world.

He should have felt relieved that she knew him so well and saw through him so easily. Instead he wanted to kiss that happy, content, I-don't-give-a-damn smile off her face.

Without a word, he leaned forward and took her face between his palms.

"Alex? What are—?"

He ravished her mouth, sealing his lips to hers, battling her tongue with his, giving her no quarter, no space to breathe, seeking to brand her so that she would never be able to dismiss him so easily again. She didn't fight or stiffen as he might have expected. Instead, her hands clutched at the front of his coat and little moans issued from her throat, urging him on, speaking for her pleasure.

Alex tore his mouth from hers, unable to catch his breath. No other woman had ever made him feel so demanding, so possessive, so *desperate*. He'd always been able to enjoy the moment and charm the woman, then walk away. Not now. Not with her.

Forcing a smile to his face, he pulled his hands away only with the greatest amount of discipline. "You're correct. You don't taste like a debutante, either."

She blushed, lifting her hands to right the hat he'd set askew. "Thank you for the appraisal. I'm almost afraid to ask what that means. Do I taste old and wise?"

His gaze lowered to her lips, and when he spoke, he spoke to seduce, to arouse. It came easily now, his intention not to manipulate but to show her his desire. He could give her that, at least. "On the contrary. You taste like the sweetest nectar, beautiful and ripe. I believe you could quickly become an addiction, Willa, if a man weren't careful."

He slid closer to her. Deftly removed the pins of her hat and laid both hairpiece and accessories at his other side. Lifted her from the seat and settled her over his lap, one arm braced around her back and the other settled across her thighs. "Tell me you don't want me to kiss you, and I'll let you go," he said, noting the flutter of her pulse at her throat. He rubbed her back in small, soothing circles.

She stared at him with her large blue eyes, stray wisps of hair floating above her head where the pins had once helped to tuck them down. She sat rigid in his arms, so different from the woman who'd opened herself to him last night with such generosity and desire. "I don't want you to kiss me," she said.

"Liar."

He kissed her, anyway.

There was, Willa decided, such a thing as an Alex kiss. Whether he was slow or savage, passionate or teasing, whether it was a peck, a brush, or a long, consuming kiss, he made her feel that she'd been nothing more than a dry piece of kindling waiting for his touch, then set aflame and burning as soon as his mouth touched hers.

I need you.

Thank God she didn't say *that* aloud. Neither did she tell him how she resented him for the need. Nor how, after more than two years of trying to escape from the loneliness presented when her brother finally became a man and her father began to depend on *him* instead of *her*, Alex's arms finally felt like a place she could stay. She was tired of traveling, tired of trying to impress her father when she could never measure in his eyes as a son could and . . . tired of running. The only honesty she'd allowed herself recently was that she'd rather have a family, a home. Not because her brother had one of his own, but because she remembered her mother stroking her hair at night with her fingers and singing her lullabies. She wanted love. She wanted to love and to be loved. Safety, security, permanence . . . and this.

Alex's arms were strong about her. He wouldn't let her fall. He would protect her.

For now.

Suddenly the meeting of their lips was too much, and Willa tilted her head back. She wouldn't break away, but she knew she would give herself away in a kiss. He would understand her desperation and her need.

"Alex." She sighed his name as his lips glided down her neck, a hot, sensuous trail ending in the hollow of her throat. She waited for him to descend farther, to try to kiss her breasts, but he stayed there, his breath warming her skin, his mouth resting on her skin. "Alex?"

He pulled away, not meeting her eyes, and gently set her aside. "I'm sorry, Willa. I can't kiss you again."

A deep humiliation ached in her chest as she drew herself together, her chin rising. "If you'll recall, I told you I didn't want you to kiss me."

"I know. I apologize."

He handed her the hat and pins, and Willa stared down at his long, masculine fingers holding the flimsy feminine headpiece. She glanced up into his eyes. He was watching her intently, tracking her movements. "Very well, then." She didn't ask why he'd stopped; she didn't need to know.

"I respect you. I am going to marry another woman, and you are going to marry another man. I respect you too much, and I respect my future wife too much in order to continue this—" He paused, closed his mouth, and swallowed. "This . . ."

She took a deep breath and waited.

He stared at her for a moment longer, then smiled. And then it was as it had been before, and there was nothing between them that mattered. He was harmless. She needed to be watched to ensure she didn't mess with something he wanted. And they were both charming and beautiful.

She smiled at him. He smiled at her. And all was well with the world.

Chapter 20

Willa stared out the window. Pressure built inside her chest, a burning, aching hollowness that swelled in her throat, in her nostrils, and in her eyes. She would not cry.

Damn him.

She would *not* cry.

An hour passed by. Two. The entire day, until the sun faded behind the horizon and they sat there in the darkness of the carriage side by side, not speaking.

When they finally arrived in London at the Mivart Hotel, he held his arm across the door so she couldn't exit. Willa stared at his arm, clenched her jaw, then dragged her gaze toward his face.

There was nothing left to say.

Don't look back.

Don't look back.

Don't look back.

This time, she didn't.

"Where have you been?"

Alex glanced up from his desk, his eyes bleary. Jo stood half hidden by the open study door, one hand planted on her hip.

He hadn't been able to go to sleep after taking Willa to the hotel.

"You know where I've been," he said.

"I've been waiting for you to return. It took you a long time to check on the testing."

"I took Miss Stratton with me. The nonsaturation works." Those were the main points. He was sure she'd have liked to hear the entire story, but he was too weary to oblige.

"The nonsaturation works? Alex, congratulations! That's wonderful!"

"Thank you." He stared at the list and blinked. He was so tired, his vision clouded.

"Well, I'm relieved to hear how thrilled you are," she said drily.

He looked up then. She smiled.

"I have something to tell you," Jo said.

Alex stood, scrubbing his hands over his face. "You've become betrothed to a lord."

"Good God, no. Allow me to begin again. I have something *exciting* to tell you."

The image that had kept him awake after returning to Holcombe House flashed again in his mind. Willa, walking away as he stared after her through the carriage window. Again and again the scene repeated itself.

Alex strode around the desk toward the sideboard. "Whisky?" he offered.

"If you're not going to oblige me by acting curious, then I suppose I won't torture you by dragging this out. I terminated your bookkeeper."

Alex stilled, the bottle in his hand frozen midair. He slowly set it down and turned around. "You fired Mr. Swarthing?"

"I found the books where you hid them and went over everything while you were gone. Only a few months, Alex, and he'd made a mess of it."

The fog of sleep had cleared away instantly. Alex narrowed his eyes and strolled forward. "How did you fire him? He's my employee."

Jo shrugged. "I threatened to summon the law. There were inconsistencies—glaring inconsistencies that even you wouldn't have been able to miss if you'd taken the time every now and then to look over the accounts. Instead of chasing after Willa. Or is it Lady Marianna you're chasing after? I become confused sometimes."

Alex gritted his teeth. "I'm no longer courting Lady Marianna. As for Miss Stratton—"

"I should also mention that I went through your letters while you were gone. It appears Willa has been a very busy little bee on your behalf."

He stilled. "What do you mean?"

Jo stepped away from the door, revealing a large sheaf of papers in her hand. "Letters from various people. Some lords and relations to lords, so I know you'll be pleased. Some from businessmen—in England, Europe, and even America. All asking about your nonsaturation process."

"She told them my secret."

Jo slapped his shoulder with the papers. "She told them to invest in Laurie and Sons for the greatest textile invention this century. They all mentioned her name, wrote about how she recommended they contact you for more information."

Willa had tried to help him, even though they were rivals, even when she could have been the one to inform her father about the process for the benefit of Stratton's company. But most important, he'd been wrong. Idiotically wrong. Arrogantly wrong. He'd never been so happy to be wrong in his entire life.

Alex whooped and picked Jo up. He spun her about, just like their father once had.

"I'm thrilled that you're excited," she drawled once he put her down. "Truly, I am. But aren't you going to congratulate me for getting rid of Swarthing? Compliment me on how clever I am? Or are you just going to ignore my accomplishment of keeping the man from robbing our company and family blind?"

Alex inclined his head. "Well done, Jo."

"I want the books," she said.

"No."

Her mouth gaped, and Alex smiled. "You didn't think it would be that easy, did you?"

She pursed her lips. "Actually, I did. I just gave you two pieces of good news. I expected something in exchange."

"You deserve more than hours spent hunched over the accounts. I'm not refusing you to make you upset, Jo. I'm refusing you because I want to see you happy."

"You say you want me to be happy. I want the books *because* they make me happy. They're a piece of him, a piece of me that won't get lost in this huge house. You can have the rest of the business, the nonsaturation, your aristocratic bride or whomever you choose. I want you to have those things. I *want* you to be happy. But let me be happy, too, Alex." She paused a moment, then asked, "Have I made you feel guilty enough yet?"

Alex sighed, raking his hand through his hair. "As if I didn't already feel like the biggest bastard in the world tonight."

She smiled. "Wonderful." She held out the letters to him. "I did hide the books before I came to see you, just in case you said no."

"I assumed you did," he said. "And, if you must know, I rather look forward to having someone competent to review the accounts again. It's true I should have taken more time to look over them myself, but I did see there were quite a few errors from Swarthing."

She quirked a brow. "And yet you still refused to let me have them."

"I know, I know. But he came with the highest recommendation. I'm not sure what to say, other than that I should have listened to you from the beginning. Though you're older and thus at times I do fear for the workings of your mental faculties, you're much wiser and—dare I say it—usually much more intelligent."

Jo scowled and turned away. "Stop trying to charm me. I know your tricks."

"Aren't you going to tell me what a wonderful, marvelous brother I am for giving you the books now?"

"You're very adequate, thank you."

Alex chuckled as she disappeared through the doorway. "Good night, Jo."

Her voice drifted back. "Good night, Alex."

He *wouldn't* let Willa go. Not yet.

Chapter 21

As Willa sat before her dressing table while Ellen worked on her hair, a knock came at the door. Willa groaned and waited for Ellen to halt and step away so she could rise.

Willa opened the door with a smile. "Oh. Hello."

Half her hair hung down her head, she wasn't wearing her slippers yet, she was fairly certain a smudge of chocolate stained the corner of her mouth, and Alex Laurie stood on the opposite side, fist still raised. He returned her smile and bowed. "Good evening to you, Miss Stratton."

Willa rubbed a knuckle at the corner of her mouth. "What are you doing here?"

Alex shook his head and leaned toward her. "You missed it." He touched his thumb to her lips.

Willa narrowed her eyes. "If you're trying to help

me with the chocolate on my face—and I assure you I don't welcome your help—may I point out that it is on the *other* side of my mouth." Her lips moved against his thumb as she spoke, and it was almost like a caress.

Ridiculous, she corrected herself. *It was nothing like a caress; it was simply an unmoving thumb.*

Or rather, it *had* been an unmoving thumb. "Aha!" Alex said, his smile growing wider as he slowly traced the line of her lips to the other side of her mouth. His eyes grew dark. "Yes, there it is. All gone now." Lowering his hand to his side, he added, "Glad to see you're enjoying the presents you asked me to stop sending you."

Willa scowled. "Again, I ask you: what are you doing here?"

"I wanted to see you."

She stared at him, then started to close the door. His foot caught in the space between the door and the frame.

"I love you."

She stared at the door, her mouth still open.

"Willa, is everything all right?" Sarah poked her head around the corner into the antechamber, frowning at the foot in the opening.

Willa waved her away.

"Would you mind opening the door again?" Alex asked. "I'd like to give you your present."

He loves me. He loves me. He loves me.

"And my foot hurts, too." He paused. "Just a little, though."

"You said you loved me."

"I did. I must confess I was sort of hoping you would say you loved me, too."

Her heart slammed against her ribs, and she noticed her breath was coming fast as well. "And if I don't?"

"Then I will make you love me, of course, with my charming ways and handsome face. But first you have to open the door, Willa."

She did, swinging it wide until they were face-to-face. Or rather, nose to shoulder until she looked up.

"There you are." He smiled at her, although it didn't quite reach his eyes. "Do you remember when we were at the inn in Northamptonshire and you asked me who I was?" His voice was low, almost hoarse.

"Yes." Only now did she take the time to study his face, to see the dark skin beneath his eyes, the weary lines creasing at the corners of his mouth. Her hands itched to smooth over his face, to erase the tiredness etched into his skin, to pull his mouth down to hers.

"I am still a man who wants you. I will never stop wanting you."

Willa stepped forward. Her breasts brushed against his chest.

He sucked in a breath and raised his hands to frame her face. He kissed her. Softly, gently, reverently. "But I would be lying if I said that wanting you is enough. I love you, Willa Stratton. More than I could express in any letter, more than I can tell you, standing here now. Don't leave me," he whispered against her lips. "Don't leave me."

He wrapped his arms around her and pulled her tight against his chest, opening her mouth to stroke inside. Coaxing her, wooing her. And Willa let herself surrender to him there in the doorway, his kiss consuming every thought and every doubt, every fear.

Too soon he pulled away, chuckling breathlessly. "I actually came here to give you a present, not to tell you that. That was to come later." Bending down, he lifted a white box from beside his feet, then handed it to her with a crooked smile. "A thank-you gift. I promise I have no ulterior motives, although it may seem like I do when you open it."

"A thank-you? For what?" The box was light in her palms, as if it contained nothing but air.

"For helping me to see past my own fear. Go ahead. Open it."

Willa held the box in one hand and opened the flaps with the other. She peeked inside, but it was too dark, and she put her hand in the box. Her fingers smoothed along something soft, a cloth that felt like satin or silk. She met Alex's eyes, blushing at the look in his gaze, as if he were remembering their time at the Three Crows, as if he were undressing her in his mind now.

She drew out her gift. "A pink chemise." She smiled. "At the opera—"

"Yes. I remember everything you say, you know. As I said, this is a thank-you gift. Thanks to you, I now have twelve investors who have already agreed to help Laurie and Sons with our move into developing the nonsaturation process on a large scale. You, my darling, are holding 'one of the greatest inventions of this century.'"

Willa laughed softly as she returned the chemise to the box. "I hope you don't intend to make it a habit of quoting my words back to me all the time."

"Only the ones where you continually compliment me and my inventions. And when you tell me you love me, too."

Willa looked down. She closed the box. "Thank you, Alex. I'm glad I could help you. Truly. Hopefully in some small way it makes up for the deeds of the evil princess in the past."

His hand touched her wrist. "You sound as if you're still intending to leave."

"I can't stay." She ached all over, her chest and belly. No, she was numb, her limbs heavy and almost unable to move. "Good-bye, Alex."

Tugging her wrist from his hand, she stepped back and shut the door.

Chapter 22

As Alex stayed in Holcombe's bedchamber, at first he thought the image at the foot of his bed was the dead earl's ghost, finally come to fulfill all of Kat's predictions and haunt him.

"Alex."

He came fully awake at the ghost's whisper, blinking against the shadows. "Willa?"

She moved toward him, sliding her palms along the edge of the bed. "You screamed a little. Are you all right? I didn't mean to scare you."

Alex snorted. "I didn't scream. And what are you doing here? I'm not complaining, mind you; I'm just curious how you came to be in my house, in my bedchamber, in the middle of the night."

"Thomas let me in," she whispered, and Alex knew

he loved her without a doubt when she didn't say anything more about him screaming at a ghost.

"I think I like Thomas the best of all the servants." Alex sat up and scrubbed his palms over his face, then looked at her again. "Holy God."

She smiled, smoothing one hand down the side of the chemise, its color the shadow-kissed pale gray of the night. Alex's gaze followed the slide of her hand past her hip, then returned to the scalloped oval of her bodice where her breasts threatened to spill out.

"Thomas didn't see you like this, did he?"

"No."

"Good, because even if I liked him best, I'd have to dismiss him if he saw my wife dressed in nothing but her shift."

She stilled, standing beside him. "You truly want to marry me?"

He reached for her hand, pulled it to his lips. "More than anything, my love."

Her breath hitched. "Even though I'm not part of the *ton*?"

He kissed the back of her hand, the valleys and hills of her knuckles, then turned her wrist over and kissed her palm. "You have to realize that you'd be accepting my family in addition to me. Even if the nonsaturation process failed now, even if I lost everything I had, even if your father burst through that door with a gun in his hand. You might not want me then, but I—"

"I love you, Alex."

His throat got caught on the rest of his words, and he swallowed. She'd said it. It must be true. She couldn't take it back. "I love you, too, Willa."

They stared at each other in the shadows, her hand in his, until he finally laid his other hand upon her hip and leaned forward. "Come here," he said, and pulled her toward him.

She climbed onto the bed and leaned over him, the braid of her hair gleaming white over her shoulder. Alex lifted his hands to her face and stared. A tease of a smile played at the corners of her lips, and her eyes shone in the darkness. Alex released a long breath. "My God, Willa."

Her smile widened. "What?"

"You're beautiful." He pulled her down to lie across his chest as he captured her mouth. His hands worked at her braid to loosen her hair. He'd only seen it unbound once before, and suddenly to see it that way again was all he wanted in the world.

That, and to stay like this with her, forever.

With a laugh he broke their kiss, then appeased her when she protested by placing brief kisses against the corners of her mouth, across her cheeks. "I'm afraid you've turned me into a hopeless creature who doesn't want to live without you," he murmured. "You won't leave now, will you?"

"No," she replied quietly. "I'll never leave you."

No other words were needed. The soft sound of sighs and gasps punctuated each movement as he helped her to remove the chemise and straddle his hips. Alex arched beneath her and moaned at the brush of her hot wetness over his cock. She leaned over him, teasing his mouth with her breasts as she slid down his length, her spine warm and supple beneath his palm.

A low hiss, a long moan.

Her loose hair flowed down on either side of his vision until all he could see was Willa, rocking steadily above him, her head tilted back, shadowed with her own pleasure. He met her downward stroke with a push of his hips and she gasped. "Alex."

Willa paused, bowed over him, her body still vibrating from the sensation.

"Ahhh." She slid down again, a sinuous movement.

She loved this position, loved watching his face below her. Sometimes he stared up at her, his gaze locked with hers. Sometimes he watched her breasts hungrily and caught them in his hands, driving her pleasure higher. Other times he closed his eyes and pressed his lips together, as if he couldn't handle any more.

Willa stroked a finger down his cheek. His eyes opened and met hers. Smiling, she rode him faster, harder, until only breathless staccato moans mingled with the creaking groan of the bed broke the night's silence.

The first acute pinpoints of ecstasy fled to her fingertips, her toes, and Willa cried out, clutching his shoulders. He urged her on, his hands firm on her hips, and she shuddered over him, then collapsed onto his chest as he spilled his own release inside her.

Not on the bed or the sheets. Finally, he made her his.

He wrapped his arms tight around her back afterward. Willa breathed in the scent of his skin at his throat: warm, male, salty with sweat. She wondered at the sweetness inside her chest, a fullness she couldn't name. It had been building ever since she met him, but was only now complete.

"I love you, Alex Laurie," she whispered.

"I love you, Willa, though we're going to have to see about changing your surname very soon."

"I agree."

A few minutes later, she said it again: "I love you." Then she sighed and mumbled, "I'm afraid you're going to have to push me off. I don't think I can ever move again."

The low rumble of his laughter vibrated beneath her, and suddenly she knew:

Joy.

Read on for a peek at another
enchanting Victorian romance
from Ashley March

Romancing the Countess

Available now from Signet Eclipse

London, April 1849

*A*s on most every other night, Leah lay in the center of the bed and watched the shadows cast from the firelight flicker across the canopy. The steady lash of rain and wind rattled the windows in their cases, a buffer against the usual silence.

Lightning flashed through the room, and her breath caught as she stared at the illumination of silver--threaded flowers overhead. Even if the bedchamber had been suffused in darkness, she still could have recited each detail of the bed's rococo-style construction. The fluted mahogany posts with their serpentine cornices. The shallow frieze of interwoven palmettes and draperies of lush, midnight velvet. The feet fashioned as lion heads below and the domed canopy above.

When the lightning came again, Leah measured her breath, anticipating the accompanying growl of thunder.

She imagined the women who had come before her: her husband's mother, his grandmother. Had they, too, stared at the canopy so long that they began to dream of its embroidered ribbons and flower garlands, of shimmering, silvery threads and roses turned black by the shadows? Had hours and hours passed until they imagined they could see each impeccable stitch, counting them only to forget the number when a sound downstairs erupted from the silence, startling them into awareness?

With her heart pounding, Leah waited for the sound to transform into footsteps up the stairs, to distinguish itself into the pattern of Ian's steady, swaggering gait. How foolish she'd once been to admire the way he walked—to admire his easy grin, the golden shine of his sun-swept hair . . . anything about him. And how even greater a fool she was now to dread his arrival into her bedchamber, when she knew he would easily accept her plea of a headache. He might even be glad for the reprieve.

Still, as the echo of footsteps climbed within her hearing, she remained in the center of the bed. Neither on the left nor the right, but rigidly in the middle, as if the few feet on either side could serve to sufficiently delay the moment when he leaned across her and began stroking her breasts in solicitous, husbandly regard. He could have spared her that, at least.

Leah's breath hitched at the sound of footsteps in the corridor. Then, slowly, she sighed with relief. It wasn't her husband. These footsteps were too hasty, the stride too short. Her gaze retreated from the door to the canopy overhead, her fingers released their stranglehold on the counterpane, and she began counting the stitches again.

One, two, three, four . . .

"Madam?"

Leah's gaze stumbled over the width of the ribbon and flew toward the direction of the housekeeper's voice.

"Mrs. George? I apologize for disturbing you . . ."

"No, no. Not at all," Leah called. Tearing the covers aside, she hurried across the room. Anything to leave the bed. She had already opened the hallway door and raised her arm to invite Mrs. Kemble inside when she froze, arrested by the housekeeper's expression. Gone was the woman's usual implacable cheerfulness; in its place was a face worn with time, each wrinkle sagging with the weight of her age. Her brows were lowered, her teeth buried in her upper lip, and the hands clasped at the front of her waist trembled as she met Leah's eyes.

"I'm sorry, madam. There's . . . there's been an accident."

Leah blinked. The housekeeper's mouth seemed to

be moving at an extraordinarily slow pace, as if each syllable struggled to escape. "An accident?" she repeated. And somehow, simply by saying the words, she knew that he was gone.

"Yes, Mr. George . . ."

They stared at each other for what seemed an impossibly long time, until Leah was certain she could have counted at least a hundred canopy stitches.

Finally, she forced the words out. Not as a question, but a blunt, sure statement. "He's dead."

Mrs. Kemble nodded, her chin quivering. "Oh, my dear, I'm so sorry. If there is anything—"

Gone. Ian, her husband, was dead. Never again would she lie awake at night, waiting for him to return from his lover's arms. Never again would she listen for his footsteps or count the stitching or bear his torturous, sensual lovemaking.

He was gone.

And Leah, who had vowed never to cry for him again, sank to her knees, her hands clutched in the housekeeper's skirt, and wept.

"Rook to queen. Check."

Sebastian nodded and considered the whimsical dance of the fire's shadows as they played across what little remained of his ivory army. He slid a lonely pawn forward.

His brother uttered a low oath and planted his bishop near Sebastian's king. "Checkmate. Damnation, Seb, that's four in a row. Do you even realize you're losing?"

Lifting his gaze from the chessboard, Sebastian raised an idle brow. "Yes. And I thought you'd be happy."

James swept aside the pieces and began arranging them anew. "I'd be happy if you found a new role. Something other than heartsick lover. At least condescend enough to pretend to notice my presence. It's only been half a day."

"Fourteen hours." Sebastian rolled the ivory queen between his thumb and forefinger.

Precisely fourteen hours had passed since Angela left for their country estate in Hampshire, but already he was going mad without her. In three years of marriage, they'd spent only a few nights apart. Even though their lovemaking had been sporadic since she'd taken ill in the autumn, he was still accustomed to their usual domestic routine: sitting before the fire together as she brushed her hair, discussing the day's events. If she didn't feel well, a kiss good night before they separated for their individual bedchambers.

James paused in the act of replacing the last ebony piece. "Fourteen hours . . . And I suppose you also know exactly how many minutes and seconds?"

With a small smile, Sebastian settled his queen upon her square and refused the urge to glance at the mantel clock over the sitting room hearth. Instead, his fingers reached below to the note he'd tucked away in the chair's crevice. There was no need to unfold it; he'd already read the words a dozen times, enough to memorize the few short sentences she'd written.

If he breathed deeply enough, he imagined he could smell her perfume rising from the well-worn paper, the same blended scent she used for her bath.

Lavender and vanilla.

Memories wrapped around him, warm and soothing and arousing. It had been a long time since Angela had allowed him to watch her bathe, but still he could remember the heady scent of lavender and vanilla upon her naked skin, the slosh of the bathwater over the sides of the tub as she bucked beneath his touch.

The corner of the note twisted between his fingers.

James nudged the first pawn into play. "I know you have Parliamentary duties to attend to, but surely they would understand if you made it a priority to see to your wife's health first."

"They'll have to." Sebastian led his own pawn out. "I'm traveling to Hampshire in a week, whether the bill's resolved or not."

One week. Compared to fourteen hours, it seemed a hellish eternity.

Still, he looked forward to surprising Angela; she wasn't expecting him to arrive with their son for at least a fortnight. He might bring her a gift as well, perhaps a little house spaniel to keep her company when the weather forced her to remain indoors.

Something to cheer her, to keep her from her melancholy. Regardless of how much he tried to attend to her, she seemed so lonely at times.

Her health had never been the same after Henry's birth, but recently she'd become more and more withdrawn. She continued to act the role of generous hostess while they were in Town, smiling and flirting as usual, but privately he could tell the London air was making matters worse. Sebastian could see it in her eyes when she looked at him. In the way the lightest touch of his fingers sometimes made her flinch, as if her skin was too fragile.

He didn't regret allowing Angela's departure to the countryside, but damned if he could stay away for even a week when she needed him.

Sebastian considered the row of ivory casualties at the side of the board, pieces fallen beneath James' advance. He moved his queen's bishop to counter James' rook. For the first time that evening, he actually felt like making an effort to win. "Make that three days instead."

James glanced up with a knowing look. "The night's young yet. I'm sure given a few more hours you'll be calling for the coach."

A crash of thunder outside echoed the anticipatory clamor of Sebastian's heart. He smiled. "Perhaps," he murmured, and captured one of James' knights.

The horses would have to ride hard through the storm, but he could very well reach the Wriothesly estate the next afternoon. It would be only a short while after Angela would have arrived, and to think he would be able to see her again so soon . . .

In a matter of minutes, Sebastian managed to eliminate piece after piece of the ebony set, including the king's bishop. "Check."

James tapped the table. "I seem to recall asking you to pretend to notice me. I never asked you to win."

Sebastian edged his chair away. "Hurry and make your move."

"Leaving so soon, are you?" James asked with a grin.

"Yes, damn you. Now take my rook so I can—"

A knock sounded at the sitting room door.

"Enter," Sebastian called, glaring at James as he took his merry time in lifting his queen into the air, then slowly moved it toward the remaining white rook.

"My lord. A message has arrived for you."

Sebastian gestured absently in the direction of the butler, then, realizing how late it was, lifted his gaze to the doorway with a frown. "Who is it from, Wallace?"

"A Mr. Grigsby, my lord. I beg your pardon. I wouldn't have interrupted your game, but the messenger said it was most urgent."

"One moment." Sebastian turned to find his rook gone. With one last move, he shifted his queen across the board to trap James' king. "Checkmate."

"Yes, it's a great surprise—that one is," James muttered. Then with a wave of his hand toward the doorway, he added, "At least find what your mysterious message is about before you go."

"You're very generous as a loser, aren't you?"

With a faint smile at James' retorted oath, Sebastian beckoned for the folded parchment. It was cheap, the material coarse beneath his fingers, and spattered with raindrops. "A Mr. Grigsby, you said?" he asked without looking up.

"Yes, my lord."

"Hmm." Unfolding the letter, Sebastian bent it toward the light. He read slowly, his mind distracted by thoughts of Angela.

And then he saw her title.

Lady Wriothesly . . .

He read again, and again, and each time the words refused to coalesce into any meaningful coherence.

. . . identified by crest . . . carriage accident . . . coachman injured, man and woman killed . . . coachman informed . . . Lady Wriothesly . . . Mr. Ian George . . .

The letter began shaking before his eyes. No, his hand was shaking. The letter . . .

He must have said something, because he could hear James calling to him.

Angela was dead. His beautiful, sweet, beloved wife.

And Ian, too. His closest friend.

They were dead. Together.

Fragments of thought collided, then fused into a numbed comprehension. Sebastian stared at the letter, his thumb rubbing the ink until it smeared. He heard James' voice: "Sebastian, what is it?" Then the letter was gone.

And all he could think was:

She hadn't been lonely, after all.

Ashley March

Romancing the Countess

Sebastian Madinger, the Earl of Wriothesly, thought he'd married the perfect woman—until a fatal accident revealed her betrayal with his best friend. After their deaths, Sebastian is determined to avoid a scandal for the sake of his son. But his best friend's widow is just as determined to cast her mourning veil aside by hosting a party that will surely destroy both their reputations and expose all of his carefully kept secrets...

Leah George has carried the painful knowledge of her husband's affair for almost a year. All she wants now is to enjoy her independence and make a new life for herself—even if that means being ostracized by the Society whose rules she was raised to obey. Now that the rumors are flying, there's only one thing left for Sebastian to do: silence the scandal by enticing the improper widow into becoming a proper wife. But when it comes to matters of the heart, neither Sebastian nor Leah is prepared for the passion they discover in each other's arms....

"A glorious new voice in romance."
—Elizabeth Hoyt

LOVE
ROMANCE
NOVELS?

For news on all your favorite romance authors,
sneak peeks into the newest releases, book
giveaways, and much more—

"Like" Love Always on Facebook!

f LoveAlwaysBooks